THE MONARCHS

A novel by

STEPHEN MARK RAINEY

Crossroad Press

Other Books by Stephen Mark Rainey

The Last Trumpet
Balak
Dark Shadows: Dreams of the Dark (with Elizabeth Massie)
The Lebo Coven
Blue Devil Island
Other Gods
The Nightmare Frontier
The Gaki & Other Hungry Spirits
Legends of the Night
Song of Cthulhu
Evermore (with James Robert Smith)
Deathrealms
The Gods of Moab

Cover by Aaron Rosenberg and David Dodd

Interior design by Aaron Rosenberg and Stephen Mark Rainey

ISBN 978-1-937530-19-8 — ISBN 978-1-937530-13-6 (pbk.)

www.crossroadpress.com

First edition

Dedicated to David Niall Wilson,
Longtime friend, fellow writer, and keeper of proper wine temperatures,
without whom I would never have found myself lost in the Dismal Swamp,
the experience that inspired me to write this novel.

Chapter 1

In late August, the tidewater lowlands should not have been cold, but the first storm of the new hurricane season brought a wind that roared through Fearing like an arctic gale. Courtney Edmiston felt its belligerent caress the moment she slid out of the Jaguar's passenger seat and came face to face with the Blackburns' plantation house, which looked as if the winds of several centuries had tried, with partial success, to batter it down. It was a sprawling, three-story mongrel, mostly Victorian, half-hiding behind a barrier of centurion oaks, obviously built to convey grandeur but reduced almost to grotesqueness by the ravages of time and the elements. Its peeling gray walls and warped roof looked as if they might collapse with the next big gust. Several large drops of rain smacked Courtney rudely in the face without registering, and only when Jan Blackburn emerged from the behind the wheel, calling, "It's going to be a big one," did she turn her attention from the hulking mansion to her bags in the backseat. With some difficulty, she tugged out the two large suitcases and started up the flagstone walkway to the porch, one in each hand, until Jan rushed to relieve her of the heavier one.

The footlocker in the trunk could wait until later, since there was nothing in it she would need right away. Still, she hesitated to leave it, for these three cases contained everything left in the world that she owned. For anything else she might need to survive, at least for the foreseeable future, she would be relying on the generosity of this house's inhabitants.

They reached the shelter of the massive, wraparound porch just as the bottom fell out and the wind rose to a train-like roar, the likes of which Courtney had heard only once, many years before — when a tornado had swept across the north Georgia landscape less than a mile from her parents' home. Her family had fared all right, though some of their neighbors had been less fortunate. The memory of that storm gave her a shudder. Jan, however, appeared to take the weather's mounting fury in stride and shoved open the front door, through which Courtney could see a warm and inviting oasis of golden light. With a last shiver, she stepped across the threshold into the Blackburn family's ancient keep: the closest thing to home she might know for quite some time to come.

"Just leave your bag here," Jan said, setting down her burden and brushing back a few dripping blonde locks. "We'll take them back to your room in a few. First things first. Drinks are calling."

“Good plan,” Courtney said, carefully placing her suitcase next to the other on the hardwood floor and glancing around at her surroundings. Whatever the exterior’s dilapidated condition, the interior appeared very much the opposite. Quaint electric candles illuminated the rich gold and crimson wallpaper, and a profusion of hanging mirrors turned the relatively small foyer into an expansive, multifaceted chamber. Above, an ornate crystal chandelier hung on a polished brass chain, its brilliant aura lending the impression that, inside the house, gold was the predominant color. Courtney followed Jan down a narrow, maze-like hall, through an elegantly appointed dining room, to a warmly lit great room, one end of which had been converted to a full bar, larger than most of those in the Atlanta restaurants and taverns Courtney once frequented.

Jan stepped behind the counter and produced a tall bottle. “Still partial to Cabernet Franc?”

Courtney smiled and slid comfortably into one of the tall, swiveling chairs. “Absolutely.”

Jan uncorked the bottle and selected two glasses from the overhead rack. As she poured, Courtney pulled off her rain jacket, laid it over the back of the chair next to her, and ran a hand through her shoulder-length sienna waves to break up the clinging droplets. Outside, the wind buffeted the house with the sound of a giant’s fist pummeling overstressed wood, and rain clattered on the roof two stories above like a barrage of machinegun fire. “That sounds killer,” she said, glancing at the ceiling. “I hope you don’t have any leaks.”

Jan smiled, handing over a brimming glass. “Don’t let the façade fool you. This house has stood up to hurricanes, twisters, floods, and storms in general for over a hundred years. If it starts leaking now, I’ll have to blame you. Cheers.”

She stiffened a little before her face broke into a smile. “Just like old times. Blaming me, I mean.”

Jan took a sip from her glass and glanced at the ceiling before coming to sit beside Courtney. “I want you to be comfortable here,” she said, her face turning earnest. “You’re my guest, so don’t feel obligated to do anything but relax and enjoy yourself. Worry about getting back on your feet later.”

Courtney felt the blood rushing to her cheeks. She didn’t want get teary, but with even a little wine, it was almost inevitable. “Thanks,” she said, cupping her hands around her glass, as if it contained something precious. “You know I hate to impose. But right now, I’ll take any help I can get. And I do appreciate it.”

“You’re not imposing. I invited you. And tonight, we’re going to forget everything but this.” She lifted her glass and drained it.

Courtney couldn't help but laugh a little. "Tell me you don't still drink like that all the time."

"Only with you."

"Now I'm worried." She took a modest sip. "So where's the rest of the household?"

Jan's face darkened a little. "David's around somewhere, who knows. And Aunt Martha, she'll be where she always is — up in her room. She almost never comes out anymore except at mealtimes." Jan glanced at her watch; it was almost seven o'clock. "Arlene left a while ago. She's our housekeeper. Lives in the cottage at the back of the property. We couldn't do without her anymore."

"Just how much property do you have?"

"Oh, a hundred acres, give or take a few. You know, Mom and Dad farmed it all their lives — up till the end. David and I have threatened to try starting it up again, but…well, we just haven't had the motivation."

"I understand. Believe me."

"Someday." Jan's eyes turned inward for several long seconds.

The wine was delicious, and Courtney resisted the urge to down the last half of her own glass in one gulp. She knew Jan harbored deep wounds from the not-so-distant past. Both her parents had been killed the previous year, and only a few months earlier, her fiancé. All in automobile accidents.

But Jan still had a home, at least.

Courtney and Jan had met during their freshman year at Duke University, almost fifteen years ago. Since then, Jan had visited her in Atlanta several times, but this was Courtney's first trip to Fearing. She had met Jan's parents and younger brother, David, at their graduation ceremony, but that had been only a day-long encounter, and her attention had been divided between too many people to take in much beyond the superficial. She remembered them as very sweet, unassuming people, and had she not been aware of their status, she would never have guessed that the Blackburns were the wealthiest family in Fearing, North Carolina. Jan, certainly, had been a fairly typical college student, unmistakably well-bred, but untainted by the almost prerequisite snobbishness of kids whose families' blood ran blue.

Courtney had noticed a large, framed portrait of Jan's parents over the huge fireplace at the opposite end of the room. She glanced over at it and was struck by the couple's rather sad smiles, and particularly Jan's mother's eyes, which seemed to be fixed on some unhappy future moment. Mr. Blackburn was an attractive, slender man with silver-blond hair and a long, aquiline nose. His violet eyes were warm, but they appeared somehow haunted, as if he, too, foresaw some great tragedy. "When was that taken?" she asked, pointing to the photograph.

"About a year before they died," Jan said, giving the portrait a wistful look. "That was the last picture they took together."

"It's nice. You favor your mother." She gave Jan a thoughtful glance and noticed that she, too, wore a distant, preoccupied look. "You've got your dad's eyes, though."

"Yeah. And his big feet."

She chuckled, and Jan refilled their glasses. Courtney went at this one with a little more gusto, for sitting here with her longtime friend, she could almost pretend that these past, turbulent years had been illusion, and that she and Jan were as young and carefree as when they had shared drinks at the first Tri-Delta mixer. Still, though she loved seeing Jan again and had always longed to visit the Blackburns' opulent home, the reason for being here now was a bitter pill, and it burned too virulently in her stomach to ignore.

As ever, Jan could sense the darkening of her mood. "Have you talked to Frank's parents lately?"

She shook her head. "They still blame me, believe it or not. And I'm beyond even wanting to reconcile anything with them. It's just not going to happen."

"This is you I'm talking about. You can't go on thinking someone you were close to hates you. It'll eat you up."

"No. I'm beyond caring about them. At all."

"You don't mean that."

She took a long swallow. "Pretty much."

"Well. Let's not dwell on that." Jan sighed and glanced over her shoulder. "I know David will want to see you. No telling what he's up to."

"You sure he's home?"

"No. But there aren't many places around for him to go."

"So I figured." Courtney smiled a little. The drive from the Newport News Amtrak station had been easy enough, but once they had turned off U.S. 17 toward Fearing, they were in the most desolate country she had ever seen. The town's population was a mere two-thousand, and the Blackburns lived a couple of miles out from the town proper, on a tiny, two-lane road that only led deeper into the Great Dismal Swamp. Fearing's little downtown, with its trio of stoplights and handful of antique buildings, looked like a picture postcard from the 1940s, sleepy beyond belief, and devoid of attractions for anyone who sought more excitement than fishing in the Moratok River. To Courtney, such a place seemed a refreshing novelty, though she could hardly imagine growing up in such an isolated, lethargic environment.

She finished her second glass of wine and Jan wasted no time refilling it. By now, the alcohol was warming her blood and loosening the restraints on her inner rage. She gave her friend a long, searching look, and said, "You know, there's something in me that isn't all that sorry about Frank. I loved him — you know that. But he could be so cold. Colder than anybody I've ever known." Her voice softened as the pain of old memories took hold of her heart. "He used to hit Sheila sometimes. When he'd get frustrated with work, or me, or anything, he'd take it out on her. I called the police once, but he managed to smooth talk them. Nothing ever happened to him. Nothing."

"I remember," Jan said. "But that was so long ago, and from everything you've told me since, it seemed like things were going okay."

"Mostly, they were. When Sheila started first grade, he seemed to mellow out — almost as if that were some benchmark, some catalyst for him to straighten himself out. He knew he had anger issues, and I really think he worked at getting better. Until he lost his job. That was the end of everything."

She had seen the flashing lights outside her house first. Somehow, she knew what had happened before she even turned in the driveway.

"That would send a lot of people over the edge," Jan said, touching her knee sympathetically. "And for somebody with problems like he had…"

She could no longer even see a blue flashing light without having a panic attack.

She didn't want it to happen, but she felt the burning at the corners of her eyes. A tear began to well, and a moment later, it trickled down her cheek. She wiped it away quickly, even though it was her best friend here with her.

"And those people said it was my fault. That I somehow drove him to it. To kill my child. How could they not know what was wrong with him? They were his parents. That son of a bitch killed my little girl, and they blamed *me* for it."

"They were just so distraught," Jan said, bringing her hands up to Courtney's shoulders. "They just couldn't believe it was in him. Parents can be like that about their children."

"'Distraught' passes. It hits you hard and then goes away. But they still hate me. They said so. It must have been festering there, I don't know how long. And after they said I was so good for him. That I helped him, that I did what *they* never could."

"People can be blind when it comes to their loved ones," Jan said, her eyes again turning inward. "Some people *have* to blame someone else, or they simply can't deal with their own pain. They implode."

The dam had crumbled, and Courtney's tears were pouring now. "I'm almost glad he killed himself. I *am* glad he's gone. But it was too easy an out for him. Too, too easy." She wiped her eyes, but it didn't staunch the flow. "You know, his father said he should have done it to me as well. How could anyone say something like that? How could they?"

Jan held her close now, and whispered into her ear, "They loved their son too much. That's all. I know it hurts. But if they truly meant what they said, it's because they never really knew you. Not on the inside. And that only makes the tragedy worse."

She had been reining in her emotions for months, and now, swept up in the cataract, she wept with her face buried in her friend's neck. Jan's arms encircled her firmly but tenderly, transmitting both sympathy and strength. Long ago, when a kitten they had taken into the Tri-Delta house had been hit by a car, Jan had held her the same way. Jan's grief was no less intense, but her ability to comfort others was a gift she offered freely and generously. But even with Jan, Courtney could only release so much, and after another moment of drawing reassurance from her friend's embrace, she pulled away, wiped her eyes again, and reeled in the pain.

She picked up her glass and sipped the wine, again with reserve, her hand trembling only slightly. Then, looking back at Jan, she said, "You know, with me, men have never been anything but raving assholes. Even my dad, bless him. He could be such a son of a bitch." Jan smiled darkly and wiped a last tear from Courtney's cheek. "From the beginning, I knew Frank had problems. I almost didn't marry him. But I did. Now, I regret the day I met him."

"I know. I'm so sorry."

"Men," she said, holding up her glass. "Fuck the lot of them."

Jan's eyes had adjusted their focus over her shoulder, and her lips began to widen into a wry grin. "I'm sure you don't *really* mean that."

Slowly, Courtney became aware of the subtle change in the air that signaled the presence of another person in the room.

She grimaced slightly and gave Jan an apologetic look. "David?"

Jan nodded.

"Hello, David," she said without turning around, trying to stifle any expectations she might have regarding Jan's brother. Consciously, she knew he would no longer be the gawky, somewhat sullen teenager who had behaved crudely around her all those years ago, but that impression lingered so stubbornly that when she did swivel to regard the young man standing in the doorway, she could barely keep her jaw from dropping.

"Hello, Ms. Edmiston."

A sardonic humor lit his brilliant blue eyes, and the thin, almost cruel smile on his finely drawn lips suggested more disdain than respect in his greeting. A thick crescent of dark hair hung low over his forehead, casting a shadow that accentuated the brightness of his eyes. He was tall, something over six feet, she thought, very slender, but graceful rather than gangly. He wore jeans and a silver-gray button-down shirt, which bore numerous dark splotches from the rain.

"I take it back," she said softly, just for Jan to hear, as she rose to her feet. Then, to David, she said, "I was wondering if I'd get to see you tonight."

"Wonder no more." He stepped forward and took the hand she extended to him, gently clasping only her fingers. "Nice to see you again. I'm sorry if I caught you in a moment of…frustration."

He looked more amused than apologetic. But if circumstances had been reversed, she thought, her reaction might not be so different. "Sorry about that," she said with sincerity. "Long story. Things haven't gone so well lately."

His expression softened a little. "So I understand. What a shame." Then, giving her hand a final squeeze that she interpreted as compassionate, he stepped around the bar, dropped a few ice cubes into a tumbler, and poured himself a tall scotch on the rocks. He pointed to the near-empty wine bottle. "You two look to be well on your way."

Jan ignored the remark. "Where have you been?"

"Down at Arlene's cottage. She was having computer problems and asked me if I'd help her out with it."

"Did you?"

"Yeah. Spyware. All clean now."

Jan pressed a hand to her chest. "You mean you actually made yourself useful?"

"Only briefly."

Jan glanced at Courtney. "It's against his religion to at least act like a decent human being for more than a few minutes every day."

"It's a constant struggle," he said. "But I like Arlene. Thought I'd make an exception and try to behave for an hour or so." He looked at Courtney. "Arlene's a senior, not very tech-savvy. You'll meet her tomorrow, no doubt."

"Okay."

"How about you? Are you spoiled for modern technology?"

"Well, my life doesn't revolve around electronic gadgets, like most of the people I know, if that's what you mean."

"Good. There isn't much around here to rely on. But you can get on the Internet, and if you climb out on the roof on a cloudless day, you might get cell phone service."

"That's good to know."

"I've got an extra laptop you can use anytime you want to," Jan said. "In fact, I'll leave it with you tonight once you're settled in your room."

"That'd be great. Thanks."

David took a long swallow of his scotch and said, "Well, I think I'll scrounge up something for dinner. Courtney, have you eaten?"

"We stopped in Elizabeth City for Japanese on the way in," Jan said, before Courtney could answer. "But Arlene left a pot of shrimp in the kitchen for you and Aunt Martha."

"Ah yes, she mentioned that." David gave Courtney a long, appraising look and then his wry smile returned. "It'll be grand having you here. I trust you'll enjoy our company."

"Grand?"

"Yes, grand."

"Even the fucking men?"

"Some of them, anyway."

"Then I'll see you later." He bowed mockingly and disappeared into the hallway.

"Sweet, isn't he?" Jan said, crinkling her nose.

"Well, he's not as crude as when I first met him."

"I guess that's something."

"So what's your Aunt Martha like?"

"She's actually Great-Aunt Martha. Goes back a couple of generations on Dad's side. The third floor belongs to her. She is — how shall I put it? — a bit eccentric."

"I don't recall you ever talking much about her."

"She's been around forever. I mean forever. But we almost never see her. She lives her life and we live ours. She usually shows up for meals and that's about it, so I doubt your paths will cross much. But just to warn you — she may be a bit crotchety. She's like that."

"So am I."

Jan chuckled and drained the last of her wine. "Well, shall I take you to your room? You can freshen up, go to bed, watch television, anything you like. Or we can always open another bottle."

"I think I'll pass on the latter. I've had twice too much."

Jan raised an eyebrow. "You? What, are you getting old on me or something?"

"No, I'm just delicate. You know that."

"Yeah. Delicate like a wildcat. Well, come along, dah-ling."

Courtney followed her out to the foyer, where they picked up her bags, and then — rather than upstairs, as she might have expected — down a long hall toward the back of the house, past the kitchen and several closed doors, to a wing that in recent years must have been used infrequently, if at all. The ancient wallpaper was stained and peeling, the air smelled faintly musty, and a few cobwebs hung in the corners, which thrilled her not at all. However, when Jan came to the end of the hall and opened the last door on the left, Courtney stepped inside to find a small but comfortable-looking suite, with a neatly made single bed, a small television on a stand at its foot; a chest of drawers with a large mirror; a well-used fireplace; a nook with a microwave and coffeemaker; and tiny, private bath with a shower stall. Wide, louvered windows took up most of two walls, and outside, in the dying daylight, she saw only the close-pressing woods and a tiny patch of purple sky overhead. The storm had blown through violently but quickly.

"This used to be Arlene's suite until we decided to let her have the cottage. I figured you might appreciate the privacy."

"It's nice," Courtney said, shoving her suitcase into the corner next to the bureau. "I was beginning to wonder if you were leading me down to a dungeon."

"Sorry. We haven't kept this wing up since Arlene moved. But the room is in good shape, and I think you'll have everything you need to stay with us a while. There's no AC back here, but you've got a ceiling fan." She pointed upward. "The room stays pretty comfortable, even in the summer."

Courtney smiled gratefully and wrapped her arms around Jan's shoulders. "You don't know how much I appreciate this. I'll never be able to repay you."

Jan returned her embrace and whispered, "You know better than that." Then, as they parted, she said, "Well, make yourself at home. If you need anything, just shout, and we'll get you fixed up. If you change your mind about that bottle, or just want to sit up for a while, I'll be in the great room."

"Okay. I think I'll just freshen up and maybe read a little bit before bed. I am about worn out."

"I know. It shows." Courtney scowled indignantly, and Jan laughed. "Don't worry, you're still ever so beautiful."

She gave Jan a little shove toward the door, and when her friend had gone, she closed it and hefted her smaller suitcase onto the bed to unpack her most necessary items. Once she had hung some clothes in the closet and stowed the rest in the chest of drawers, she started to undress, only to realize then that the one thing missing in the room was curtains or blinds for the windows. Night had fallen completely now, and the light in the room would make her plainly visible to any eyes on the other side of the glass. Well, there was nothing out there but woods, she thought, and the only eyes that might see her belonged to animals and insects that couldn't care less about spectacles unfolding inside her room. She went ahead and stripped off her clothes, but as soon as she did, she realized that the trees pressing so close to the house actually made her uncomfortable. The shadows seemed too deep, the sounds of chirping and buzzing a little too loud, and she could almost feel the gaze of countless eyes that seemed more curious, more *intent,* than they should have.

She wasn't accustomed to being surrounded by true darkness. In the city, even in the dead of night, lights shone brilliantly from far and near, and for most of her life, it had been all she could do to shut *out* the light that crept incessantly from the world outside.

She was just about to step into the bathroom when a sound rang from outside that froze her in mid-stride. It sounded like an old woman shrieking, she thought, and she stood motionless, listening for the sound to come again. No further screams came, but after a long, almost disturbing silence, a sharp, feminine voice began babbling, nonsensically but rhythmically, its timbre shrill and piercing, as if someone was calling out in panic in a foreign language.

Hesitantly, she moved closer to the windows and soon realized that the sound was coming from above.

Aunt Martha?

It must be, she thought. But what in God's name did such caterwauling mean? Was the old woman truly in anguish up there, or was this some random outburst of a sort that Courtney had better get used to?

"A bit eccentric," Jan had said by way of warning. Christ, if that actually was Martha making such noise from her third-floor sanctuary, it was much worse than that. The woman had to be stark, raving mad.

She debated throwing her robe on and going to find Jan, just to be on the safe side, but then she decided against it, certain that if there really were a problem with the old woman, Jan or David would already be aware of it.

Her shower didn't last long. The day's travel and the dredging up of her most intimate pain had exhausted her — not to mention more wine in the course of an hour or so than she had consumed in months. After she had dried off and finished her nightly ablutions, she pulled on a long T-shirt that doubled as a nightgown and slid beneath the sheets of her bed, which she found firm and reasonably comfortable. She usually read for about half an hour before bed, but tonight, her eyelids were on their way down before she had even turned off the bedside lamp.

As consciousness slipped rapidly away, she heard a few distant babblings, which might have been the voice from upstairs, but by then, she was too far gone to care. Her last waking thoughts were of her dead daughter, whose image followed her into her dreams.

Unfortunately, they were not pleasant.

#

Chapter 2

"Well, fancy you!"

Startled, Courtney didn't drop the glass of orange juice she had just poured, but she did slosh a portion of it over her bedroom slippers. She managed to stifle an expletive before it could fully emerge, but as she turned, an electric arc of pain zoomed through her neck and skull, rudely reminding her that her tolerance for alcohol was a fraction of what it had been when she and Jan used to close bars on an almost nightly basis. Still, accustomed to rising early, she had gotten up with the sun, counting on being the first to the kitchen. But when she had stepped through the door, she discovered an old steel percolator already hissing and bubbling on the counter, filling the room with a delicious aroma.

The raspy voice had come from a spindly, featureless wraith, backlit by the brilliant sun framed in the east-facing window. The silhouette cocked its head in birdlike fashion, briefly revealing a pair of narrow violet eyes that regarded her quizzically. Finally, the figure stepped forward so that Courtney could observe it without shielding her eyes.

Withered was the word for old Aunt Martha. Rail-thin, no more than 90 pounds, with skeletal arms that protruded from the sleeves of her drab housecoat like twigs bent at awry angles. The gray bun at the back of her head pulled her wrinkled skin so taut that her eyes looked Chinese.

"Good morning," Courtney said, softly, so that her voice would not trigger another wave of pain. "You must be Martha."

"You think?" the old woman barked, her appraising stare never wavering. "Well, I know who you are, too. I daresay there was advertisement aplenty of your arrival."

Courtney offered the woman a wan smile. "I guess Jan's been as excited about it as I have."

"I'm talking about the racket till all hours, which some of us do not appreciate." Martha's eyes bored into hers and didn't blink.

Courtney raised an eyebrow. "Actually, I went to bed fairly early. I'm afraid I don't recall us making much noise. Sorry."

"A wine drinker like that young Jan, I'd hazard, and a silly one, from the sound of it. Are you a drinker, Miss Edmiston? I have to tell you that drinking is no credit to a young woman, and my niece is living testimony to the fact. Anyone with half an eye can see that. How are your eyes, Miss Edmiston?"

Courtney's hackles started to rise, but she held to the path of diplomacy, if only to thwart another onslaught of pain. "Jan and I haven't seen each other in several years. It was something of a special occasion."

Martha pressed too close to her now, her eyes still unblinking. "I suppose you had a lot to catch up on, then. Three years is such a long time — to a child."

She shrugged. "I hope I can look at the passing of time from your perspective someday. I'm sorry if we disturbed you."

"How kind. I suppose you're sincere, but for the young, sincerity is a means to a self-serving end. If I were you, I should be wary of falling into that trap."

"I'm watching out for it as we speak," Courtney said, testily now. "Is Jan awake?"

"I heard a stirring in yonder, so she may be. Do you take coffee, girl?"

The obviously disparaging "girl" rankled, but she knew better than to let the old woman intimidate her. "Yes, ma'am," she said, using her thickest southern accent.

"It'll be ready in a few minutes. That black woman never gets here early enough to start the first pot. I'm sure she's happy as the devil to find it waiting on her when she gets here to work. She *works* for us, you know."

"So I understand."

There was a long, uncomfortable silence. Finally, Martha said, "So. You had trouble at home, did you?"

She took a tense breath and nodded. "Yes."

"A shame. But people are too soft, you know that? Folks think they should be happy all the time. So when trouble comes, they make it worse by dwelling on how miserable they are. It's a matter of misguided expectations. If you accept the fact that suffering is your lot in life, then your brief moments of happiness are transcendent. This is a very simple fact, but most people don't understand it."

"Let me guess. You're a Woody Allen fan."

"Eh?"

"Schopenhauer?"

"What?"

Courtney shook her head. "Never mind."

"I don't appreciate sarcasm."

"No, I'm not…" She waved a hand, as if to brush away her remark. "Sorry. Anyway, about late last night — were you by chance shouting…or anything?"

"Shouting?"

"I heard sounds. Yelling. Babbling."

"That was just Aunt Martha singing."

Courtney turned and was almost relieved to see David standing in the door, dressed in a loose-fitting satin robe, his sardonic smile firmly in place. He came to Courtney and gave her a shoulder a little squeeze.

"Good morning."

"Good morning to you."

"Coffee ready yet, old woman?"

"Two minutes. The first cup is mine, you know." Martha glared at Courtney with her unblinking eyes. "Singing is a healthy way to cope with unhappiness. It releases endorphins and elevates the spirit." She snapped her head back toward David. "You should sing more."

"I sing all the time. That's why I don't have any friends."

Courtney snorted despite herself, and a piercing lance drove through her temple. David gave her a knowing look and chuckled.

"You'll be back in practice in no time. My sister gives excellent tutorials."

It took her a moment to realize he was referring to their drinking. "There are some things I'd just as soon not get too accustomed to." She downed the last of her orange juice, which helped the cottonmouth a little. But two pairs of eyes peered intently at her, as if their owners expected her to elaborate or share some morsel of timeless wisdom. Hoping to escape Martha's scrutiny, she turned to David and offered him a faint smile. "So, David, what do you do? Do you work at an office or anything?"

"Yes, if you call my studio upstairs an office. You're more than welcome to."

"What kind of studio?"

"David fancies himself an *artiste,"* the old woman said, shaking her head with clear disdain. "He shuts himself up there with a bottle of scotch and splashes paint on a perfectly good canvas until it's ruined. I'll tell you this, girl, he's no Norman Rockwell."

David's sapphire eyes gleamed with humor. "To my dear great aunt, there was only ever one true artist."

Martha's head was still shaking. "Norman would never have taken a bottle with him."

"I'd like to see your work," Courtney said, trying her best to ignore the old woman.

His eyes dimmed a little. "I'll show it to you. Sometime. It's not particularly good."

"The artist isn't always the best judge."

"Or the best artist." He glanced at the old percolator on the kitchen counter. "Looks like our go-juice is ready. Old woman, how about we let our guest have the first cup this morning?"

"What guest?"

"No, no. Please go ahead," Courtney said, gesturing at the pot, already exhausted by her exchange with Martha and loath to absorb many more of her quirky barbs. She had to admit, if the old crone did spend most of her time closed up in her own rooms, then so much the better for this visit being a pleasant one.

The skeletal figure ambled to the coffee pot, carefully poured a cup, and tentatively sipped it, finally giving it an approving nod. Then, somewhat to Courtney's surprise, Martha filled two more cups and handed one each to David and her. She pointed to the kitchen table and gave Courtney a sour look. "There's sugar and fresh cream over there, if you're the kind who likes to ruin a good thing."

"Don't mind if I do," she said, going to the table, where she very deliberately scooped two spoonfuls of sugar and poured a large dollop of cream into her cup. She felt David's amused gaze as she stirred it noisily.

"You're going to fit in perfectly here," he said. "Arlene will be here in fifteen minutes or so, and she'll make us breakfast. Do you usually eat in the morning?"

"Actually, no, not often," she said. "Sometimes on weekends. You know what, though, I do like to get in a good run most mornings. It'd be okay for me to run out here, I take it?

To her surprise, David's face darkened, and he gave Martha a thoughtful glance. The woman's eyes narrowed slightly, but she offered nothing in return. He mulled over the prospect for several moments, and finally, his smile returned. "I don't see why not. I would advise you not to stray from the road, though. They don't call it the Dismal Swamp for nothing."

"I don't suppose you like to run?"

He chuckled. "As little as possible, my dear, as little as possible."

He did *something* to keep in shape, she thought, for his slender figure was well-hewn, his skin lightly bronzed by the sun. In his obviously expensive, elegant robe, she had to admit that he looked rather dashing, even this early in the morning.

"Maybe I'll go for a short one after I finish my coffee," she said. "I don't think I'm up for anything more than that."

"That's what comes from partaking of bottles," Martha said, putting one haughty hand on her bony hip.

"I appreciate your concern," Courtney said with an exasperated sigh, giving David a hopeful look. "I think I will go out for a quick one — if that's okay with you?"

"Whatever you like," he said, somewhat stiffly, as if he didn't quite approve, though his expression remained pleasant. "I'm sure Jan will be up by the time you get back."

"Well, then. I'll see you in a little while." She gave him a final smile. To Martha, she said, "It's been a pleasure meeting you. Your wisdom is inspiring."

"It ought to be."

Without further word, she took her cup and made her way back down the hall to her room, waiting until she was out of earshot before muttering, "'I don't appreciate sarcasm.'" Well, apparently, certain old women could find plenty where there was none, but didn't recognize it when it came. Martha was obviously not senile, nor did she appear insane; merely eccentric, as Jan had claimed. Nevertheless, the previous night's disturbance — the wailing and babbling from upstairs — still preyed on Courtney's mind, and she decided to make every effort to avoid antagonizing the woman. She was a guest here, after all, and it was not her place to judge or insult any member of Jan's family.

Martha's admittedly excellent coffee had begun to have a revitalizing effect, so Courtney slipped out of her nightshirt, changed into a pair of shorts, a T-shirt, and running shoes, and headed out the back door, into the cool but humid morning air. She found herself on a small, concrete stoop facing the dense woods, the nearest branches of which hung so low and close to the house that she had to duck to get past them. The previous night's storm had drenched everything, and from the shadowed depths, the steady patter of water on leaves sounded like a herd of forest creatures, both great and small, marching past unseen. A thick, mossy odor permeated the air, not quite unpleasant, but nearly overpowering.

As she rounded the side of the house on her way to the road, she picked up speed, feeling as if she were in her element again, away from the woods' uncomfortable stare. At the end of the driveway, she turned left, opting for the more familiar route toward town. Jan had told her that, to the right, the road led to only a handful of neighboring farms before dissolving into a network of rural byways, mostly unpaved, which wound into the depths of Dismal Swamp. Before her visit was over, she decided, just for curiosity's sake, she would have to go that way and explore; for the time being, however, it seemed more prudent to head toward whatever passed for civilization here.

To her left, the woods flanked the road for as far as she could see, while to her right, fields of soybean and tobacco extended toward the western horizon until they merged with a dark, distant tree line. Occasional barns rose from the fields like crumbling citadels, and eventually she passed a few farmhouses relatively close to the road. At one of them, she spied an elderly gentleman, dressed in overalls and a checkered flannel shirt, standing on his front porch, eyeing her with a thoughtful frown as she jogged by. She sent him a curt wave, and, to her amusement, he returned it, only to duck inside with a guilty look, as if afraid he had committed some kind of heinous crime.

He must know every person, car, and animal that ever passed this way, she thought. To him, an unfamiliar young woman running alone by his house would be quite the novelty.

By the time she turned back, she reckoned she had gone just about a mile, and not a single car had passed in either direction. To the south, the sky had turned purple, and the breeze was picking up. Very likely, they would be in for another storm today.

When she came to the break in the woods that revealed a corner of the old gray house in the distance, she heard the first low rumble of a vehicle on the road — coming from behind her, approaching slowly. A few moments later, a rusty, aging pickup truck with windows so dirty they appeared translucent rattled past at little more than a crawl, and she glimpsed distinct movement within — thc occupants turning to eye her curiously. The truck continued moving until it reached the Blackburn house, where it pulled off to the left side of the road and stopped, its driver cutting the engine. For a moment, she thought surely someone would get out, but the doors remained closed, and she saw the vague silhouettes inside turn to watch as she steadily closed the distance.

Her instincts whispered darkly that these new arrivals could mean trouble. As she drew nearer to the truck, she tried to make out its license plate, but a layer of caked mud obscured the numbers. Through a relatively clear patch of glass, she could see the face of the man in the passenger seat, his nose pressed against the dirty surface, his eyes glaring at her with unconcealed lust. She hadn't thought to bring pepper spray, or any such deterrent, and her eyes automatically searched the edge of the woods for sharp sticks, rocks, anything she might use to fend off the men if they attempted to assault her. She spied nothing useful.

The eyes were still ogling her when she reached the driveway, and as she made the turn, she put on an extra burst of speed, her heart and lungs laboring with more than just exertion. Any second now, she expected to hear the truck's door creak open, a voice calling after her, or the sound of pursuing footsteps, but as she sprinted toward the house, nothing happened, and she began to breathe a little easier. Maybe she'd had nothing to fear in the first place; maybe they were just a couple of harmless local hicks who thought it would be fun to stare at the new girl in town and maybe rattle her a bit before driving off, guffawing. She paused before making the turn into the wooded backyard for a last glance at the truck, to see if the men were still peering after her.

They were. And as she stood there, panting and dripping cold sweat, she realized with awful certainty that the grim, silent truck on the far side of the road wasn't carrying a couple of crude but fun-loving local boys. She could no longer see them, but she could *feel* the pair of icy gazes, cunning and calculating, like the hypnotic stare of vipers poised to strike the moment her attention wavered.

And having seen her turn unthinkingly into the Blackburns' driveway, those men knew exactly where to find her.

#

Chapter 3

She could tell by the expression on Jan's face that her description of the pickup truck had struck a familiar, unpleasant chord.

"They stopped right in front of the house, so I guess they counted on me coming here. Do you know who they are?"

"Not for certain," Jan said, her face too pale for Courtney's liking. "But there are a few rednecks around here that like to cause trouble every chance they get. They're jealous of anyone with money, and they're not embarrassed to show their asses every chance they get. I doubt it's anything to worry about."

Courtney and Jan had claimed the pair of rattan rocking chairs on the front porch, which overlooked the tree-shaded lawn, the balmy breeze having swept away the sticky humidity from earlier in the day. Distant gray clouds still threatened rain, but for now, it was a pleasant morning, and the comfortable surroundings helped ease Courtney's mind after the traumatic climax of her run. However, she couldn't escape the feeling that Jan was holding something back from her.

"Nothing like having my first good run spoiled."

"Maybe you can get David to go with you next time. Don't let him fool you. He's a decent runner. He'll jump at the chance, too."

"He didn't exactly seem enthusiastic this morning."

"He's got just enough of Aunt Martha in him to enjoy being obstinate."

Courtney smiled thinly. She could warm to the idea of David accompanying her. For one thing, he didn't seem the kind to be easily intimidated.

And since this morning, she found him frequently in her thoughts.

"So, it's like that, is it?" Jan said with a smirk.

"What? Oh." Courtney shook her head. "No, I was just thinking. Yeah, I guess I would feel better if someone came with me."

"I'll talk to him, if you'd like."

"Sure. That would be good." Uncertain whether to press the subject further, she said, "So, how does a woman of means occupy herself in a place like this?"

"I actually spend a fair amount of time in Elizabeth City. I volunteer at the hospice there three days a week."

"Oh. That must be…difficult."

Jan nodded. "It is, but it's also very gratifying. I've met the sweetest people there. It's hard to explain, but somehow it helps me deal with Mom and Dad's deaths, even though their circumstances were very different."

"I guess I can understand that."

"I've taken off this week so I can be here with you. After that, though, you'll be on your own. I'm sure you can manage."

Courtney had given little thought to the coming days and how she might occupy herself when Jan was away. The idea of being alone in the house with David — well, alone but for Aunt Martha — now seemed as intimidating as it did alluring. Maybe it wasn't such a good idea to invite him to run with her, she thought. Realistically, it wouldn't do for either of them to get too interested in the other. "I'll make do," she said, a bit distracted by an agreeable image of David that seemed to have emblazoned itself on a number of her brain cells.

Jan's eyes glinted knowingly, but after a minute, her face turned grave again. "So. Tell me about your job. What happened there?"

At those words, Courtney felt a little twinge of anger. "At first, they claimed to be understanding. But they're one of those companies that will use any excuse to get rid of someone who's got problems. As soon as I went back to work, my boss started claiming I was making too many mistakes. 'If you can't keep your mind on your work, then maybe you'd better go,' he said. That's when I knew my number was up."

"How long had you been there?"

"Almost six years. Then some customer complained that his claim had been mishandled, that we had violated HIPAA regulations, which is a major deal. It wasn't even my account, but they decided that I should have been the one to follow up on it. Thus ended my illustrious career at Sterling Med-Health Services. I couldn't cut it with just Unemployment. So three months later, the bank foreclosed on the house."

"I'm sorry. I know how hard it's been on you."

"Maybe your aunt Martha is right. If you don't expect to be happy, you're less apt to be disappointed."

"Martha's not right. She's just a bitter old woman."

"So, was that actually 'singing' I heard last night, or does she have serious problems?"

Again, Jan's face went a little pale. "Martha lives in her own world. I don't profess to understand it. Look, do me a favor. Don't interact with her any more than you need to. Try to be pleasant with her when you do. It'll make your life easier. She has her point of view, and that's all there is to it."

"I kind of got that."

"Seriously. If you don't cross her, you'll get on with her well enough. That's the best you can hope for."

Courtney nodded, her eyes having turned to the distant road. For a few seconds, she thought she heard a telltale rattle beyond the trees, but nothing appeared at the far end of the driveway. She listened intently, feeling Jan's curious eyes on her but ignoring them.

"What is it?"

"A motor. That truck."

"Everybody on this road has a truck. You're just sensitive to it."

"I guess," she said, unconvinced. "But it stopped somewhere up there."

Jan's gaze followed hers. "I didn't hear anything."

She glanced at her friend. "You sure you don't know who those men were? If it's somebody dangerous, maybe we should let the police know."

"Or not," Jan said with a frown of distaste. "There's only a handful of officers and the chief. And the chief is a drunk. The county sheriff is the serious law here. But it's a big county, and he's understaffed too. If there's trouble, you pretty much have to handle it yourself."

Courtney gave her a dubious look. "You have a very different life here than I expected."

Jan waved dismissively. "Stop worrying. It's not as if we're in a major hub for crime. We've lived here a long time, you know."

Courtney tried to be reassured, *wanted* to be reassured. When she thought about it, back in Atlanta, every time she set foot on the street, she had faced a greater risk of harm than this place probably posed at its worst. At bars, on the road, even at work, she had dealt with far more egregious advances and had never suffered any lingering anxiety. But that was back in her old, familiar environment, and in these different surroundings, she felt out of place. Vulnerable.

She realized then that the birds, which had been singing cheerful choruses in the woods, had all fallen silent, and her apprehension came rushing back.

Even Jan now seemed pensive, her eyes studying the trees that marched toward the road at the edge of the yard. A distant crunching sound — footsteps, certainly — drifted out of the deep-shadowed woods, and Courtney's heart began to race.

"I know what I heard," she said.

Jan cracked a smile, but it was a mask. "Well, if you'll be more comfortable, we can go back inside."

Courtney nodded, rose from her chair, eyes darting back toward the trees, and followed Jan into the cool, dim interior of the house. As they retreated toward the great room, a very tall, very slender black woman appeared in the hallway and gave Jan a respectful nod. "Good morning."

"Arlene, this is my friend, Courtney. Courtney, meet Arlene Owen."

She guessed that the housekeeper must be in her mid-forties. Her hair was long and black, entwined with a few strands of gray. Her stern but attractive features brightened as she gave Courtney a lingering look of appraisal. "Well, now. I've heard so much about you. Glad you've come to stay with us."

"I'm glad to be here."

"I hear they've put you back in my old room. Very comfortable, that."

"Yes, it is, thank you."

She leaned close to Courtney's ear, but spoke loudly. "Those two are completely lost without me. So don't expect them to take care of you. Now, look. I'm here every day till six or so. If there's anything at all you need, you just call me. Okay?"

Courtney chuckled. "I'll do that. Thank you."

"Arlene's the best cook in the state," Jan said. "As long as we have her, we won't go hungry."

"I've tried to show Jan her way around the kitchen, but she can't tell the difference between fatback and chitlins," Arlene said, with a little roll of her eyes. She gave Courtney a pat on the shoulder. "Don't forget. You call *me*."

"I'll do that."

"Pleasure to meet you, Courtney."

"And you."

As Arlene went on her way toward the front of the house, Courtney said, "She seems very sweet. But I am *not* going to eat chitlins."

Jan laughed. "Fear not. She hates chitlins. And yes, she's wonderful."

"I thought David said she was a senior."

"She's nearly seventy."

"You're kidding."

Jan shook her head. "She's a strong woman. Been through a lot in her life. And she's very loyal."

Somehow, the way Jan said "loyal" seemed to ring with resentment, and Courtney gave her friend a questioning glance. But Jan remained oblivious as she led the way to the great room, where she surprised Courtney by going to the window and peering out at the northern expanse of yard and the dense woodland beyond.

"You heard it too, didn't you?"

"I heard something moving in the woods. Probably just an animal."

"What if it's not?"

"It was."

"Then what are you looking for?"

Jan turned away from the window and gave a little shrug. "I don't know. Nothing, I guess. You've about got me spooked in my own house, you wretched thing."

"That reminds me. Would you by chance have any extra curtains for the back room? I feel kind of exposed back there."

Jan opened her mouth in a silent "Oh," as if she had just remembered something important. "Damn. I meant to do that for you. Arlene had some nice ones that she made herself, but she took them with her to the cottage. I didn't think to hang any new ones for you. I'll take care of it."

"Thanks. I'd be more comfortable."

"I don't blame you. You never know when David might be prowling around looking to spy on you."

"It's not David I'm worried about," she said, but then wished she hadn't when Jan huffed noisily and threw her a distinctly annoyed glare.

"Just wait here, my paranoid princess. I'll go see what I can find."

#

The curtains were a little too short and didn't pull together fully, but they were better than nothing. Thankfully, Jan's annoyance with her had passed quickly, and she had gabbed cheerfully while they hung the slightly yellowed sheets of fabric on rusty old rods over the windows. Jan left, smiling, saying that they would plan on going out for dinner in the evening. Still, despite the return of her friend's good spirits, more and more Courtney felt certain that Jan was concealing something from her — something darker, more invidious, than just lingering grief. Courtney could understand grief; my God, no one could understand it better.

For a few moments, she entertained the disagreeable notion that Jan's motive for inviting her here might involve something other than helping her recover from her own life's ruin. If that were true, then it was a kind of betrayal, for in their long friendship, they had shared so much, always with total honesty.

At least, she had always believed so.

No. For God's sake, this was just her own wounded psyche conjuring up sinister intentions where none existed.

Anyway, what possible ulterior motive could Jan have?

She heard a shuffle behind her and looked around to see David standing in the doorway, his smile a tad less wry than usual. "I understand you're accepting applications for a running partner."

"I might be."

Too late to back out now — not that she would have changed her mind.

"I hear you had a bit of a fright this morning."

"It was unnerving, yes."

"Just so you know, I don't think anyone around here would actually bother you. It was someone just trying to spook you. I guess they succeeded."

"How about you? Do *you* have any idea who they were?"

He shook his head. "Not specifically, but like my sister told you, there are a few cretins around here with too much time and too few brains. You'd be just the thing to bring them out of the woodwork."

"What do you mean?"

"A young woman they've never seen before, out running alone on a near-deserted road. A lonely pervert's dream."

"So they're perverts, are they?"

"An educated guess."

"You really know how to make a woman feel at ease."

"Well, if it will help ease your mind, I accept. I'll run with you. But you'll have to make allowances for my rusty old framework. It's out of practice."

"Old, right. I've got, what, four years on you? And you look healthy enough."

"Appearances can be deceiving."

"In your case, I'm betting not."

"I don't start before nine AM."

"Lazy bones."

"Take it or leave it."

"You drive a hard bargain."

"That's why I'm rich."

She gave him a sharp glare. "I thought it was your parents who were rich."

He didn't flinch, and his grin was infuriating. "They helped."

She sighed, wondering if he realized just how callous he could be. "Leave now. Nine sharp in the morning."

He gave her a long, searching look, which she met with equal wryness, her arms akimbo, and finally, he nodded with a look of genuine good cheer. "I'll look forward to it. We can talk more at dinner tonight."

"If we must."

"We must, we must," he said. "So, until then."

She gave him an intentionally weary nod and turned her back on him, hoping it showed sufficient disdain. But he quickly reached out, smacked her soundly on the backside, and then was gone in a flash, though his retreating footsteps in the hall sounded steady and relaxed.

Courtney swore under her breath. She found that her heart was thumping with excitement, which she had to admit distressed her, but not all that terribly.

#

Chapter 4

Out on the highway, there were several familiar franchise restaurants and shops, but in the town of Fearing proper, a prospective diner had two choices: Woodard's, a country inn that featured an elegant, four-star restaurant; or Tall Ships, a somewhat less picturesque bar and grill whose star rating was, at best, indeterminable. Jan had recommended the former but left the choice to Courtney, who opted for Tall Ships because, despite her friends' wealth, choosing an extravagant outing seemed like an abuse of their generosity. Anyway, even when she could afford such things, lavish dining held only marginal appeal.

The tavern's warm lighting and nautical décor struck Courtney as quaint and appealing, the mélange of scents — frying fish, hickory smoke, and a tang of citrus — singularly inviting. Early in the dinner hour, only a smattering of patrons lurked in the shadowed booths and at the bar itself. From a jukebox in a corner, Johnny Horton's "Battle of New Orleans" brayed at low enough volume to be almost innocuous. To Courtney's relief, David led them to a secluded booth as far from the noisemaker as possible. She slid into the seat first, expecting Jan to sit next to her, but David took the liberty, leaving Jan to sit across from them. A blonde waitress wearing a very tight Tall Ships T-shirt materialized almost immediately to take their drink orders. Her eyes lingered uncomfortably on Courtney when she asked for a glass of Cabernet Franc.

"I guess David's got himself a new one," she said, her tone clearly disapproving. "So where do you come from?"

"She's my friend," Jan said, reaching across the table to touch Courtney's hand. "And I think I'd like a Guinness, if you please."

Courtney gave the waitress her most charming smile. "I come from Atlanta. You must be Brandi. Or is it Barbie?" Jan barely held back an explosion of laughter.

"Red wine and a Guinness," the girl said, ignoring her. Then, without looking at David, she added, "And a scotch on the rocks." As she turned to leave, she flung a parting glance at Courtney. "The name is Deena."

"That was my next guess."

She felt David's amused stare and chose not to meet it. She leaned toward Jan, who was still choking back a laugh. "One of your brother's broken hearts, I presume?"

"Please. Deena's not *that* hard up."

She sent David a scornful smile. "Forgive my presumptuousness."

"Ah, jealousy," he said. "I'd hate to see you and Deena get into a fight over me."

"May I harm him?" she asked Jan.

Jan's eyes didn't stray from her menu. "Be my guest."

"Well, maybe after dinner," she said with a sigh. "I'm hungry, and I don't want us to get thrown out of here."

"It wouldn't be unusual, believe me."

"What — getting thrown out of here or somebody harming David?"

"A fight breaking out."

Courtney snickered, uncertain whether Jan was exaggerating. After a couple of minutes, Deena brought their drinks and, with cold looks to go around, asked to take their orders. Courtney settled on a calamari salad, which struck her as positively cosmopolitan for such a backwater pub. Jan and David both ordered fish and chips.

"She's not going to spit in our food or anything, is she?" Courtney asked, after the blonde had left.

"No," Jan said with rather surprising firmness. "She wouldn't risk her job over anything so petty. She'd have a hard time finding anything else around here."

Courtney raised an eyebrow and David nodded knowingly. "Yes. A *very* hard time."

"I see," she said, a little disconcerted by David's smugness, though she figured she ought to be used to it by now. However, after another moment, she became aware of a dark shadow behind her left shoulder that seemed to press uncomfortably close, and when she finally looked around, she saw a very tall, heavyset man, forty-ish, with a dark, scraggly beard and deep, penetrating eyes standing just behind their seat. She noticed then that David's gaze had turned to the man, and his jaw was clenched in obvious consternation.

The big man stepped forward, placed his huge hands on the table, and leaned down to address David. "Hello, Mr. Blackburn," he said with a nod of mock deference before offering Jan and Courtney a barracuda smile. He spoke in a soft tone but his voice rumbled deeply. "I guess y'all are obliged to leave your castle now and then to mingle with the commoners."

"Mr. Surber," Jan said with a smile that failed to mask disgust. "How nice to see you. A pity it has to be before we eat."

Without invitation, the man slid into the seat next to Jan, forcing her to scoot over reluctantly. His dark eyes fell on Courtney and glared. "Who might you be?"

"I might be a good friend of Ms. Blackburn. Thank you for asking."

"Dwayne Surber," he said, thumping his chest with his index finger. "So what's your name?"

"Courtney."

"Well, nice to meet you, Courtney, who ain't from around here." He then focused his attention on David, indicating that, to him, the two women were no longer present. "Okay, Mr. Blackburn, I think it's time to discuss our arrangement. You've had more than plenty of time to make good on it."

"Perhaps we should talk outside," David said, his eyes hardening. "This isn't the place for it."

"Whether it is or it ain't, it's where we're going to."

He glanced at Jan, whose face had gone chalky. "All right. Talk."

"Well, now. Near as I can tell, it's your responsibility to carry out your parents' instructions, ain't it, Mr. Blackburn? And you ain't done it. So you might say that some people's patience is wearing thin."

David drew himself up with an indignant scowl. "Mr. Surber, you know my parents were killed, right?"

"Yessir. Shame about that."

"Well, I have to tell you. That particular fact has made me somewhat reluctant to carry out all their wishes. Truth be told, it's led me to believe that some of the parties involved in this 'arrangement' may not have acted in good faith."

"The only party not acting in good faith is you."

"That's your opinion. Which you're entitled to, of course."

"It ain't just my opinion, Mr. Blackburn. It's the opinion of quite a few folks around here."

"That doesn't change anything."

"It might ought to."

David gave him a long, thoughtful look. "All right. Tell you what. I'll take the issue under advisement and get back to you."

"Don't you bullshit me, Mr. Blackburn. Now, you listen. I'm reasonable man, but some around here…well, I can't promise nothing about them."

"You're not threatening me, are you, Mr. Surber? You know that I don't give in to threats."

"I ain't threatening you. Just bringing you a message. One you better take damn seriously."

"Then consider your message delivered. And let us have dinner in peace."

"No sir. I come to get a commitment from you. 'Cause it's high time you gave one."

David leaned close to the man. "You look here, Mr. Surber. I just told you. I'll take your message under advisement. That's as much commitment as you will get from me tonight."

"Like that means a damn thing."

David shrugged. "Take it or leave it."

Surber now looked across the table at Courtney. "Where you from, young lady?"

"Atlanta."

"Well, Atlanta. Maybe you oughta pack yourself up and get on back there."

To her surprise, David reached over and placed a firm hand on the bigger man's wrist. "You've overstayed your welcome, Mr. Surber. I suggest you leave. Right now."

The man's dark eyes studied David's for an agonizing time before disengaging his wrist with a little jerk. Finally, he said, "Okay. I see how it is. I come to reason with you, Mr. Blackburn. I never wanted no trouble, and I didn't think you did, either. But you and me ain't the only ones involved. I guess I've done my part."

"I appreciate your candor," David said, putting on his charming smile.

"Bullshit," Surber said, slowly rising from his seat. "I don't think you appreciate much of anything."

"Good evening, Mr. Surber."

The big man gave the three of them an icy stare before turning and striding away in the direction of the front door. Courtney watched after him, and for a second, beyond the glass door, she thought she glimpsed a grotesque, half-familiar face leering at her. It disappeared when Dwayne Surber pushed his way into the night, and as she lifted her glass of wine to her lips, she found her hand trembling.

Jan's hand came down reassuringly on hers. "Don't let that man upset you," she said. "He used to work for my parents, and they had some disagreements. He's been taking it out on David, since they're no longer here for him to harass."

"Disagreements nothing," David said. "He and his family tried to extort money from Mom and Dad. When they died, he decided to try collecting from Jan and me. I've got news for him. It's not going to happen."

"Um, you insinuated that he might have had something to do with their deaths," Courtney said. "Is he that dangerous?"

"Please don't worry," Jan said. "None of this involves you in any way. Whatever he said, he was just trying to intimidate David. It's not going to work, and you don't have a thing to be afraid of."

"Is he one of the men I saw this morning?"

David shook his head. "I doubt it. Not his style. He wouldn't waste his time coming out to our place just to intimidate a guest."

"I thought I saw one of them at the door just now."

Jan and David exchanged glances. Finally, David said, "I doubt it."

A moment later, Deena arrived with their food and another round of drinks, and they fell silent as she served them, Courtney so frustrated with David's sketchy answers and patronizing tone that she felt halfway compelled to shove his plate into his lap. But when he briefly raised his eyes to meet hers, she saw in them a faint glimmer of fear — and perhaps grief — which drove her ire into partial retreat. His confrontation with Dwayne Surber had not only rattled him, it had churned up painful memories of his parents. Yet he had stood up to the man without flinching. She had to give him some credit for that.

They ate for a while without speaking, and Courtney found her dinner excellent, which helped boost her spirits. Jan finally began to tell her about some of the things they could do to enjoy themselves over the next few days — such as going to the beach, which was about an hour away. Courtney responded cheerfully, heartened by the prospect of putting some distance between them and potential troublemakers, at least for a time. Besides, she had always loved going to beach, and it had been way too many years since the last time.

Back when Sheila was just a baby.

When Frank, in a drunken fit, had gotten them thrown out of their hotel.

Don't even start thinking about that.

As she finished her meal, she glanced around at the patrons, whose number had increased significantly since her arrival, and she discovered several pairs of eyes casting furtive, suspicious looks in her direction. At first, she thought she must be overreacting to the night's stress, but several times, she raised her eyes quickly, only to catch numerous pairs shifting away from hers, and one man, sitting alone in the adjacent booth, began to blush so fiercely that there was no question as to the object of his attention.

She could barely suppress a little shudder. No one had any reason to take a particular interest in her, she thought. Except for one thing: the fact that she was with the Blackburns.

David threw back the last of his scotch, gave Jan and Courtney a quick, searching look, and said, "Well, are we ready to go?"

"Is Deena bringing us a check?" she asked.

"It's covered," he said.

"It's covered," she echoed, almost inaudibly. "Then I guess we're ready to go."

As they vacated the booth, Courtney dug into her pocket for a couple of her few remaining bills and left them on the table. A lanky bus boy quickly materialized and began cleaning the table, and when she glanced back, she saw the young man pocket the money. His eyes met hers, and he threw her a snaggletoothed grin.

"I suppose I should have warned you," David said, leaning close to her. "I'm afraid that tip will never get to Deena."

For a second, she considered marching back to the booth and yanking the bills right out of the young fellow's pocket, but she knew it would only draw more unwanted attention. She shook her head in disgust and followed David and Jan as they headed for the door. One middle-aged man, seated close to the door with his wife and young son, sent David an obsequious nod and said, "Evenin', Mr. Blackburn."

"Good evening, Bill."

"G'night, Mr. Blackburn," someone called from a couple of tables over.

"Good night, George," David replied.

"Have nice night, Mr. Blackburn."

"'Night, Mr. Blackburn."

"Later, Mr. Blackburn!"

Without looking around, David raised a hand, waved, and then led the way into the cool night air. As they went around the building to the dark parking lot, where David had parked his BMW M3, she nudged Jan and asked, "Are those people for real?"

"Oh, make no mistake, they respect us. It's just that none of them particularly like us."

"In this town," David said, as he unlocked the doors for them, "people view wealth and education as both enviable and despicable. They do downtrodden very well."

Jan put Courtney in the front seat and slid into the back. "Mom and Dad owned a couple of large farms in the county," she said. "A lot of these people used to work for them. Dad owned the bank here, too, until he sold it to a national chain — just before he died, as a matter of fact. Some people resented the fact that he allowed it to go to outsiders."

"People are bitter about *that?*"

"This was always a tight-knit community. It's not so much anymore. Some people blame Mom and Dad for bringing 'progress' to the area."

"Yeah," David said, as he started the car, shifted into gear, and pulled out of the parking lot. "Dad started up the first of the corporate farms here. Before that, it was just families and individual farmers. He provided a big share of jobs in this community, but a lot of folks conveniently seem to forget that."

"Shame," Courtney said. "And your friend Surber tried to extort money from him?"

David nodded. "That whole family is bad news. I hope you won't have to see any more of them than you already have."

Courtney hoped the same thing. But Dwayne Surber's business with David appeared unfinished, and she could not forget her brief glimpse of the homely face ogling her through the tavern door. It was the same leering face she had seen in the pickup truck that morning. She was certain of it.

One other thing she knew: from now on, she intended to keep her canister of pepper spray with her — whether out in public or in her room at her hosts' house.

#

Upon their arrival home, David retreated to his studio, so Courtney spent the rest of the evening in the great room with Jan, drinking wine and making small talk, the television providing mindless background noise. She paced her intake more carefully than she had the previous night, determined to avoid a second uncomfortable morning. Jan's drinking, however, was anything but measured — due, no doubt, to the incident with Dwayne Surber — and she laid to rest an entire bottle of Shiraz before bidding Courtney goodnight and shuffling off to her room, though promising they would still plan to be off to the beach bright and early the following morning.

Courtney retired feeling vexed and disappointed, for in her brief time here, she had scarcely found relief from the stress of her own life's collapse. She had committed herself to her old friend's hospitality, and even if she wanted to leave, she no longer had anywhere else to go. Somehow, Jan and David's explanation for Dwayne Surber's enmity seemed to her contrived, or at least incomplete. Would someone intent on extorting money confront his target so blatantly in public? No, there had to be more to the story. Tomorrow, she would demand the truth. She could believe that David might lie to her, but not Jan.

As she readied herself for bed, she glanced frequently toward the wide gap in the curtains, through which it seemed that unseen, baleful eyes in the pitch-dark woods glared in at her. Insects and night birds chattered and chirped their passionate chorales, much louder than any she had heard in Atlanta, and so intrusive that the idea of getting earplugs hardly seemed outlandish. Here in this remote suite, she felt totally isolated from the rest of the house and its people, and for several minutes the impression of being alone and vulnerable almost overwhelmed her. The men in the truck knew they could find her under this roof, and it would take only cursory reconnaissance for them to locate her quarters.

"Stupid," she muttered, tugging her mind away from her fears, which she knew were more than half paranoid, driven solely by anxiety and unfulfilled expectations. Chances were that those men had simply stumbled onto a golden opportunity to exhibit their raging immaturity, done so, and then gone on their way, never to be seen by her again. Most likely, they had forgotten all about her and were already plotting their next act of juvenile brilliance.

From far away, somewhere beyond the sounds of forest life, the breeze blew a sorrowful dirge, its voice a soft, feminine moan that rose and fell rhythmically, the trees rustling as they danced beneath its breath. Then a muted train whistle rose in melancholy harmony, and Courtney shivered, not from the slight chill in the air but from the exotic blend of sounds, which suggested wildness, or ancientness. The distant whistle, rather than signifying the presence of other human beings, seemed too lonely, intensifying her impression that that the dense, urban world she had always known had been swept from existence and replaced by a vast, primal sphere in which she was no more significant than an ant. In her life, she didn't think she had ever felt so *small*.

Then she heard something new: a low whimper, like a dog in pain, gradually growing louder, rising to a pitiful yet unnerving wail. Even as her senses sharpened to analyze the noise, the wail modulated itself into a warbling aria, which grew shriller and wilder every second, until it sounded like *"Gyah, gyah, hikari oh nyah,"* repeated in a demented refrain. Her heart lurched and began to race.

Then realization dawned, and she sighed heavily as her tension broke with an almost palpable jolt.

"Aunt fucking Martha."

For some time, the old woman howled, her voice plaintive, piercing, and maddening, impossible to shut out. And Courtney thought that if she had a gun at this moment, she would be oh-so-tempted to go upstairs and use it.

Trying hard to concentrate on the comparatively soothing voices of the night creatures in the background, she turned out the light and slipped into her bed, its sheets pleasantly cool until her body heat began to warm them. As she lay there, the old woman's voice gradually became less jarring and more hypnotic, having settled into a bizarre but rhythmic trilling, like a recording of an operatic solo played in reverse. The notion that Martha might have once overindulged in LSD or some such mind-altering substance revived a touch of Courtney's humor.

Martha's insane voice began to wind down like an old phonograph, and Courtney had actually managed to relax a little when something snapped her back to her senses.

A low, masculine mumble, just outside her window.

The old woman's voice revved up again, issuing a staccato burst of nonsensical syllables.

And the other voice answered.

A deep, rumbling gush of glossolalia, coming from so close behind her head that the speaker might have been in the room with her.

Her heart slammed into overdrive, and she sat up, throwing back the covers, uncertain exactly what she intended to do. For many tense seconds, she sat rigidly, dreading the idea of looking out the window into the unfathomable void, but knowing she could not restrain herself.

The voice seemed too *big,* too voluminous, to come from any man, yet she knew it was no animal. The indecipherable syllables could only be the product of a human tongue. And the voice responded to Martha as if the speaker understood her. Courtney couldn't claim to know any languages other than Spanish and a smattering of French and German, but she would wager everything that the utterances flowing from beyond the window belonged to no language that any sane human being had ever spoken.

At last, silence fell, and, for uncountable minutes, neither voice spoke. Unable to resist the compulsion, she steeled her nerves, propped herself on her elbows, and peered through the gap in the curtains, wondering if the darkness of her room were sufficient to conceal her from the view of anyone watching her window. As her eyes adjusted, she made out the vague shapes of tree trunks and branches limned by pale moonlight, and a few stars in the tiny purple patch overhead. She could see nothing else — for which she was mostly grateful — yet her tingling nerves assured her that the masculine speaker still lurked close to the house.

She had just about resolved to give up and try to get some sleep when she detected movement off to the left. Nothing distinct; just a slow, subtle shifting in the darkness. She focused her eyes on that spot, and after several seconds, she made out *something* there — a thin sliver of pale mist hovering above the ground, drifting from left to right at the edge of the narrow strip of yard. Very slowly, the thing began to expand, to widen, and now she could make out some pale mass, almost shapeless, but possessing unsettling contours that came gradually clearer as the thing moved toward her window.

A tall, milky blob, with two dark, suggestive cavities in its center.

Jesus God, it was a face, a fucking face, and it was getting closer and bigger, its dark sockets fixed on her like the empty eyes of a skull.

She jerked herself away from the window and collapsed on her backside, stunned, revolted, disbelieving. After many moments, when the keening of her nerves had dulled a little, her rational mind goaded her to look again, to accept that something had fooled her senses, to understand that the thing could *not* have been what it appeared. Shock, however, refused to release her muscles, holding her frozen in place, while her thundering heartbeat and labored breathing drowned any further sounds from outside.

So this is terror, she thought. She had never felt such a thing, not even when her husband had murdered her daughter and destroyed her life. Back then, she had known horror, bitter sadness, helplessness, and — ultimately — a deep-rooted, long-lasting rage. Whatever fear she had known, it had been an altogether different brand; a grim but recognizable product of events spiraling out of control and dragging her with them.

Here and now, something dark and frigid had touched her soul.

No. This had to be a trick. A mirage. A joke.

David.

Yes. Even less mature than he seemed — or as demented as Aunt Martha — he must have undertaken to prey upon her already fragile nerves. A childish prank. Or a willful act of cruelty.

Men were so often cruel.

Rage. A fury born of fear, yet much more potent, restored her volition, her mobility. It was her demon, but also her lifeline.

She rose from her bed and stumbled toward the fireplace. She knew there was a poker in the metal stand on the hearth, and she felt her way around until her fingers closed on its cold, solid handle. As she removed it, she jostled the stand, which made a hideous rattle, but it didn't fall over, and then she was rushing recklessly in the direction of the door, now absolutely determined to face — and punish — any soul with the wherewithal to even think of victimizing her again.

She tore open her door, the hallway beyond illuminated only by an anemic light that threaded its way from the distant kitchen, and headed straight to the back door, swearing in her heart that she *would* use her weapon, whether it was David out there or one of those bug-eyed hicks who had taken such an interest in her this morning.

She fumbled with the latch for a moment, and then she was standing on the narrow stoop, facing a barrier of near-total darkness, the shimmering light from the crescent moon and ember-like stars barely filtering down through the dense tree branches. A chill had seeped into the late summer air, and that perpetual, distant gale still whispered through the forest.

Nothing and no one appeared to be moving nearby. But now she realized that if she felt exposed inside her room, out here, even if not wholly defenseless, she was susceptible to assault by any predator, human or otherwise. Fear surged up again to displace her rage, her power.

My God, she thought, I'm out here with *it*.

Bravado gone, her entire body seemed to wilt, leaving her once again small and ineffectual in a vast, lightless chasm.

What could she have been thinking?

Her hand reached back for the door handle and fell on its cold, reassuring surface. Shoving it open, she backed into the vaguely lit hallway, only then realizing what a perfect silhouette her body presented to any eyes watching her from the darkness.

She was just about to close and bolt the door when she heard a slow thumping in the yard, only a few feet away. A deliberate and insanely heavy tread, like sledgehammers pounding the earth, moving steadily toward her, but she could make out nothing. *Nothing*.

"Courtney?"

She whirled around to see David standing in the hall, his eyes on the poker clenched in her dread-tensed fingers. Her immediate reaction was relief that he was not the one outside. She could hear the heavy footsteps retreating in the darkness.

How could she have even thought he might be responsible?

"Did you hear it?" she asked.

"Hear what?"

"Something outside. Someone."

"I heard you at the door." He pointed to her weapon. "You looking to build a fire out there?"

"There were terrible noises. Voices."

He raised an eyebrow. "In the backyard?"

"Right outside my window."

"Martha was at it again. I was afraid she might have disturbed you."

"Not just Martha. Someone else. I heard another voice. And there were footsteps."

He took a step toward her and placed a gentle hand on her shoulder. "You're shaking."

She could tell from his expression that he was both concerned about her and a hair's breadth from making a wise remark. "I did hear someone else.

Calling out gibberish just like Martha."

He shook his head dubiously. "I don't see how anyone could match Martha in the meaningless noise department."

"I saw something, too," she blurted and then wished she hadn't. How could she describe the misty thing that had drifted through the darkness, so indistinct and yet so awful, and make him believe her?

David just stared at her questioningly.

She waved her free hand in agitation. "I don't know what it was. A shape. I thought it was a face."

"A face."

She nodded. "Big. Indistinct. I don't know what it was. But I saw it."

"Look, Martha's carrying on would rattle anybody's nerves. I'm sorry about that. One of us should have warned you that she goes off the deep end sometimes."

"David, what's wrong with her?"

"Dementia, I guess. Most times, she's quite lucid, even if she's a pain in the ass. But sometimes…well, you've heard it for yourself."

"Then someone else is just as demented as she is."

"You're sure about this?"

"You didn't hear another voice?"

"All I heard was Martha. And you, going out the door. Look, I was in the kitchen. If someone else was shouting out there, I'd have heard it."

Her shoulders slumped, and she sighed heavily. She believed he was telling the truth. *Why would he lie?*

"It must have been one of those men from the truck."

"Let's not get paranoid. Look, if it'll make you feel better, I'll check outside the house and make sure no one's hanging around." He pointed to her poker. "And I can do better than that to protect myself."

"No," she said. "Whoever it was, they went off into the woods."

"In the pitch dark?"

"I heard their footsteps. Just as you came to the door. And you didn't hear them? Are you serious?"

He gave her a long, thoughtful look. "All right. I'll take your word for it that someone was out there. But they're gone now."

"I think so."

"Well then. I guess you should try to get some sleep."

"Sleep. Right."

"Try."

She sighed again. "I'll try."

He turned slowly toward the kitchen, then stopped. His eyes met hers and for the first time, she saw something resembling true compassion. He took a deep breath. "I don't suppose you'd want me to stay…with you…tonight… would you?"

Her heart clanged deafeningly in her ears, and for so many long moments, it thudded *yes, yes, yes*.

At last, she shook her head, and very firmly said, "No. I would not."

Unfazed, his typical wry smile returned. "Then I'll see you tomorrow."

"Good night."

"You're quite safe here, you know."

She watched him walk down the hall and noticed that he snickered a little bit to himself, perhaps at having worked up the nerve to invite himself into her room in the first place, but more likely in egotistical surprise at her refusal.

Yes. The latter did seem the more probable explanation.

#

Chapter 5

"David said you thought you saw something outside last night."

"I didn't think it. I saw it."

"Okay, you saw it. A big misty face?"

"It looked like a face."

"Turn around."

Courtney complied, and Jan squirted a generous blob of suntan lotion into her palm and began rubbing it onto Courtney's back. Its moist coolness and the warmth of Jan's hands felt heavenly, and she breathed a little sigh of ecstasy as Jan massaged her shoulders, methodically working her way down to her middle back. Rolling clouds occasionally obscured the sun, but just now, its gaze was roasting hot, and the combination of heat and Jan's touch nearly sent her swooning.

When Jan said, "All done," she settled herself on her stomach, her fingers scrunching the soft sand beneath her blanket, sensual pleasure crowding out most of the dread that had lingered like unmelting ice in her gut since the previous night. After the initial disturbing events, the night had passed quietly, but she had slept little, and so decided against running this morning — rather to David's chagrin. She had nearly forgone the beach trip as well, hoping to catch up on some rest, but Jan had convinced her to come as planned, and now she was glad she had. It was Jan's favorite spot: a little strip south of Nags Head, where only a few houses peered out from beyond the dunes and a scant handful of people populated the beach. From somewhere nearby, techno music thumped rhythmically from bass-heavy speakers, but it was smooth and mellow, and Courtney found it nearly as soothing as Jan's massaging fingers.

"You know," Jan said, propping her chin on her hands as she lay on her blanket, "not to trivialize your experience, but the ground mist coming out of the woods at night can be disconcerting. With Aunt Martha yowling at the same time, your senses might be…fooled."

"Not to trivialize your rationalization, but I did hear *another* voice. Not just Martha's."

Jan stared at her, pursing her lips in either contemplation or frustration. "All right. Let's say for argument's sake that those men from the truck did come back. They go around the house and hear Aunt Martha squalling. They mimic her just to be cruel."

The way Jan related it, the scenario sounded so improbable that even

Courtney felt inclined to dismiss it out of hand. Yet in the absence of logical alternatives, it seemed the explanation that most closely matched the evidence of her senses.

Except for the footsteps. Those slamming, heavy footsteps, which had retreated into the woods at the end of it all. She could hardly buy that even someone ill-intentioned enough to come prying around the house would stomp into that unplumbed darkness with no light to see by. It was so beyond foolhardy as to be implausible.

"Okay, I know it sounds silly," she finally said. "But I heard what I heard."

"I'm not doubting that. I see your gears turning, though. You have some other explanation?"

"Um, that your place is haunted?"

"But you don't believe in ghosts."

"I guess that's a problem."

Jan chuckled. "Look, don't dwell on it. I know you were scared. But David told me he's going to do some checking around. If anybody's looking to mess with you, then he'll get to the bottom of it. Trust me on this."

"I guess I'll have to."

"Yes, you do."

Courtney smiled, knowing that Jan had her best interests at heart. Here in the bright daylight, with the cheerful sound of rolling waves and mellow music playing in the background, last night's dread finally seemed far away, almost unreal. In her life, she had never doubted her senses or her convictions, but in the past few months, so many things had changed, and all so horribly, that she wasn't certain whether she could still rely on the foundations her old perceptions had built.

After a time, Jan said, "I know you probably haven't given it much thought yet. But I think you'll be able to find decent work in Elizabeth City. The economy's pretty good there. It's only twenty miles from our place. If you find a job there, you can stay with us until you can afford your own place."

"I appreciate that," she said. "Maybe in the next day or two I'll go up and start looking around. See what the prospects are."

"Well, it's not Atlanta, of course. But at least here you have a place to stay and you won't go hungry. We might even be able to help you out with an apartment for a few months, if necessary."

"God no, I couldn't ask that," Courtney said. "You've done so much for me, just taking me in like this."

Jan gazed at her warmly for a few moments. "It's because I love you."

Courtney couldn't keep from blushing a little. "Yeah. You too."

"Hey," Jan said, her eyes narrowing. "I really shouldn't say anything. But I think you've got David pretty well captivated."

"Oh," she said with a deepening frown. "I'm not sure that's good." But her heart sped up a little.

"Well, I can see why you'd be hesitant. Still, rest assured, he wouldn't take your safety lightly. He said he was going to make sure nobody bothers you. You can depend on his word."

"That's good to know."

"David has a good heart," Jan said. "But he's got a lot of growing up to do. Before Mom and Dad died, he was really spoiled. He's used to having his own way, and he does what it takes to get it."

"Somehow, that doesn't surprise me."

"Well, not that it's entirely my business...but I'd strongly recommend you don't encourage him. Otherwise, you're liable to get in over your head."

"I can see that too."

"Bear in mind, I didn't say the first word to you about this."

"Not a word." Courtney smiled and laid her head on her crossed forearms, closing her eyes as divine warmth poured down on her from above. Jan was probably right; last night, her perceptions had been skewed, her eyes deceived by shapes in the evening mist. However, none of that changed the fact that someone, almost certainly those two in the pickup truck, had come calling for purposes that couldn't have been benign. Jan wanted her to trust that David could put a stop to any further such incidents, and she wanted to believe. She almost did believe.

Only almost. Too many wrongs in too short a time had crushed her faith in others, even those who cared about her. Though she didn't like to think about it, in reality, David probably cared more about her body than about *her*. Such was the way of men.

"Hey."

It was an unfamiliar voice. Male. Courtney and Jan lifted their heads at the same time to see a young man with dark, unkempt hair and too many tattoos standing before them, his murky chocolate eyes fixed on something at sea.

"Hello back," Jan said.

He smiled, somewhat nervously, and tugged at the scruffy growth on his chin. "Hey, um, my friend and me, we just wondered if you'd liked to come hang with us. We got our towels and stuff over there." He pointed down the beach a short distance, where another character, slightly more heavyset but otherwise nearly identical, offered them a perfunctory wave. Both looked to be in their early twenties; Courtney guessed that the heavyset fellow had dared his friend to approach the pair of slightly more mature women.

Courtney and Jan exchanged amused looks. Then Jan smiled coyly and said, “What’s your name, hon?”

“Tim. Tim Hoffman.”

“Well, Tim, that’s nice of you. But my friend here tends to be a corrupting influence on young men. I’m not sure you want to be exposed to that kind of negative energy.”

Courtney’s jaw dropped, uncertain whether to laugh or cringe. The lines rolled too glibly from Jan’s tongue.

Tim Hoffman’s eyes focused briefly on Jan’s, then returned to staring vacantly. “Huh?”

“She’d be bad for you.” She gave Courtney a stern look. “Very bad. Come to think of it, she’s bad for me, too.”

“We wouldn’t really have a problem with that,” Tim said with a little snicker.

“Oh, you’d have a problem. Several, even.”

Half to play along with Jan and half to do anything but encourage the young man, Courtney glared sullenly into the distance, avoiding eye contact with either him or his friend. She did not intend to speak, if she could help it.

“So what’s y’all’s names?” the fellow asked.

“I’m Sunny and she’s Dreama.”

“Sunny and Dreama? That’s not for real.”

“It is too. She’s my much older sister.”

“Really?”

“Really.” Jan nudged Courtney. “Aren’t you, dah-ling?”

She nodded desultorily, wishing Jan would just brush off the young man and not play games with him. At the same time, she had to bite her lip to keep from bursting into laughter.

“So you wanna come hang out with us? We’re cool.”

“I’m sure you are. But we’re not going to be here too much longer, so I think Deena and I will just keep each other company. Thanks for asking, though.”

“I thought her name was Dreama.”

“Yeah, that’s what I said.”

“It sounded like…ah, never mind.”

“All right.”

“So, like, you’re sure you don’t wanna? We got some beer and stuff…”

“No. But thanks just the same, Tom.”

“It’s Tim.”

"I said Tim. Didn't I?"

"Nah. You said Tom."

"No way." She looked back at Courtney. "Tippy, what did I just call him?"

Rolling her eyes, she sighed and then said between gritted teeth, "Fred. You called him Fred."

Jan snorted. "Oh. Damn."

For a long, uncomfortable moment, Tim stood wearing his most puzzled expression, but finally, with an embarrassed laugh, he started shambling back toward his companion. "Whatever. You two aren't right. But that's cool. Y'all are cool."

"Thanks, hon. Enjoy yourselves." She gave him a parting wave before turning back to Courtney. "Let 'em down easy, I always say. You know, I — hey, what's wrong?"

As she had pulled her gaze away from Tim Hoffman and set it on the houses beyond the nearest dunes, Courtney noticed a flash of red — a vehicle moving on the road on the other side of the houses. It was just a flash, but in that moment, a distant pair of eyes met hers, and she recognized them, and saw a glint of recognition. Then they were gone.

No. She was mistaken. She *had* to be mistaken. It was an hour's drive back to Fearing, and nobody could have followed them here. Her mind had transformed a quick glimpse of someone inside a truck into something more ominous. That was all.

"What is it?"

She shook her head absently, listening to her pulse thudding in her ears. Since arriving at the Blackburns, her perceptions had all gone topsy-turvy. "Nothing."

"That's not a nothing look."

"Red truck went by. Bad association, I guess."

"This has really messed up your mind, hasn't it? It's so not like you."

"Yeah, I know. I guess I'm just still on edge. I'm sorry."

"You're here to relax. Get off it, will you?"

She smiled weakly. "All right, all right. I'm off it."

Jan rolled her eyes in exaggerated irritation and, with a deep sigh, laid her head back onto her crossed arms. "You're still a mess. I can see that my work is cut out for me."

"Your back's getting cooked."

"Good," she mumbled. "Better than being rare."

"Your brain is cooked, too."

"Not until later tonight," Jan said with a little laugh

Courtney also laughed, but she noticed that, now and again, Jan's eyes flickered toward the road, and her tanned knuckles paled as her fingers occasionally clenched and unclenched on the towel. Her laughter had sounded a tad nervous as well.

Jan was brushing things off perhaps too adroitly, she thought. And after the way her friend had handled Tim Hoffman, Courtney couldn't help but wonder whether she might have recently taken up acting.

#

On the drive home, they barely spoke to each other. Courtney couldn't stop glancing back, ever anxious to glimpse a red vehicle following some distance behind. When she actually did catch sight of one, her heart clambered up to her throat — though the truck turned out to be a much newer, brightly painted Dodge Ram. However, she could not fail to notice that Jan also kept one eye on the rearview mirror, and her silence seemed more a sign of nervousness than of merely being tired, as she claimed when Courtney asked if everything was all right.

When they arrived back at the Blackburn house in the late afternoon, Jan immediately retired upstairs and Courtney went to her suite to shower away the clinging sand and freshen up for the evening. Jan hadn't indicated whether they had any special plans for dinner, but Courtney hoped they could just stay home and relax, the day in the sun having sapped much of her energy. A chilly wind had begun blowing again, possibly threatening a new storm, and she didn't care for the prospect of going out in bad weather.

She pulled on jeans and a T-shirt and then went out to the great room, half-expecting to find Jan waiting for her, with a drink already poured. The room was empty, however. The whole house seemed abnormally quiet, as no sounds of life drifted down from the upper floors. Evidently, David had gone out somewhere, and of Martha, naturally, there was no sign. Curiosity now impelled Courtney to climb the stairs and check out the second floor. She had only been up here once, when Jan had first shown her around the house, and she didn't remember whether Jan's door was the first one on the left or on the right. Softly, she called Jan's name. When she received no answer, she went to the door on the left and knocked.

"Jan?"

Only silence replied, so she took hold of the knob and gave the door a tentative push. It opened with soft groan, and she realized immediately that she had discovered David's room. It was large, easily the size of her entire suite, its décor the definition of masculine. The walls were painted pale gray, trimmed with white. The bed was full-size, with a heavy, dark wood headboard and footboard, the mattress covered by a black, satin-finished comforter, the pillows wrapped in shimmery silver pillowcases. A black leather recliner faced a huge, widescreen, high-definition television, and there was a desk in the far corner with a large computer monitor atop it. Bookshelves occupied one wall, and she felt a moment's compulsion to steal inside and take a closer look at his preferred reading material, but she forbore. All in all, a very tasteful room, remarkably neat for a young man's living quarters.

Arlene's work, no doubt.

Okay, she thought, Jan's had to be the *other* door. She crossed the hall and tapped softly, expecting no answer. Without hesitating, she pushed the door open and saw Jan, naked except for her underwear, lying on her stomach atop her gold-quilted, four-post bed. Her face was turned toward the door, her eyes closed, her still-damp hair spilling over the pillow and off the edge of the bed. She looked to be in deep sleep, so Courtney decided not to disturb her. But as she stepped backward, just before drawing the door shut, she noticed a little glimmer on Jan's cheek, and realized that tears were leaking from her eyes and pooling on the pillow beside her face.

Dreaming of her parents, perhaps, or her fiancé — or both, Courtney thought. She had wondered about the severity of Jan's emotional wounds, her humor having seemed so forced, particularly since yesterday. Two separate accidents, three deaths; all the people who meant the most to Jan, in so short a time.

More than coincidence?

Given the distinct atmosphere of hostility that seemed to surround the Blackburns, the idea seemed anything but farfetched.

She returned to the stairs and started down, thinking a little catnap of her own might do some good, but then something stopped her. As she stood there, she looked up, into the shadows of the ascending staircase, which led to Aunt Martha's floor, and before she realized what she was doing, she had climbed up to the third floor. She found herself facing a short, windowless hallway with three doors — one on each side and one at the end. The only light came from the downstairs windows, and shadows as dark as night swallowed the far end of the hall. The air felt stagnant and reeked of mothballs and Listerine.

Martha, no doubt, was sequestered behind one of these doors, but not a single creak or whisper betrayed any living presence on this floor. Maybe she was one of those old people who slept all day and rambled around at night, Courtney thought; she certainly knew how to make an abominable racket during the wee hours. For an instant, Courtney entertained the idea of standing outside one of the doors and breaking into one of her infamous barroom impersonations of Lady Gaga, just to see how the old woman enjoyed having her sleep disturbed. Better judgment prevailed, but the idea did appeal to her sense of the perverse. Perhaps more than it should have.

A thin, barely discernible strip of light split the shadows at the base of the far door, which, to the best of her reckoning, led to a room that faced the rear of the house —Martha's living quarters, most likely. Again, almost of their own volition, her feet carried her down the hall to the door, where she stopped and pressed herself against the wall, ears keen for any sound from the other side. She half-expected to hear the old woman snoring, but after many long seconds, the silence remained unbroken.

Good sense pleaded with her to march right back downstairs, but impulsive curiosity — which she recognized as an unwelcome and virtually irremediable holdover from her youth — was guiding her hand toward the door handle, and no effort of will could pull it back. Her fingers closed on the cold metal and tentatively twisted it.

The door swung open to reveal a dim chamber, lit only by the feeble sunbeams that struggled in through dingy diaphanous curtains over a pair of small, leaded glass windows. The most striking thing she noticed was a grandfather clock whose case resembled nothing so much as an intricately carved coffin standing on its end, tucked into the corner nearest the door. She could also see an ancient, rickety-looking Boston rocker, covered with moldy, threadbare cushions, and a huge, dust-filmed dresser backed by a tall mirror. Taking a deep breath to steady her nerves, she craned her neck and peered around the door, half-certain she would find Martha standing there, glaring at her with those watery, unblinking eyes, but to her relief, the room was unoccupied. However, two other things stood out as extraordinary: the bed, which was a huge construct of dark wood paneling and red silk curtains, the mattress supported by a web of thick, knotted ropes; and a collection of empty soft drink cans that Courtney could only regard as staggering. Dozens of them, of all varieties, on the nightstand, on the mantelpiece above the fireplace, on the windowsills, on the bookshelves. She took a few steps into the room and noticed a stale, sour odor, like old urine, which briefly caused her stomach to lurch.

She knew she had no business in the old woman's room, but she couldn't deny an almost juvenile exhilaration at having crossed a forbidden threshold and found something unique, even if relatively unspectacular. She didn't know what she might have expected to find, but the ungodly number of empty cans around the room was enough to convince her that Martha might be even less stable than she had guessed. Obsessive-compulsive, perhaps — and very likely hyperglycemic.

She listened intently to the dead air to assure herself no one was approaching, then moved to Martha's huge bureau, taking stock of the ancient personal items cluttering its top: an ivory-backed hairbrush, its bristles choked with gray, web-like strands; a closed jewelry box, its tarnished silver top in dire need of polish; and a cluster of perfume bottles, so choked with dust that she couldn't even read the labels. When she raised her eyes, the smudged, slightly warped mirror above the bureau reflected an image of pure foolishness.

Oh, this is wrong. This is not me. Why am I doing this?

Her every nerve screamed at her to leave now, while her crime was nothing worse than simple trespassing. The impulse that had brought her here, however, seemed more than loath to release her.

She went to the nearest window and brushed aside the old, brittle drape to peer through the thick glass. From here, she could see the roof of her wing, which extended away to the left, and the dense woods that encircled the rear of the house. If Martha were to open this window and "sing," her voice would easily carry as far as Courtney's suite.

So what did the old witch have in her head when she babbled and wailed to the dark night? If some stranger had crept into the backyard and begun jabbering back at her, would even an addled woman not consider it peculiar?

She could still barely accept that as an explanation for what she had heard.

"Well, if it's not a blooming busybody."

The old woman's voice jolted her for a second, but then her shoulders slumped and she sighed heavily before turning to face the chamber's oddball inhabitant. It should not have been such a struggle to bring a contrite look to her face.

"I'm sorry," Courtney said, bowing her head slightly. "I knocked, but curiosity got the better of me. I apologize."

The old woman stood framed in the doorway, her narrow eyes studying Courtney as they might an unusual-looking insect. "I should have known a fancy girl like you would have no respect for closed doors. I'd wager that if you found me rummaging around in your room, you'd have yourself a nice little snit, wouldn't you?"

"I suppose I would."

"No 'suppose' about it."

"Anyway, I wasn't rummaging. I was just looking out the window."

Martha's face split into a grotesque grin, exposing a too-perfect row of pearl-white teeth. Courtney heard a sloshing sound, and the woman held up a bulging hot water bottle, from which long white tube extended and curled around one thin hand. "Don't get wise with me, girl, or I will administer this enema. To you."

Courtney's stomach quivered. "Um, no, thank you."

Martha took another step toward her, glaring with her terrible violet eyes, the grin never leaving her face. "You'll learn not to trifle with me. One drop of your name to the Monarch, and, oh, what a sad day it will be for you. I'll do it, you know."

"Excuse me?"

"Oh, yes. A sad day it will be. It wouldn't be the first, either. You know that, don't you?"

Courtney backed up, increasingly unnerved by Martha's stare. "No, I don't know what you mean. Look, I'm sorry. I shouldn't have come here."

"And why did you? To wish me good day, perhaps?"

She shook her head, unwilling to lie to the woman. "Because I heard you calling out from your window last night. I was curious about why."

"David told you that I enjoy singing. Did that not satisfy you?"

"I just thought there might be more to it than that."

"There is. Much more. But the point remains — your intentions were not honorable, girl. Were they?"

Tears were actually beginning to well in her eyes. She shook her head again. "No. I'm sorry. I'm very sorry."

The grin left Martha's face. "Not as sorry as you will be. Now get out."

Without another word or last look back, Courtney turned and went out the door, heading quickly for the stairs, cursing under her breath at her own stupidity.

Behind her, the old woman's door slammed shut with the force of an explosion.

#

Chapter 6

With tears blurring her vision and her shame-reddened face lowered to the floor, Courtney nearly collided with Arlene as she rounded the corner of the hall that led to her suite.

"Whoa there, Ms. Edmiston," the older woman said, whirling out of Courtney's path and throwing out a hand to keep her balance. "Careful! My bones are more brittle than yours."

"Oh, excuse me," she said, looking up in surprise and wiping her eyes with the back of her hand. "I didn't expect anyone to be back here."

"Had some dusting to do. Hey, what's the matter with you?"

Courtney drew a deep breath to steady herself. "Nothing I can't deal with. Thank you."

Arlene's eyes narrowed. "Only old Martha could make anyone that upset."

"It was my fault," she said softly. "I was stupid and upset her."

"You don't have to do anything stupid to upset that old biddy, Ms. Edmiston."

She gave Arlene a weak smile. "Oh, it was stupid, all right. I should have known better. What am I saying? I did know better."

"Oh, my. You went up there, didn't you?"

She nodded. "I guess nosiness got the better of me."

"Old Martha doesn't take kindly to anybody trespassing on her floor, no ma'am."

"It was worse than that. I went into her room."

"Oh, Ms. Edmiston. Oh, no."

"Please. Call me Courtney."

"All right, Courtney. From the looks of you, Martha must have had a rectangular spasm."

She couldn't help but chuckle. "If you mean did she let me have it, I'll say she did."

Arlene frowned, but her eyes were kind. "Listen. She's a temperamental old thing, as you've well discovered. I'd steer clear of her, or she'll go out of her way to make your life miserable. Don't think she won't."

"I believe it. Like I said, it was my fault. I knew better, and I went on and did it anyway." She laughed wryly. "Not like I haven't done *that* before."

"I'm sure you've learned your lesson."

She nodded and then gave Arlene a searching look. "Hey. Martha said something about 'the Monarch.' Do you know what she was talking about?"

The black woman's eyes widened. "She said that to you?"

"Yes."

"Mercy. She wouldn't do that unless she was some kind of angry."

"So what's it mean?"

Arlene took a deep breath. "The Monarch. It's an old folk tale. Supposed to be something…something terrible…that lives out in the swamp. She used to tell stories about it to frighten David and Jan when they were just young'uns. Nowadays, she brings it up when something has her all upset. It's a bunch of nonsense, but if she's carrying on about it, that woman's on the warpath."

"She said that if she told it my name, it would be a sad day."

"My goodness!"

"I know she's a bit oddball," Courtney said. "But I couldn't help getting the feeling she was completely sincere."

"Yeah, she's sincere. Sincerely hateful. Like I said, you'd do well to avoid her. She'll be happier and so will you."

Courtney nodded thoughtfully and started toward her room. "You're not the first person to tell me that. Well. Thanks for listening. You're a nice person."

"So are you, I'm sure," Arlene said with a smile. "I expect you should try using better judgment, though."

"You can count on that."

Arlene went on her way, and Courtney returned to her room, feeling somewhat less burdened now that she had confessed her sin to Arlene. The old housekeeper seemed very sweet — the Anti-Martha, she thought with a little giggle.

Then, as she glanced out her window toward the deep woods, her mood turned somber, for shadows were falling fast, and the wind was picking up again. She pulled the drapes together as far as they would go. It wouldn't do to have "the Monarch" looking in at her, now would it?

She froze at the thought, remembering the weird voice that had seemingly responded to Martha's gibberish, the indistinct but ghastly "face" that had peered in through her window, the absurdly heavy footfalls heading into the woods at the end of it all.

What kind of incredible thing was loose in this place?

There was another prospect, far less incredible but hardly more comforting: that certain twisted individuals were perpetuating some horrific trickery, for purposes she couldn't fathom. If so, Martha was not acting alone.

While Courtney could not desire for one instant to return to the conditions from which she had fled, neither could she have anticipated stumbling into such a daunting, perhaps even perilous environment as this one. She could never doubt Jan's intentions for bringing her here, but she did have to question her friend's timing and prudence. Surely, whatever was happening had commenced before her arrival, and now, like it or not, events had overtaken and ensnared her.

Trespassing in Martha's territory certainly hadn't helped; if anything, it had served to bring her into the light of the old woman's scrutiny, where she might have otherwise passed unnoticed.

"God, stop the bus, I want to get off," she whispered to herself.

Usually when she was upset she preferred to be alone, but now, under the circumstances, she hoped Jan would wake up and come downstairs soon. With any luck, she could tell her side of the story before Martha spun it her own way. At any rate, Jan would be the first to understand, for they had both committed their share of indiscretions — oftentimes together — back in their glory days. Such as sneaking into the Pike fraternity house and depositing a few exotic undergarments in strategic places, resulting in more than one serious relationship turning precarious. In the grand scheme of things, her latest offense seemed so trivial; yet this was the Blackburn's domain, and Courtney was a guest, who had no business upsetting any member of the household, no matter her personal feelings.

She heard footfalls and some rustling somewhere down the hall, probably in the kitchen, and she started out the door, thinking it might be Jan, or even David. But the possibility that Martha had ventured forth stopped her, and she stood at threshold, indecisive, absolutely unwilling to face that old woman and her temper again so soon. It wasn't dinnertime yet, though, so it was unlikely she would have already come down. Probably just Arlene, preparing to start dinner.

How silly to be so intimidated. If anything, she should just carry on as if nothing had happened, behave pleasantly around the old woman, and maintain a semblance of good humor. It was the best way to get past any bad feelings.

But her feet wouldn't move.

Somewhere beyond the door, the floor creaked. Someone was coming down her hall. It *must* be Jan, she thought. Martha had absolutely no reason to wander this way.

Gathering her nerve, she stuck her head out the door and, to her relief, saw David coming toward her, his smug little smile an oddly welcome sight. He was wearing black jeans and a gray button-down shirt, the top two buttons open, and his lightly bronzed face looked as if he had gotten some sun today. Her heart leaped just a little.

"Good afternoon." He glanced at his watch and raised an eyebrow. "Or evening, I should say. I hope I'm not intruding."

"No," she said, "not at all. What's up?"

"I noticed my sister was sound asleep. Wondered if you were awake or if you had crashed and burned as well."

"I'm awake. Doesn't mean I haven't crashed and burned."

"Well, you don't look much like a heap of charred wreckage." Then he gave her a long, thoughtful look, and she realized that her face probably still bore the traces of her tears. "Is everything all right?" he asked.

"Fine," she said, offering him a little smile. "It just wasn't the world's best afternoon ever."

"Sorry to hear it. You feel like feeling better?"

"How so?"

"Go to dinner with me."

"I take it you mean something other than sitting across from you at the dining room table."

"Something other, yes."

"Such as?"

"You have two choices."

"If we eliminate Tall Ships, that leaves one, right?"

"I didn't figure you'd want to go back there two nights in a row — especially given certain of the clientele. How does Woodard's grab you?"

"That's fancy, isn't it?"

"Fancier than Tall Ships. Not that that means a whole lot, as you might guess."

She tugged on the sleeve of her T-shirt. "I'd need to wear something nicer than this, right?"

"Wouldn't hurt."

"That sucks."

"Do it for me."

"What about Jan? Does she like Woodard's?"

"Jan is asleep."

"Doesn't mean I want to leave her behind."

"You could do that for me, too."

She could feel her face flushing. "I'm her friend. What would she think about me running off to have dinner without her?"

"She's a big girl. I'm sure she'll understand. Besides, once she's down, she's down for the count. She might not get up before tomorrow anyway."

"She would if one of us woke her."

"Now, this is just me, but if I were really her friend, I wouldn't want to wake her because disturbing her sleep would be unthinkably rude."

"Unthinkably, huh?"

"Yes."

"You're terrible. Do you know that?'

"Yes, I do."

Her face turned serious. "I don't know, David. I'm not sure it's such a good idea, just you and me."

He clasped his hands behind his back and stared at the floor for a moment, mulling things over. Then he nodded to himself and raised his eyes to hers. "Tell you what. I am going to have dinner at Woodard's tonight. I'll be ready to leave in forty-five minutes. If you decide you'd like to go too, meet me in the foyer, and we'll have an excellent dinner together. If not, then I'll have an excellent dinner without you. Your choice. No pressure."

"Forty-five minutes?"

He nodded. "Don't be late."

"Don't wait for me."

He offered her a curt bow, smiled, and then turned and disappeared down the hall in the direction of the kitchen.

"Damn it," she whispered. If she had one lick of good sense, she would go upstairs, wake Jan, and insist that she accompany them to dinner. That was the smart thing to do. However, it would also be rude. Unthinkably.

No pressure. Right.

She went to the closet and began to rummage through her clothes, thankful that she still possessed a reasonably decent wardrobe. After a full five minutes of indecision, she settled on a comfortable, floral-print wrap blouse and plain white cotton skirt, and then spent two more minutes pondering whether to go hose or no hose. *No hose*. Dressy casual was probably more than sufficient for fine dining in Fearing, North Carolina.

Confronting her surviving collection of shoes, after another couple of minutes' deliberation, she finally chose her pair of Ellen Tracy dress sandals.

"Stupid, impetuous twit," she muttered to herself.

#

Woodard's dining room wasn't busy — she would have been surprised if it was — and its sophisticated décor and menu struck her as dramatically out of place in a town whose number of wealthy residents could be counted on one hand and whose tourists numbered no more than could fill the tiny inn's guestrooms. Still, a dozen or so diners occupied other booths and tables, so dinner promised to be an intimate, though not entirely private affair.

Which suited her just fine.

Dark, Tudor-style beams and glowing sconces above the tables gave the dining room an old-world flavor she appreciated, and a single rose in a tall vase on the tabletop added a romantic flair. David had ordered a bottle of Cabernet Franc because he knew she preferred it, and she took an approving sip from her glass. "So," she said. "How does this place make money? Does your family have a hand in it, too?"

He chuckled. "No. Old man Woodard was in the shipping business. He made a fortune in Newport News, back in the sixties. This was how he occupied himself after retirement. He died a while back, but his sons keep the place running just because they enjoy it. They don't need to turn a profit."

"I see. Around here, the rich are really rich and the poor are really poor, aren't they?"

He shrugged. "Like a lot of places."

She sighed. "I never thought I'd be one of the poor."

"Courtney, as long as you're with us, you've got nothing to worry about. I promise you, Jan would never let you hurt for money." He smiled. "*I* wouldn't."

"How can you say that? You barely know me."

"That's not entirely true. You don't think Jan and I ever talk?"

"It's not the same."

"Still. You're more special to Jan than you know. So to me, you're special by proxy."

She laughed, but then gave him a solemn look. "You know, I don't want to be somebody's project. I've been self-sufficient for a long time. This is all still a blow to me."

"Look. I know you're not a charity case. But we're here to help you get back on your feet. You've got a cushion beneath you."

"And I appreciate everything you've both done." She then drew a long breath. "Though I don't guess I've shown it very well."

"Why do you say that?"

This was her chance to come clean about her run-in with Martha, and a cold lump rose slowly in her throat. Still, it was better for him to hear it from her first. After a bracing gulp of wine, in a measured, matter-of-fact tone, she proceeded to relate all that had happened since she and Jan had returned from the beach that afternoon. By the time she finished, her mouth was parched, and she drained her glass in a single swallow.

David stared at her for so long that she became uncomfortable, and the lump began reforming in her throat. Finally, he smiled reassuringly, though something in his eyes let her know he was troubled.

"You're right," he said. "It was a foolish thing to do. Aunt Martha values her privacy, maybe more than a rational person would understand. But it's easy to see why you'd be curious. Big house like ours, a secretive old witch upstairs. Given some of the things I've heard about you over the years, I'd say snooping was a foregone conclusion."

"Look, I came clean with you about today. Anything else you've heard about me, I deny it."

"How do you know it's bad?"

"Because I know your sister."

"Okay, so it's bad. Big deal."

They fell silent as their server — a young man with far better manners than Deena — approached to take their orders, and Courtney used the moment, with a little help from the wine, to allow her nerves to settle. At David's suggestion, she ordered a petite filet mignon, while he chose the heftier cut. When the waiter finished jotting the orders on his pad, he gave her an earnest smile and said to David, "Thank you, Mr. Blackburn. You two have a wonderful evening."

"Let me guess," Courtney said, as the young man left, "this dinner is 'covered' too?"

He grinned and patted his wallet. "Covered by American Express."

"I get the impression they like you better here than down the street."

"They're just paid more to be friendly here."

She shook her head in bewilderment. "This is so different than what I'm used to — the way you know everyone, and they know you. Even if they don't like you. That would bother me."

"They'll know you in no time, too. I can introduce you to the whole town in about an hour."

"I'm not complaining. I've always preferred anonymity."

"It may be too late for that."

She sighed, unhappy about the direction of the conversation. "So, David. Tell me about Aunt Martha's Monarch. Arlene was surprised she would bring it up to me."

"It's just a crazy story that woman used to tell us as children, to frighten us," David said, quickly and somewhat defensively. Then, with a little more reserve, he added, "She's just hoping to rattle you. In her eyes, you're no more than a child. Hell, Jan and I too, for that matter."

"Why is it called the Monarch?"

"Because it ruled the swamp, of course. A horrible, horrible thing. If it came for you, it would drag you away and impale your body on a tree, just to show everyone who was boss. It's probably some campfire story Martha herself heard when she was young." He chuckled. "As if she ever was."

"So what makes her so spiteful? Did she have issues with your parents?"

"She actually got on pretty well with Dad, though she never much liked Mom. Mom wasn't afraid to stand up to her."

"I guess she wouldn't like that, would she?"

"In Mom's case, it was a recipe for disaster," he said, his eyes taking on a faraway look. "There were many unpleasant nights in the house, not long before the end."

"I'm sorry. I didn't mean to bring up anything painful."

He made a dismissive gesture. "No, it's all right. All that is past now."

"Were you close to your parents? I know Jan was."

"We were once. In the last few years, things had gotten a bit…strained. Dad always expected me to carry on the business, but that was never for me."

"So, David, what is your calling? Or do you have one at all?" She challenged him with her gaze.

"Art. Computers. Graphic design in general. Despite what Aunt Martha says, I've done rather well with my commercial art. It's my fine art she doesn't get."

"How fine is it?"

"I dabble in abstract expressionism. I'd like to exhibit it someday. For the moment, though, things are kind of bleak on that front."

"That's a shame."

"Do you like art?"

She shrugged. "Not particularly. Certainly not abstracts. I prefer something that looks like something."

He chuckled. "I'll have to show you a few things. Maybe you'll change your mind."

"I wouldn't hold my breath."

David looked a tad bemused, but before he could say more, their server arrived with their salads, and the conversation died abruptly. Their entrées followed almost immediately, and Courtney forgot about everything else to enjoy one of the finest meals she'd had in years — certainly since Frank had destroyed everything in her world that meant anything to her. She had to admit that she was glad she had come. So far, David's company had been anything but unpleasant.

When they were finished, he asked if she cared for coffee, but she declined, too full for even a small cup. So he called for the check, and once he had paid it, they rose, and he escorted her to the door, one hand tentatively on her arm. As they stepped into the fresh, evening air, facing a picturesque inlet of the Moratok River, he gave her a hopeful smile.

"So, it wasn't so terrible having dinner with me, was it?"

She smiled back and shook her head. "No, it wasn't terrible."

"I didn't think you were going to come. What made you decide to chance it?"

She glanced down at her feet. "These shoes," she said. "They haven't been out for months."

"I hope they enjoyed themselves."

"I think they did."

He started to lead her around the building to the parking lot, but Courtney abruptly froze, one hand shooting out to grasp his arm.

"Jesus."

In the first parking space at the corner of the building, she saw a filthy red pickup truck and, next to it, two figures silhouetted by a streetlight at the far end of the lot. One was leaning against the truck, arms crossed belligerently, while the other — a shorter, huskier fellow — was chugging away at a bottle of beer. When he realized that Courtney and David were standing a few yards away, he tossed the bottle over his shoulder, and it bounced away in the parking lot with a sharp *bang-clank*. The two men exchanged brief glances and then began to advance.

Courtney's heart nearly exploded when she confirmed that the wide, leering eyes of the shorter man were the same lascivious eyes that had peered at her through the grimy windows of the pickup truck the morning before.

"That's them," she whispered.

"Take it easy," he said in a calm voice. "Nothing to worry about."

The taller of the two men stepped up to David, while the other circled around behind them, and she could feel his eyes crawling over her body. She saw that the first man had a long hunting knife sheathed at his belt. He was lanky, his clothes and face grimy. Probably in his early 20s.

"Evenin', Mr. Blackburn," he said, his voice as grating as a chainsaw. His eyes shifted to Courtney, and he gave her the lewdest of smiles. "Ma'am."

"And how can I help you gentlemen?" David asked, his voice soft but steady.

The man nodded at Courtney. "Who you got here? She's a new one, ain't she?"

"That's none of your concern."

"Well, now, I don't think that's quite for you to say, Mr. Blackburn. Let me tell you about my concern. Seems to me we had an agreement, and you've not done your part to honor it. Now have you?"

"I've got news for you, Ben. You and I have never had any agreement."

The man named Ben looked over David's shoulder at his companion. "Hear that, Hank? Now he says we got no agreement."

"Well, I reckon he's mistaken," came the voice from behind Courtney, a low tenor with a sharp nasal twang.

"Yeah, that's it. He's just mistaken. Well, then, Mr. Blackburn, we gonna have to get a few things straight. Right here and now, aren't we?"

To Courtney's horror, Ben reached for the knife at his belt. At the same time, she felt a hot, moist hand clutch the back of her neck, and a second later, something cold and sharp was pressing urgently against her right cheek. For a split-second, something glinted brightly at the corner of her eye.

A blade.

She felt pressure in her abdomen as her bowels knotted. My God, these men might kill her where she stood. It was happening so fast, she couldn't take it in.

"We gonna give you one chance to rectify your mistake," Ben said to David. "But one chance only. And if this bitch means anything at all to you, you ain't gonna want to blow it."

Terror was setting in rapidly now. *But faster and harder came the rage.*

"Relax," David said to the men, his voice still steady and under control. "Let's not be hasty here. You don't want to be hasty."

"But Mr. Blackburn, we've been the picture of patience for quite some time now. The waiting is over." Ben smirked at him.

The blade pressed a little more insistently against Courtney's cheek. A little voice was telling her to release her demon.

What did she really have to lose?

Hank must have felt her muscles tensing because he leaned in close and whispered in her ear, "You just stay real calm now, bitch. Don't even think about moving."

Her upper body relaxed a little, but her leg muscles remained coiled like tight-wound springs. If she could break his grip without him cutting her, even wearing her heels, she figured she could easily outrun the stubby little freak.

What about David? Could he escape as well?

"This is quite a mistake you're making," he said to the man named Ben. "You have no idea what you're getting yourself into."

Ben laughed harshly. "I think you got that exactly backwards."

Her rage now a blazing pyre, Courtney had almost convinced herself to make a move on the man and damn the consequences when the world around her seemed to become a blur.

Before she even realized what was happening, David had spun around and, from behind, delivered a powerful kick to the short man's knee, which dropped him like a sawn oak and sent his knife clattering away on the pavement. She felt David's hand grab her bicep, and with one seemingly effortless tug, he pulled her toward him, away from the fallen man and well out of Ben's reach. Then, in one smooth motion, he knelt, picked up Hank's knife, and brandished it at Ben, whose eyes now bulged in disbelief, his mouth agape.

"As I said," David said, his voice now so cold that Courtney barely recognized it, "you have no idea what you're getting into. I would suggest you go home now, and don't ever let me see you again." To punctuate his point, his right foot lashed out and connected solidly with Hank's gut, just as he was beginning to rise. The man collapsed again, this time with a deep grunt as the air gushed from his lungs.

Ben clutched his knife in one hand, and Courtney could see in his eyes how desperately he wanted to use it. But he apparently possessed only a fraction of David's nerve because his hand was trembling.

"Yeah," David said, mockingly. "You're one tough fellow when it's two of you against an unarmed couple. How about now? You want to come at me?"

Ben's surprise was giving way to anger. "You're gonna regret doing that, Mr. Blackburn."

"If anybody's going to regret anything, it's you. Now. I don't care what kind of arrangement you *thought* you had with me. You were wrong. So I suggest you take your sack of shit brother with you, and don't let me see you again. If I do, I won't be responsible for what happens to you. Are we quite clear on this, Ben?"

"You think you're gonna get away with this?"

"You think I'm not completely serious?"

At David's feet, Hank was groaning and beginning to rise. David backed up a few steps, pulling Courtney with him, to make sure Hank had no chance to make a surprise move on them. With a whine of pain, the short man pulled himself to his feet, his face a grimace, his eyes glaring hatefully at David.

"Give me my fucking knife back."

David snorted a laugh and gave the hunting knife a long, thoughtful look before slowly holding it out to Hank, haft first. Then, as Hank reached for it, David deftly flicked it up in the air, caught it by the handle, and jabbed its point deeply into Hank's palm. The short man screeched and jerked his hand away, spraying blood into the air, a few drops splattering Courtney's shoes. For a second, she thought Ben was going to charge them, but he remained in place when he realized David was still holding the knife, his eyes daring the other to make a move.

"Any questions?" David asked.

Hank remained doubled over, his punctured hand tucked under one arm, and he began to back away, evidently accepting his defeat. Finally, Ben slid his knife back into its sheath, grasped his brother's shoulder, and jerked him upright.

"Get your ass back in the truck," he growled. Then he looked at David. "You know this ain't over, Blackburn."

David's eyes narrowed. "For your sake, it had better be."

With a look so venomous that Courtney felt her gorge rising, Ben backed toward his truck, practically tripping over his brother, who was fumbling at the passenger door handle with his uninjured hand.

David leaned toward Courtney. "Let's head toward the car. Keep on the other side of these cars — just in case he gets reckless."

She nodded, her head reeling with delayed shock as they took a few steps toward David's car. His eyes remained locked on the pickup truck as Ben climbed in and started its engine. "Let me guess," she said. "You have rage issues too."

"Maybe a few."

"You were set to kill them, weren't you? I mean…if you had to."

"I don't think it would have come to that."

"You would have, though."

He gave a little shrug. "From where I was standing, I'd have said the same about you."

She watched the pickup truck with some apprehension as it slowly backed out of its space, its two occupants still glaring vengefully at them. "I don't know," she said. "I don't know about killing. But I think maybe I was ready to die, if it came down to it."

He turned his eyes to hers and studied them intently. "Talk about issues," he said at last. "I wouldn't have expected that from you."

"Why not? You know what I've lived through."

"Well, you don't know what I've lived through, and I can tell you with certainty that you're nowhere near ready to die."

David opened the passenger door for her, and when she fell into the front seat and tried to grasp the seatbelt, she found her hands trembling violently. As he slid behind the wheel, she said to him, "David, I don't care what the cops are like around here, we have to call them. We have to."

"Well, it sounds reasonable. But I'm going to advise against it."

"Why?"

He pointed toward the far corner of the parking lot, near the single streetlight. "Take a look over there."

Her gaze followed his pointing finger, and her heart nearly stopped when she saw, tucked into a space between a van and an SUV, a parked police cruiser, its occupant a mere silhouette but obviously watching them intently. She whipped her head back to David and said, "He was there the whole time, wasn't he? He saw everything that happened."

David nodded grimly. "That he did, my dear. That he did."

#

Chapter 7

"You knew who they were the moment I told you about that truck," Courtney said, pointing an accusing finger across the bar at David. "You knew exactly who they were."

David had poured himself a better-than-hefty tumbler of scotch, and he held it to his lips for a long moment to avoid answering her. When he did, he turned his eyes to the window. "I'm sorry. I didn't figure anything would come of it, and I didn't want to upset you needlessly."

"Yeah, well, consider me upset." She had already downed a full snifter of brandy and was working on her second.

Jan sat on the stool next to Courtney, her hands encircling a near-empty pilsner glass. She pulled one hand away from it to touch Courtney's shoulder. "Honey, those guys are mostly bluster. And it sounds like David taught them a lesson they're not soon going to forget." Her tone was heartening, but she turned to glare at her brother, plainly infuriated with his conduct.

"Bluster my ass," Courtney said. "I had a knife at my throat. Do you know what that feels like? That son of bitch was going to cut me."

"Not a chance," David said, ignoring his sister's withering stare. "They were out to scare us, that's all. They don't have the balls to do more than that."

Courtney heaved an exasperated sigh and clenched her fists atop the bar. "So, just who are those men? Would you tell me that?"

Jan said softly, "You met their father at Tall Ships last night."

"Surber, right? Dwayne Surber? Ben and Hank are his sons?"

She nodded. "They're all in it together."

"And Ray," David added. "Don't forget Ray."

"Dwayne's brother," Jan said.

"Oh. Anyone else out to get a cut of your fortune as well? Their cousins? In-laws, maybe?

"Let's not get riled," David said, rolling his eyes to the ceiling. "We came out in one piece, didn't we? I'm glad I could be of service to you."

Courtney lowered her eyes and nodded. "I'm sorry," she said. "You did get us out of that...better than I might have expected." She looked at Jan. "It's just that I can't believe there was a cop there the whole time, and he just sat there. He just watched."

"I warned you," Jan said. "We can't rely on the law here."

"I'm beginning to wonder about a lot around this place."

Jan gazed at her, seemingly close to tears. "I'm sorry things have turned out this way. I just wanted things to be better for you."

"I know." She gave Jan a guilty look. "I'll admit, I haven't made it easy for you."

"Yeah," David said, cutting her a smile. "You upset old women wherever you go."

"Oh, for God's sake." She couldn't help but chuckle. "Yes, that's my mission in life."

"And you do it so well," Jan said, grinning weakly.

With that, the tension in the room eased noticeably. Courtney studied David thoughtfully for a moment. "So, how did you learn to do what you did? I mean, disarm that freak like that?"

"Attribute it to panic. And a bit of martial arts training."

"What's a bit?"

"Red belt in Tae kwon-do," Jan answered for him. "And a green belt in Judo."

"Is that impressive?"

"Reasonably," Jan said. "Of course, it's taken him twice as long as the average moron to earn them."

"Can you break bricks with your head?"

"I would never harm a hapless brick."

Courtney laughed. But after a long silence, her serious mood returned. "So, David, if you can't go to the law, what do you plan to do? You made what sounded to me like a serious threat if those men come back."

He raised an eyebrow. "A threat?"

"You said you wouldn't be responsible for what happened to them if you saw them again. What did you mean by that?"

His eyes wavered a little. "Oh, come on. I just meant that if they go playing with fire, they're likely to get burned."

She felt a pang of apprehension. "Well, I think you're going down a dangerous road."

"We've had to deal with twisted people before, and I doubt these will be the last. We'll be fine."

"I'm glad you have so much faith in your own resources."

Jan pushed her brandy glass toward her. "Here. Finish your medicine. You'll feel better."

"No doubt." She tilted back the snifter, the burn in her throat far from unwelcome but ultimately unsatisfying. Alcohol could not drown the problems they faced. "Well. I think I'm going to retire shortly. I could use a good night's sleep. Any chance your noisy great aunt will give it a rest tonight?"

"I'll see that she does," David said, giving her a serious look. "Her first peep will be her last."

"That sounds ominous."

He smiled. "I'll gag her with duct tape."

Jan snickered. "Maybe you'd better let me handle any dealings with Aunt Martha."

"Whatever you think best, dear sister."

"Whichever one of you, I don't care," Courtney said. "Thank you. Thank you so much."

"It's covered, dah-ling."

Thus reassured, she drained the last of her brandy and stood up, only to find her knees wobbly. She braced herself against the bar until the weakness passed. Between the alcohol and the lingering shock of her ordeal, her body had borne about all it could for one day.

"Would you like me to walk back with you?" David asked.

She held up a hand and shook her head. "No, thank you. I'll see you tomorrow."

"Good night, then."

"Good night."

Jan stood up and gave her a motherly hug, which she had to admit felt warm and sincere. "Thanks," she said, returning the hug. "I'll be fine."

"I know you will."

She made her way down the long hallway to her suite, strangely happy just to be free of Jan and David for a time. Yes, they were trying to comfort her — she truly believed that — but she *knew* Jan was still withholding information from her. And David. Well, he remained inscrutable, and his continual assurances somehow rang hollow. Even though he had likely saved her life tonight, he was a long way from having earned her trust.

It wasn't paranoia that led her to make sure every window in her suite was closed and locked, the back door dead bolted. After a moment's consideration, she decided to lock the door to the hall as well. Despite David's nonchalance, she had no faith that the Surber brothers would easily forget their humiliation, and if they had already been brazen enough to trespass on Blackburn property in the middle of the night, then it was no stretch to believe they might return with even more malevolent intentions.

As she readied herself for bed, she became aware of the inevitable singing, chirping, clicking, and scrabbling from the dark woods outside. So much life out there, and so close, seemingly willful in proclaiming its presence.

Consciously, she realized that as long as the night creatures were carrying on so energetically, there were probably no interlopers in the immediate vicinity. On a deeper level, however, the cacophony still unsettled her.

After she had brushed her teeth and slipped into her long T-shirt, she turned out the lights and settled herself in bed, only to discover that the room had developed a slight case of the spins. The damned brandy, she thought; she wasn't used to sucking down so much alcohol so fast. Being with Jan again had made it too easy to lapse back into the old, not-so-responsible patterns of their college years. Still, fatigue and spent nerves had a far stronger grip on her body, and it wasn't long before consciousness went spiraling away, quietly and unmourned.

The last thing that registered in her awareness was that silence had replaced the noises of the night, but even that disconcerting fact wasn't enough to halt sleep's inexorable advance.

#

When she opened her eyes again, pitch darkness and total silence greeted her. After several seconds, she was able to make out the illuminated digits on the nightstand clock, which read just past two, and a thin wash of moonlight tinting her half-open curtains. She remembered that, just before falling asleep, the night sounds beyond her window had suddenly ceased.

Her fingers tightened on her pillow, and all her senses sprang alert, an inexplicable rush of dread melting away any lingering effects of the alcohol. She sensed no movement, heard no sound above the beating of her heart, but the impression of a presence lurking nearby bore so heavily upon her that it compressed the air in her lungs. She lay there for eons, listening, waiting, her chest so tightly constricted that her ribs felt ready to crack.

It was actually a relief when the soft, almost-melodic moan began to drift out of the darkness, for then the pent-up air in her lungs finally burst free.

The moan became the same warbling litany of meaningless syllables she had heard before, only much softer now, almost hypnotic in its rhythmic rising and falling. To her surprise, she found her hand pulling away the bedcovers, her feet sliding out of bed and working their way into her slippers. The action was so automatic that it confused her, for her mind had not willed it to happen. When realization fully set in, she remained calm, but an inner voice began to whisper more and more forcefully, *I am not in control. I am not in control!*

Shakily, she stood up and shuffled toward her door, her panic still contained by a wall of self-discipline, though she didn't know how much longer she could maintain it. She could *not* be moving against her will, yet her feet kept carrying her farther away from her bed, the only symbol of security left in her room. Her arms and legs were a marionette's, and she *knew* that Aunt Martha was pulling the strings, for as the eerie voice reached a high note, one foot moved forward, and as the note fell low, her other foot followed. Her fingers unbolted her door, and then she was in the hall, moving forward with a purpose she did not begin to understand.

"For God's sake, don't," she whispered as she unlocked the back door and tugged it open, the sharp creaking briefly drowning the voice from the abyss beyond. Then she was stepping into the humid night air, facing a bizarre, silvery web-work, which she realized were thickly entwined tree limbs catching the pale moonlight. She stepped off the little stoop and into the damp grass, which tickled and prickled her ankles as she walked toward the beckoning trees, goaded on by the disembodied voice. She seemed to be outside her body, which was all that kept her from panicking. But now she *wanted* to panic, to somehow break the spell that kept her moving, for she was certain that the power gripping her intended not to frighten her but finish her.

The fingers of a low-hanging branch scrabbled at her hair and nightshirt, and with every step she took, her feet sank deeper into cool muck. Surely, all she needed to do was assert her will. No one could master her mind; it just wasn't possible. She *pushed* with all her mental strength, struggled to make her legs to obey *her* commands, not the other's, but the signals hit dead ends and fed back into her brain, jolting her but not freeing her.

The ethereal voice abruptly went silent, and her feet stopped moving. She staggered as if a giant hand had slapped her, the thin branches still clutching her hair like groping, skeletal fingers. Then she realized she could see her shadow front of her, in the center of a pale gold rectangle. She spun around and saw Martha's window illuminated, and heard another voice speaking — indecipherable, but distinctly masculine.

David.

A bit late, perhaps, but as good as his word.

She stood frozen for a few moments, until she was certain her muscles weren't going to betray her and send her tumbling into the wet grass and weeds. Looking around anxiously, she found she had actually entered the woods, for the branches had closed around her on all sides, like gnarled arms seeking to embrace her. The light from the window penetrated only a short distance into the trees, but amid the thick undergrowth, she spied a few splotches of muddy water, some of which bubbled ominously, as if something were hiding just beneath the surface. Even if the pools weren't deep enough to swallow her, the idea of stepping into a host of unknown, perhaps venomous creatures nearly sent her into a fresh panic.

She slogged her way back to firmer earth, grateful when she felt only cool grass beneath her feet. The back door hung open, waiting for her, and she stumbled toward it, panting, trying to replenish the oxygen that terror had stolen. She had just reached the stoop when, behind her, something heavy moved.

A deep, wet *thud,* like a sledgehammer slamming into the mud.

Another. And then another. Coming toward her.

She glanced back and saw the nearest tree branches parting as something shoved its way through them. High in the branches, higher than the head of the tallest man, she saw a pale shimmer — an indistinct shape, but as large as one of her bedroom windows.

She could not hold back a sharp scream as she tore open the rickety storm door, leaped into the house, and slammed the heavier wooden door shut behind her. The stubborn dead bolt refused to move, but she wrestled frantically with the thing until it finally slid home. For too long she stood there, torn between seeking refuge in her bedroom and retreating deeper into the house. However, when she heard a heavy shuffling on the other side of the door, she turned and sprinted down the dark hall toward the kitchen, her shoulder smashing painfully into the doorjamb as she rounded the last corner. The range hood light was still burning, providing a small sphere of illumination, which seemed a welcoming oasis until she realized that the kitchen curtains were still open, offering whatever was outside a clear view of her through the window.

"Oh, Jesus," she whispered, scanning the cabinets and drawers, finally tearing open the cutlery drawer and grabbing a long butcher knife. She stood in the middle of the room, clutching the handle in bone-white fingers, her head cocked, ears keen for the first sound of movement either outside or in.

Somewhere beyond the kitchen door, from the direction of the great room, the floor creaked. A footstep, perhaps — but it couldn't have been the thing from the swamp. It was too huge, too heavy to enter the house without smashing its way through a window or door. Only silence crept in through the windows, and when she heard another creak, this one closer than before, she turned to face the great room door, knife at the ready.

A second later, David appeared, wearing his satin robe, his eyes narrowed and curious. When he saw the knife, he stopped and crossed his arms. "Courtney? What's the matter?"

"That thing is outside," she said hoarsely.

"What thing?"

"The Monarch."

He glanced at her muddy feet. "Do you sleepwalk, by chance?"

She looked down and shook her head. "I wasn't sleepwalking. I wasn't dreaming. I heard Martha starting up, and then I ended up outside. I couldn't stop myself."

He shook his head dubiously. "Well, Martha did start up, but I went and quieted her down — just like I said I would. I'm sorry she disturbed you again."

"It wasn't just her," she said. "I heard that thing coming out of the woods. I saw it. I saw…something."

"The same thing as last night?"

She shook her head. "Just a blur. But I'm sure it was the same."

"Courtney, the Monarch is just one of Martha's stories. She told you about that to upset you. It looks like she succeeded."

With deliberate care, she put the knife down on the countertop and stared at him, half-furious, half-pleading. "I know it sounds crazy. It *is* crazy. But there's something out here. And it's not the Surber brothers."

He looked at the ceiling, as if to hoping to discover a message from the heavens. "I am going to commit that woman," he said softly. Then, to her, "I'll go with you back to your room. You need to get cleaned up."

"I don't want to go back there."

"Courtney. There's nothing to be afraid of. Come on. I'll show you." He held out a hand to her.

Damned if he didn't sound just like her father, she thought. *Or Frank*. So firm in his convictions, unwilling to listen to her, even when she had obviously suffered a trauma. "Don't patronize me, you son of a bitch. You're not hearing what I'm saying to you." She immediately regretted allowing the old bitterness out of her mouth, but it was too late to take it back.

His eyes widened in surprise, but then he stepped forward and gripped her by the wrist. "I don't need that kind of talk from you. Come on." He pulled her with him as he started down the hall toward her room. She tried to free her arm, but his grip was too strong.

"David, don't," she said. "Listen to me. Something about your aunt's singing. It affected my mind. For all I know, it's affecting you too."

"The only thing affecting me now," he said, "is lack of sleep. I'll thank Aunt Martha for that. I don't want to get angry with you. But I'm going to show you that — whatever has gotten you so flustered — it's got to be in your head."

He half-dragged her down the dark hallway, past her room, and to the back door, where he released her so he could unfasten the dead bolt. She was half-tempted to run away from him and go wake Jan, but something — maybe his confidence, his *authority* — kept her at his side. He pulled open the door, took her by the wrist again, and before she could even protest, he had led her out to the stoop beneath the silver-tinted trees. Her heart hammered in protest, and with her free hand, she pulled at his arm. "You're out of your mind," she said, realizing how bizarre that sounded, coming from her lips under these circumstances. "Do you realize that?"

"So I've heard," he said distractedly, his eyes scanning the trees and grounds to either side. Then he looked at her and smiled faintly — before turning back to face the woods and shouting, "Hey, Monarch!" he called. "Come see what I brought you!"

#

Chapter 8

"What the *hell* are you doing?"

"Putting my money where my mouth is. Hey! You out there!"

"Just stop it," she said, the sting of his insult subordinating her fear. "If you don't believe me, just say so."

"Just saying so wouldn't prove a thing to you, would it?" His eyes scanned the trees, and he glanced back up at Martha's window, probably to ascertain the old woman had turned off her light and gone to bed.

She realized that, while she was inside, the night creatures must have resumed their choruses because now she noticed them falling silent at the sound of David's voice. For a brief moment, she actually resented them for failing to bear out her story.

She could feel his disdain for her apparent gullibility. "I'm sorry, David. You're wrong. What happened to me was real. I don't understand it, but it happened, just like I said it did."

He gazed at her, his expression softening a little. "I know you're upset about all that's happened since you got here. Your nerves are overwrought."

The idea that he might be right seemed intolerable. Yet the alternative was unthinkable — or should have been.

"What's this 'singing' your aunt does?" she asked, trying to suppress her anger. "It sounds almost like a foreign language. But that's no real language — is it?"

He shook his head. "God knows, Courtney. I don't know what's in that old woman's head any better than you do. She suffers from dementia. That's all there is to it."

"I don't accept that," she said. "There's got to be more to it. Tell me something. Does she know anything about hypnotism?"

"Hypnotism? Are you joking?"

"No, I'm not joking. When she started up tonight, I felt like my body was completely out of my control. That's never happened to me before. And I know that she was responsible."

He started incredulously at her. "Okay. If that's so, then what was she trying to make you do?"

She turned away from him, unable to withstand the look she knew he was about to give her. "She wanted me to come out here. Where *it* was waiting."

For a long time, he didn't say a word. Finally, he said, "I'm not sure who's the most demented."

That was all she could take from him. She turned and headed for the door. "Good night, David. Thank you for your concern."

She was just opening the door when he called after her, "Wait. I'm sorry. That was uncalled for."

"Yes, it was," she said coolly. "I'm going back to bed. But there is one thing you can do for me."

"What?"

"Make sure that woman upstairs doesn't open her mouth again tonight."

"I wish I could have stopped her in the first place."

Yeah, so crazy Courtney wouldn't have gone south, he was no doubt thinking. With a sigh of disgust, she slipped inside and returned to her room, knowing that, regardless of what she had told David, she would not sleep another minute tonight. While anger had vanquished her fear, at least for now, her body was a live wire, and there was no way she would be able to relax, even if circumstances allowed it.

She was about to close the door when she realized David had followed her and was standing in the doorway, his eyes boring through her, into her emotions. Just for a second, relief that he was still nearby overshadowed her annoyance with him. "What?" she asked, her voice still razor sharp.

"I don't want you to be angry with me," he said, lowering his head with a touch of humility. "I've tried to make a good impression on you, and I'm afraid I've blown it."

"I don't care to be treated like a hysterical, brainless bimbo. You know better. I know you do."

"You're right," he said. "It's just that you've been under a hellish strain since you got here, and it seemed to me that it had gotten to you. And don't forget — you called me names first." He gave her his most captivating smile.

She blinked, remembering ruefully that he was right. "Then I apologize for that."

He put a gentle hand on her shoulder. "And I'm sorry for overreacting."

She saw that damnable, mocking look in his eye, and she realized then that he probably wasn't sorry at all. She just nodded.

"You're still shaking like a leaf," he said. "You really are upset."

"What would you expect?" she asked defiantly.

To her surprise, he gripped her arm firmly and pulled her toward him. Then both of his arms were encircling her body, and to her surprise, she found herself melting into his embrace. One of his hands cradled her head, and he leaned forward, his lips coming to meet hers, at first tentatively, then with increasing fierceness.

She didn't want to respond, *she didn't,* but she did, and then their bodies were moving together toward her bed, and she felt him drawing her down with him, his lips never leaving hers. His touch was exhilarating, his kiss exquisite, and it was so much sweeter because she wasn't supposed to be doing this; he was her best friend's brother, she had vowed not to encourage him, and she damn near didn't even like him.

She wrapped her arms around him and pulled him tighter, working her tongue against his, alternately gently and then furiously, drawing away from his mouth, feeling the tip of his tongue slowly brushing her lips. One of his hands moved down her back, slid under the hem of her long T-shirt, and then slowly worked its way toward her breasts, his touch warm and reassuring, hot and exciting. She raised up long enough to strip off the long T-shirt and toss it to the floor. As his fingers caressed one soft breast, his lips moved to her throat, and she felt his teeth against the delicate skin, and there was pressure, and then he was biting the tender flesh just above her shoulder. Her heart skipped a beat because *it hurt*. She couldn't take pain, not this way, but somehow as his teeth and tongue worked together, nibbling and burrowing, she realized that her fingers were clenching the muscles of his back, her nails drilling into his skin, spurring him on, thrilling him. She bore the pain, and then his mouth moved lower, over her collarbone and then to her breast. His tongue gently stroked her flesh, and only intermittently did he allow her to feel the sharpness of his teeth, stoking both her desire and her fear.

Her fingers played in his hair, ran up and down his jaw, poised to push him away if he trespassed against her, but every nerve his tongue touched shivered with pleasure, and she moaned softly, which only fueled his hot kisses. Understanding the feeling no better than she had the power of Martha's voice, she found herself reveling in the horrifying knowledge that she might well be performing for the amusement of *something* watching through her window, even at this moment. The thought froze her blood, but when David's teeth pressed into her inner thigh and began to gnaw, fear melted and trickled away, and her back arched with excitement as pain and dread turned to sweetness.

On and on it seemed to go, until he pulled away from her, and the vacancy felt cold. She saw him removing his robe, his eyes gleaming faintly in the darkness, fixed on her, scanning and absorbing her body. His eyes were lustful, and yet — perhaps for the first time — she knew he was seeing *her,* not just her body, and he was captivated. For that, she felt at least a little vindicated.

As he glided back onto the bed, his weight slowly settling upon her, warm and wonderful, she dimly registered the fact that something just outside her window was moving. Something heavy.

And all the night sounds had stopped.

But she paid none of it any mind. David was here, with her, and she with him. At this moment, that was the only thing in the world that mattered.

#

She woke alone. Her room felt chilly, and outside the windows, the day was smoke-gray, the wind crying like a despairing child through the trees. She sat up, saw the impression David's body had left in her bed, and she knew none of it had been a dream; not the horror of the thing coming out of the dark woods nor the thrill of him fucking her every way but Sunday. As she moved, she realized her lower regions were a bit sore, for he had been brutal, using her for his own gratification; yet she also remembered something in his eyes, and in his touch, which insinuated that he had bonded with her on a deep, even spiritual level.

He had been brutal with her because she *expected* brutal. It was what she knew best. Somehow, he had pulled that from her brain and given her exactly what she was accustomed to. From that perspective, he was ten times the man Frank had ever been.

She dragged herself out of bed and went into the bathroom to look at herself in the mirror.

Her neck and shoulders were bruised, displaying the livid marks of his teeth. On her abdomen and thighs. Down her legs. Good God, she thought, he had damn near devoured her.

"Can't rape the willing," she said, wondering what had possessed her to be so willing. Lingering effects of the alcohol, perhaps. Vulnerability born of fear. Or — she froze at the notion — something completely beyond her own volition.

She remembered Martha's voice coiling and uncoiling in her mind, compelling her to leave her room in the dead of night, out to where something terrible and almost certainly deadly was waiting for her. The idea of someone else's will totally dominating her own seemed inconceivable. Nonetheless, it *had* happened. And she wondered: just how deeply had her mind been affected? Could she be certain at any time that she had full control of her own body and mind?

What if David was right, and she had just dreamt the whole thing? It would certainly simplify the world and, by rights, ease her mind considerably.

But he wasn't, and it didn't.

She turned on the shower and stepped under the water, wishing it could wash away every memory of the previous night. She scrubbed her skin roughly, punishing the offending bite marks, but they wouldn't fade, and she wondered what Jan would say if she knew what had happened. The idea of keeping such a secret from her best friend offended her, yet she knew that Jan would feel resentful, especially after she had just warned Courtney about the dangers of getting involved with David.

Once done with her shower, she felt refreshed, though the evidence of last night's tryst remained etched in her flesh like grotesque tattoos. The stormy weather bringing cool air struck her as fortunate, for jeans and a long-sleeved sweater would not appear unduly conspicuous. In fact, she noticed now that her room seemed quite chilly. Thankfully, they had no plans to visit the beach today.

It was just after seven, and Martha would likely be the only one already up and about. Courtney felt tempted to go confront the woman and damn the consequences, until she paused long enough to consider what those consequences might mean to her. At best, she would have to leave the Blackburns. And then where would she go? She didn't have a car or enough money to stay even a single night at a hotel.

She left her room and stood in the hall, listening. No sound came from anywhere in the house, and she wondered if Martha intended to avoid her for as long as she remained here. On that hopeful note, she headed for the back door and, after peering through the window to make sure the yard was empty, stepped out to the little stoop, boldly facing the shadowy woods as if to prove to any spying eyes that she had survived the night. Still, back here, where the trees pressed so close to the house, she felt small and exposed, even in daylight, and the memory of having come out in the dark, against her will, nearly sent her fleeing back inside. But she steeled her nerves, determined not to succumb to fears of phantom horrors.

The wind gusted fiercely through the branches, sending them into clattering motion, and thick, purple and black cumulous clouds rolled slowly overhead like undulating bruises in the sky. She stepped into the dew-frosted grass and went around the corner of the wing to stand outside her bedroom window, thinking that if her visitor from the past two nights were anything other than a dream it would have left some sign.

The grass did appear flattened in places by some great weight, though she could not make out any distinctive pattern. She took a few steps toward the woods, where the grass gave way to tall weeds and thick mud, and after a few moments' examination, she froze, her heart leaping to her throat.

If it wasn't a footprint, it was the strangest mark upon the earth she had ever seen: two semicircular impressions, forming something resembling a huge hoof, fully two feet long, with several smaller, snakelike indentations around their edges. One end was deeper than the other, as if the maker's weight had shifted forward. *As if it was walking*. Her eyes roved deeper into the woods, and six feet farther in, she found a second print. To the right, she spied another set of tracks, much smaller — her own — which stopped and reversed themselves just a few feet into the trees.

It occurred to her that the giant prints led *out* of the woods. She saw none going back in.

Taking a deep breath, she continued into the thick foliage and spied another of the huge, hoof-like marks a short distance ahead. She had no intention of venturing deeper into these inhospitable woods, but daylight and curiosity's grip had quashed most of her apprehension, and she felt no compulsion to rush back to the shelter of the house. Still, not far ahead, the dense, rustling boughs swallowed most of the day's gray light, and the rushing wind produced a disconcerting chorus of groaning and creaking from all around her.

At first, she thought it was just branches bending in the breeze, but then she realized that, some fifty yards into the woods, something was moving. An animal, or even a man, she thought, unable to make out details through the intervening trunks and limbs. An involuntary tightening in her chest, a herald of approaching dread, prompted her to start backing up, even as her eyes attempted to lock on the odd, shambling shape. For a few moments, it stopped moving, and the cold certainty that indiscernible eyes had fallen on her opened the gate for all the previous night's terror to come flooding back. As she watched, a pale, misty oval slid slowly into view from behind a thick poplar. Too indistinct to identify, but clearly enough, a face.

Not a human face.

Slowly — as slowly as if a ring of deadly vipers surrounded her — she turned around and began walking, picking her steps carefully so as not to slip in the mud and fall. A fall would be fatal. A fall would leave her helpless prey for the Monarch, but as long as she kept moving, she could get back to the house before it could reach her. She heard the heavy, sledgehammer thud behind her, then another, and she picked up her pace just a little, knowing it couldn't come into the house after her because Martha was in the house, and this was Martha's Monarch, wasn't it?

Once she broke free of the trees and found solid earth beneath her feet, she began to run.

Once back inside the house, she slammed the door and locked it, but remained at the window, peering through the glass into the trees, terrified but still determined, *desperately* determined, to view the thing that had taken such an intense interest in her.

There! There it was. Slowly approaching the house, its trunk-like body moving stiffly through the trees, its face lowering beneath the rafters of entwined limbs to peer in her direction.

Slowly, Courtney realized that the Monarch's face was a fat cluster of leaves at the end of a swaying branch, illuminated by a stray beam of sunlight that had burned its way through a gap in the clouds. The spindly body was a sapling caught in the wind, bumping and banging against the bole of a giant poplar.

"You've got to be shitting me," she whispered, realizing that she could no longer trust her own senses.

That she had lost credibility even with herself.

But the tracks. Those tracks were as real as the sturdiest oak out there, and nothing as illusory as sunlight on boughs could have made them.

She turned and went down the hall to the kitchen, where she found a dour-looking Martha standing at the counter, pouring the morning's first cup of coffee, and the old woman's unblinking eyes swiveled to regard her. Without breaking stridc, Courtney raised a hand in greeting, said "Good morning, Martha," and continued on her way, heading to the staircase that led to the second floor. She marched up, went straight to Jan's room, and, without knocking, opened the door to find her friend just sitting up in bed, rubbing the sleep from her eyes.

Her jaw dropped as Courtney came in, but seeing the look on her face, her expression changed to a thoughtful frown, and she asked, "What's the matter, honey?"

"Come outside with me, please."

"Why? What's wrong?"

"I have to show you something."

Jan looked perplexed but nodded. "Give me a minute, okay?"

"I'll be right here." Courtney stepped out to the hall, leaned back against the wall, and crossed her arms, trying to control her breathing to keep from hyperventilating.

Two minutes later, Jan appeared, dressed in a T-shirt, sweatpants, and tennis shoes. "Tell me what's wrong," she said, her tone slightly irate.

"Maybe you can tell me." She led the way down the stairs and back through the kitchen, where Martha continued to stand silently, glaring at them with unconcealed distaste.

“Morning, Martha,” Jan said as they passed through.

“Yeah,” the old woman said.

They went down the hall, out through the back door, and Courtney took Jan by the hand as she headed for the edge of the woods, more than half-afraid that the tracks would have somehow vanished.

She came to the first one, actually relieved to find it still there, and pointed to it. “Do you see that?”

Jan stared at the mark, her eyes widening a bit. “Of course I see it. What is it?”

Courtney showed her the next one, a few feet into the trees. “There are more of them back there. I thought maybe you could tell me what they are.”

When she looked up at Courtney, her face was white. “No, I don’t know what they are. Someone must have made them.”

“Someone?”

Jan looked as if she might collapse into tears at any moment. “Apparently. How else could they be here?”

“You look spooked. What’s the matter?” Courtney asked, staring hard at her friend.

“Nothing. I’m barely awake.”

“What would you say if I told you these were the footprints of a living creature?”

Jan’s mouth hung agape, her chest heaving as she breathed too fast and too deeply. Finally, she shook her head. “I’d think you had a vivid imagination. We have a prankster.”

“And who would do such a thing?”

Jan’s eyes flickered toward the house. She was barely keeping her composure and seemed on the verge of saying something significant, only to change her mind. “Maybe you should ask my brother,” she finally said.

Courtney looked at the house as well, her brain shifting in new directions, trying to fit David into some pattern she might not have previously recognized. She had always suspected he might be guileful and — now she knew firsthand — even brutal.

However, as for last night, he had an airtight alibi. She almost started to say as much, but then cut herself off.

Now it was Jan’s turn to regard her with curious eyes, and Courtney tried not to blush, but it was too late.

#

Chapter 9

Jan had not pressed her for any details, though after Courtney's foolish stumbling, she must have deduced the truth about her night with David. And Jan refused to elaborate any further about Aunt Martha's Monarch, so Courtney simply stopped asking. A wall now stood between them, and this, more than any fear of nocturnal horrors, twisted her emotions almost beyond tolerance. For all these years, Courtney had believed that she and Jan could share everything about anything, but her friend's stubborn silence and poorly preserved façade of normalcy convinced her this was no longer true.

Was it her going off alone with David last night? If so, then Jan was far more sensitive about the subject than Courtney had imagined.

Fortunately, Jan was happy enough to let her borrow her Jaguar to drive to Elizabeth City, and Courtney spent the morning and early afternoon exploring the town and filling out job applications. She targeted any place that might be able to use her considerable office management and customer service skills: insurance companies, the hospital, real estate agencies, even the local government offices. One Realtor happily accepted her application and asked her to come back for an interview the following week, to which she agreed, even though she had no experience or particular interest in the real estate business. Right now, though, she would take anything — *anything* — that would get her back on her feet and out on her own.

The silver Jag drew endless admiring looks from business owners and passersby alike, which she rather enjoyed, though she half-feared the expensive car might give potential employers the idea that she didn't really need the job. In her life, she had never desired extravagant things, but as she left Elizabeth City and hit the southbound highway toward Fearing, she realized how easily she could become accustomed to a car like this — not to mention everything it stood for.

She found herself wondering what kept David and Jan at their aging, secluded home in such a small town, one so overtly hostile toward them. In a way, she envied anyone who could claim a strong attachment to their ancestral home. Because her father had been in the Air Force, her family had moved frequently while she was growing up, and she had never had a chance to bond with any specific location. She had actually begun to care deeply for the home she and Frank had made in Atlanta, but now that place was poison, and if she never returned to Georgia at all, it was fine with her. Still, that was not the same as being surrounded by enmity, seemingly from all quarters — a situation that, to her, would become intolerable in a very short time. Perhaps, after their parents' deaths, Jan and David were discovering what it was like to bear the full brunt of the town's deep-rooted antagonism. Maybe Jan's wall was her coping mechanism, which Courtney could at least understand — yet she could not conceive of any reason for Jan to keep her on the outside.

When she pulled the Jaguar into the Blackburns' driveway, she immediately saw, parked next to the front walkway, a Town of Fearing police cruiser — all too likely, the same one she had seen in the Tall Ships parking lot the previous night. An electric buzzing began at the back of her skull, and her fingers tightened involuntarily on the steering wheel. She drove carefully around the cruiser and parked in the detached garage at the back of the house, wondering if this visitation had something to with their encounter with the Surbers. One thing was certain: given the things Jan and David had said about the local cops, one of them showing up here could mean nothing but trouble.

As if they didn't have enough of that already.

One eye on the woods, she went in through the back door and contemplated hiding out in her room until the visitor left. Her inevitable curiosity, however, refused to allow any such scheme, so she made her way down the hall, through the kitchen, and to the great room, from which low voices drifted through the door in somber tones. Just before she stepped inside, for one vain moment, she was glad she was dressed in her finest business attire rather than her typical casual wear.

The first thing she noticed was Jan and David sitting upright in their plush leather chairs at one end of the room, where the floor was elevated like a stage by a foot or so, the two of them looking for all the world like monarchs holding court. She almost went queasy at how quickly the term "monarch" came to mind. The police officer standing before them was a slender but densely muscled, gray-haired man with gunmetal eyes and startlingly large hands, one of which rested casually on the handle of his holstered revolver. His leathery skin was deeply tanned, his chiseled face ruggedly handsome. As she entered, his eyes regarded her curiously, and his other hand came up to stroke the bottom of his long chin.

"And you must be Ms. Edmiston," he said in a low, coarse voice.

David's face wore his customary dark smile. "Courtney, this is Mr. Flythe, our local police chief."

The chief nodded curtly to her, and his eyes narrowed thoughtfully. "How long you plan to be here, Ms. Edmiston?"

"I'm not exactly sure," she said, moving to stand next to Jan, a little surprised by his question. “I’m staying here while I look for a job in Elizabeth City.”

“Mr. Flythe has brought some rather disturbing news,” Jan said, giving her only a brief glance. “Apparently there was some…unpleasantness…this morning.”

“What does that mean?”

“It means murder, Ms. Edmiston.” The older man’s eyes bored into hers.

“Murder?”

“Mr. Hank Surber. He was killed sometime last night.”

“Good God!”

Flythe’s eyes refused to release hers. “I believe you’d made his acquaintance, had you not, Ms. Edmiston?”

Courtney could not suppress an irate scowl. “I would not say that, no.”

“Perhaps I’m mistaken.”

“Yes, you are. What happened to him?”

“Well, to put it bluntly, Ms. Edmiston, he was slaughtered. In fact, his body was brutally savaged.” For a second, the chief appeared deeply unsettled. “Never seen anything like it.”

“Why come here?” she asked, her voice weak. “I’m sure no one here would know anything about it.”

“Interesting you should say that.” He took a notepad from his shirt pocket and flipped through a few pages. “In fact, I have witnesses who claim that Mr. Surber and Mr. Blackburn here had an altercation last night that turned quite violent. I understand you were present at the time.”

Now a few slivers of anger lanced her burgeoning fear. “You wouldn’t happen to have been one of those witnesses, Chief Flythe?”

He raised an eyebrow. “Now, where would you get an idea like that, ma’am?”

“Because there was a police car in the parking lot when it happened. Whoever the cop was, he watched the whole thing without intervening.”

“That doesn’t sound very likely. If any of my officers witnessed a violent confrontation, they most certainly would intervene.”

“Not last night.”

“So you admit to being present at this altercation?”

“Yes,” she said, despising the man for drawing her into such a dreadful situation. “Those two men — the Surber brothers — attacked David and me, and he acted in self-defense.”

“And just how did Mr. Blackburn defend himself?”

She sent David a questioning look. His face remained impassive. “He sent them packing," she said, a little too tentatively.

"'Sent them packing.' Okay. How so? With his bare hands? Did he have a weapon?"

"Basically, the Surbers had knives, he disarmed them, and then invited them to leave. That was pretty much it."

"He didn't say anything about settling scores, or getting even, or anything like that — after he sent them packing?"

"Not exactly, no."

"Then exactly what?"

Courtney grimaced, realizing her tongue had slipped. "That's all," she said, anxious to avoid implicating David by revealing words he had uttered in the heat of the moment. "He ordered them to leave us alone. That's all."

"So, you misspoke earlier, Ms. Edmiston? You actually did know the victim."

"I would hardly call being attacked by him getting to know him. Would you, Mr. Flythe?"

He ignored her remark. "May I assume that, after you returned last night, you remained here for the rest of the night?"

"Yes, sir."

"How about Mr. Blackburn? Was he here all night as well?"

Now she felt both Jan and David's eyes on her, and her cheeks began to burn. "I believe so."

"You believe so. But you can't be certain?"

"During the time I was awake, he was here."

"And how late were you awake?"

"Nearly till dawn. I had a hard time falling asleep."

"Any particular reason?"

"Chief, I think my friend has given you as much information as you could reasonably expect," Jan said, flashing one cold eye at Courtney. "Since you're obviously not here to arrest anyone, I think it would be better if you left now."

"Maybe you should let me be the judge of that."

"You know," David said, "we're not legally obligated to answer your questions, but we've all been more than cooperative. If you want to complicate things needlessly, I'll be happy to call my lawyer. I'm sure Will Garner wouldn't mind stopping by to chat."

Chief Flythe's glare would have staggered Courtney where she stood, but David merely raised an eyebrow, evidently expecting an answer.

"No," he said at last, looking as if, for a penny, he would spit at the younger man's feet. "I don't suppose that's necessary." As he turned away, his jaw working back and forth furiously, his eyes fell again on Courtney. “I’d like to recommend, Ms. Edmiston, that you don’t leave Fearing too soon. You may yet be able to shed some light on this situation.”

“I doubt that.”

“We’ll see.” His gaze softened slightly as he looked at her. “Well. I appreciate your cooperation, ma’am. You’ve been helpful.”

As if on cue, Arlene appeared at the door to the front hall, gave Courtney a quick, reassuring smile, and said to the chief, with exaggerated courtesy, “If you’ll come this way, sir.”

As he left, Flythe’s eyes lingered on Courtney, his expression thoughtful. He ignored David, whose imperturbable gaze followed him out the door. As the chief’s footsteps dwindled in the hallway, David sent Courtney an apologetic look.

“I’m sorry you had to go through that. I’d have forewarned you if I’d had a clue he was coming.”

“I can’t believe that man was killed,” she said, shaking her head, still half-stunned. “But I can see why the police would question us. They know about the fight.”

Jan’s eyes remained locked on the door where the chief had exited. “That bastard. It wouldn’t surprise me if *he* had something to do with it — just so he could try to pin it on us.”

“I can’t believe a cop would do that. No matter how corrupt you say they are.”

“I’m not sure I’d put anything past Mr. Flythe there,” David said. “That was his car there last night, no matter what he says.”

“You’re sure about that?”

“Very.”

She thought for a moment and said, “You know, if we had gone to the police last night — whether the chief was there or not — they’d have gotten our side of the story first. It would be harder for him to blame anything on you.”

“Courtney, it wouldn’t matter one way or the other. He would just make it out as me being all the more brazen. But don’t worry — either of you. He can’t pin a thing on me. He just wishes he could.”

Jan gave her brother a stern look. “He’ll dig deep.”

“Then he’d better watch where he steps.” He glanced quickly at Courtney. “I just mean he’ll end up stumbling into a lot of empty holes. There’s nothing to find.”

“Do you know exactly what happened to him? Hank Surber?”

For a second, David's confidence seemed to waver, and his eyes flickered almost imperceptibly toward the ceiling. "It's curious. His body was… disfigured. His brother found him outside their house this morning."

"Hanging from a tree," Jan added. "Impaled on a broken branch."

Death had brushed Courtney too closely before, never more horribly than when it had taken her daughter. But now, as Jan and David both held her in their stony gazes, it seemed closer and more menacing than ever before — as if it hid in the room with her, lurking in the deepening shadows like something sentient and cruel.

She excused herself and returned to her suite, something cold and implacable following at her heels. When she closed herself in her room and turned her eyes to meet the murky, mocking stare of the woods on the other side of her window, frigid fingers closed over her and, for an interminable time, caressed her body until she was a shivering, weeping wreck on her bed.

#

Jan appeared at her door at dinnertime, and though Courtney had initially decided to skip the evening meal altogether, the little salad she had nibbled on at lunch had scarcely held her, so she reluctantly accompanied her friend to the dining room, anticipating making quick work of whatever Arlene had prepared before retreating again to her tenebrous sanctum. However, once she sat down and sampled Arlene's remarkable chicken and dumplings, a strong appetite kicked in and kept her at the table for two full servings. Fortunately, Martha came down only long enough to fill a plate and shoot her a few soul-searing scowls before returning upstairs. Jan and David displayed few outward signs of anxiety, though did she notice the two of them occasionally exchanging contemptuous glances. Jan obviously had issues with her brother's handling of the current situation.

After dinner, against her better judgment, Courtney allowed Jan to drag her to the great room for drinks, while David retired to his studio, ostensibly to attack a new composition he had been struggling with, though Courtney guessed that, under the circumstances, he had little desire to spend any more time than necessary with his sister. Jan confirmed this as they broke into a bottle of Aglianico.

"He's become so cold in the past few days," she said, with a hint of her old candor. "Ruthless, even. I know he's been under pressure, with the Surbers coming down on him all at once. But it worries me to see him become so coldhearted. Like the way he cut Hank with that knife. It's hard to feature David doing anything like that."

"But he did get us out of a damn bad situation," Courtney said. "Men like the Surbers, I doubt they would understand anything less dramatic."

She snorted derisively. "I'm sure he did what he thought was best. To me, it seems like the perfect way to ensure that they'll retaliate."

"At least one of them won't," Courtney said, taking a sip of her wine and studying Jan's expression.

Jan frowned gloomily. "No matter what those men have done, I wouldn't have wished a horrible death on any of them."

Courtney took a deep breath and another sip, hesitant to speak her mind with Jan already plainly upset. However, she could not back away. "You know, I've seen how you both react when the subject of Aunt Martha's Monarch comes up. You say there's nothing to it, but the subject obviously makes you uncomfortable. Tell me the truth about it."

For an instant, Jan's eyes turned hot with anger, but they cooled just as quickly. She sighed. "Courtney, what do you think there is to it? It's an old story. Do you honestly believe there could be more to it than that?"

"After what I've seen and been through, I know there's something going on that's beyond anything I've ever experienced. Like my 'sleepwalking' last night. That was *not* normal, and there's no way I can accept that Martha wasn't somehow responsible."

"Courtney, you had a strange experience, and because you don't understand it, you want it to be someone's fault. Look, I know how big a change all this is for you. Don't think I'm not one-hundred-percent sympathetic. But I can't accept that my great-aunt somehow mesmerized you and sent you out to be destroyed by something from a folktale. Do you understand my reasoning here?"

"Of course I do. How do you think I feel? Maybe I'm going completely crazy. But I've seen you, Jan — you and David both. When you told me how Hank Surber was killed, I could see it in your eyes. You both were thinking of Martha. You were."

Jan rolled her eyes in exasperation. "If anything, it's that these things appear to validate her crazy point of view — to someone who doesn't know better."

"You mean someone gullible. That's what you're saying, isn't it?"

"You know I don't mean that about you."

"Tell me this, then. Who do you think was responsible for killing Hank Surber?"

"How would I know that? The Surbers probably have more enemies in this town than we do. It doesn't have to be about us at all."

"Earlier, you were ready to blame the cops. Were you serious or just upset?"

Jan sighed. "Mostly upset. On the other hand, I'm not sure I'd put it past Chief Flythe. Ever since Mom and Dad died…"

"What?"

"Nothing. Let's just say he and the Surbers are cut from the same mold."

"Are you telling me he's in on trying to extort money from you?"

"Not directly. But he knows what the Surbers are up to. David thinks they intend to cut him in to keep him looking the other way."

"Jesus," Courtney groaned. "You know, it seems to me the best thing you could do is move somewhere else. Why do you even stay here?"

Jan gave her a long, curious look. "This is our home. Nobody drives us out of *our* home. I guess you wouldn't understand. You've never had the kind of connection to a place that we do."

"Still, if this life is making you unhappy, wouldn't you want to try to build a new one somewhere else? Something better than this?"

"There *isn't* anything better than this," Jan snapped. "Not for us."

Courtney lowered her head. "I'm sorry. No, I guess I don't understand."

They fell silent for a time, and she could feel Jan's wall coming up again, cold and unyielding, her mental focus turning to something deep within herself. Courtney was tempted to bring up her night with David, just to see whether it would buttress the wall or bring it tumbling down, but it seemed perhaps too cruel, given Jan's sensitivity about the subject. Still, David was her brother, not her husband, and his decisions hardly required her approval.

For that matter, neither did hers.

Then, as if reading her thoughts, Jan turned to look at her coolly. "You know, I warned you about getting involved with David. Nothing good can come of it."

"We're not exactly 'involved.'"

"It doesn't matter what you call it. You know I'd do anything in the world to help you. But if you're not going to listen to me, then you're on your own."

"Of course I listen to you," she said, knowing how lame it sounded. "I'll admit I turn a little weak around David. But I'm a big girl. You don't have to be worried."

"If that's what you think, you've got another thing coming."

"Why do you say that?"

"Because he's *my* brother."

"Earlier, you asked me to trust that he's got my best interests at heart. Was that wrong?"

"Not wrong. But maybe I should qualify that. He isn't about to let someone outside the family take advantage of you. That doesn't mean *he* wouldn't."

"That's kind of harsh, isn't it?"

"Just realistic."

"Believe me, I trust you. It's just that he can be very…persuasive…when he wants to be."

Jan laughed humorlessly and poured Courtney another glass of wine. "Oh, my dear, you have such a gift for understatement."

#

Chapter 10

As Courtney stepped into David's studio, she felt as if she had entered a tomb in which the things that lay there were not quite dead. The air was cool and sharp with the tang of solvents, and the paintings that lined the walls appeared to her grotesque, even though she could not positively identify the subject matter in most of them. Against her will, she found herself sharing Aunt Martha's disdain for David's talent, such as it was.

She had been just about to retire when he came down and invited her to view his latest work. She reluctantly agreed, earning a dismayed look from Jan, and had accompanied David upstairs, but now she rather wished she had declined. The coal-dark hues of virtually every canvas lent a gloomy ambiance to the entire gallery, even with the bright studio light blazing above David's easel near the back of the room. Indeed, many of the pieces resembled nothing more than splotches of thickly layered pigment, as if David had stood at a distance and flung globs of paint at each canvas. Yet, at the same time, certain of the compositions appeared to reveal half-hidden faces, others of strange, alien vistas, rendered in broad, abstract strokes. It was the oddly *organic* aspect of so many of the paintings that she found unsettling.

"Straight from your dark heart," she said softly, gazing at the nearest painting, the subject of which resembled nothing so much as a child with a huge, insect-like head, complete with bulbous, multifaceted eyes, nestled in a pool of curdled black ink. "Your aunt is right. You're no Norman Rockwell."

"Thank you," he said with a little smirk. "That means a lot."

She moved on to look at a few others and stopped when she came upon one that she found bizarrely recognizable. "That's Jan, isn't it?"

He nodded. The portrait, if one could call it that, showed a solitary figure surrounded by spindly, charred-looking tree trunks, all standing against a twilight backdrop filled with swirling, Van Gogh-esque stars. The face, too large in proportion to the body, distinctly bore Jan's features, the eyes downcast and mouth arched in a dismal frown. The impression of terrible loneliness seemed almost corporeal, and though Courtney hated to imagine her friend in this light, somehow the painting captured her essence more profoundly than a photographic image.

"Is she truly so unhappy?"

"Ever since Mom and Dad died — and then Phillip, her fiancé — she's suffered terribly. Very quietly, of course. You know how she is."

"I knew she was planning to get married, but she never told me much about Phillip. What was he like?"

"I didn't know him well either. He was from Elizabeth City. They met at the hospice. His grandfather died of cancer there."

"She never told me how they met. The way she talks now, you'd think she wouldn't dream of leaving here to marry someone."

"Believe it or not, he was planning to come here to be with her, not vice-versa."

"Really?" Her expression darkened. "I trust he was an honorable person? I mean, he wasn't looking to take advantage of the family wealth or anything. Was he?"

David stared at the painting. "As I said, I didn't know him well, but something about his character struck me as…how shall I put it? Somewhat dubious."

"And he died in a car crash?"

"A month after Mom and Dad. On the same road, not far from here."

"Strange coincidence."

"Yes."

"You know, I've begun to wonder if there's any such thing as coincidence anymore." She watched him staring at the painting of his sister and saw pain lurking in the shadows of his gaze. "So what did you want to show me?"

He smiled wanly, beckoned her with one finger, and led her to the easel near the back of the room, on which a large canvas rested. As she stood before it, her stomach knotted as a miasma of emotions began to seethe, hot and cold, tepid and ardent. It took several seconds for her to realize she was staring into a mirror, one that reflected *her* all the way to her soul.

"How did you…?"

"Photographic memory," David said, tapping his forehead. Then he pointed to a tabletop next to the easel, where she saw a couple of photos of Jan and her together, taken during their college days. "And a little help from Kodak."

"That's completely amazing," she said, looking up at the canvases that lined the wall. This portrait was so different that she could scarcely believe the same artist had painted it. The image was starkly realistic, yet rendered in soft, broad strokes, her face a brilliant sun amid one of his ubiquitous dark environments.

The work of a modern Goya.

On the canvas, her head, shown at a three-quarter angle, was slightly lowered, her eyes looking pensively outward — not at the viewer but somewhere beyond. Her face wore a sullen expression, yet in her eyes and tightly drawn mouth, she could see *rage,* deeply buried but smoldering, as indisputable in the pigment as it was in her spirit. She also saw gentleness, and a yearning to return to a long-lost innocence.

Any competent artist might have captured her image superficially, but David could not have rendered her energy, her passions, with more intimacy if his brushes had worked in her own blood.

"I don't know what to say. It's incredible."

"You like it?"

"I don't know if 'like' is the right word. I'm…stunned."

"Close enough." He chuckled. "Thought I'd try something different. This is what came out."

"This is what you've been struggling with the last few days?"

"Since the day you arrived."

"I'm stunned."

For a time, he gazed at the portrait with her, his eyes indicating he was pleased with her reaction. Naturally, he would be; in the short time he had known her, he had discovered her strengths, her vulnerabilities, her passions. No one before him had ever done so — at least, none so readily.

Only by virtue of the fact he was Jan's brother.

Now, when he stepped behind her, put his arms around her shoulders, and brought his lips to her neck, she merely stood there, neither responding nor pulling away. For a moment, he hesitated, perhaps puzzled; then one hand slid down her arm, around her waist, and pulled her body toward his, his lips working their way down to her shoulder. She feared his bite and nearly withdrew when his teeth brushed her skin. But they did not assail her, and as his tongue began to work gently but persistently on her flesh, her ambivalence gave way, and she melted into his embrace, gripping his arms as they encircled her, arcing her head back so his mouth could work on her slim throat.

His fingers roamed over her, gently but assuredly, and she luxuriated in his touch, keeping her hands on the backs of his arms, never releasing them to explore his body. She offered no resistance when he began to pull her toward the back of the studio, but when she saw a neatly made single bed, tucked into a corner behind a wall of easels and shelves of art supplies, her legs locked, and she finally pulled away to look into his eyes.

"Is this what you brought me here for?"

"I brought you here to share something I hoped you would appreciate."

"I trust you mean the painting."

He gazed at her with rare earnestness. "Yes, I mean the painting. But my feelings for you. I was beginning to think you appreciated them, too."

"I do appreciate them." She inhaled deeply to summon a little dose of courage. "Your painting shows that you grasp me pretty well. But I don't grasp what's inside you, David. You're selfish. You've got rage in there too — I probably recognize that better than anyone. But you're closed up tight. I don't know the real you."

His eyes remained inscrutable. After a time, he nodded thoughtfully. "You're right. But it's only been a few days that we've actually spent time together. And I do have a certain advantage on you."

"You mean your sister."

"Yes." He took one of her hands, lifted it to his lips, and kissed her fingers. "But I happen to know you've learned quite a bit about me in a short time. Not necessarily good things. I'm sorry about that."

"What, in particular, would you be sorry for?"

"When we were together before. I was so…rough…with you. At the time, it seemed right. Since then, I'm not so sure."

"I didn't tell you to stop."

"No," he said, gazing deeply into her eyes. "I think I was surprised."

"You think?"

"Pretty sure."

"What else?"

"I was very short with you when you were frightened. That was wrong of me."

"You were trying to make a point."

"Did I?"

"Maybe."

"Then I might not be sorry."

"No. Be sorry."

"Why?"

"Because I want you to be." Finally, she put her arms around his shoulders and kissed him lightly on the mouth. He embraced her tightly and returned the kiss, holding her there for an endless moment, absorbing her warmth, her energy. When he moved again and began to pull her toward the bed, this time, she didn't resist. But as she lay down beside him, she asked, "Why do you have this in here, when your room is just down the hall?"

"I actually sleep here fairly often. I like the atmosphere. I just work until I can't work anymore, and then I settle in for the night. It's handy."

She glanced around at the paintings on the walls. "They're almost… disturbing to me."

"Perhaps when you get to know me better, they won't be."

"Don't bet on it. If someone I didn't know had painted these, I might think he was disturbed."

"Ah. It never pays to judge an artist by his work. But if they affect you deeply, then I must be doing something right."

"You're very talented. But it's all so dark — even the one of me. You must have some light in your life."

He looked at her tenderly. "I think that would be you."

She laughed, not hiding the bitterness. "If you think so, then I really am worried about you. It's been a long time since there's been any light in my life. A long time."

"That doesn't mean you don't illuminate someone else's."

She stared into his gleaming, still-earnest sapphire eyes. He seemed so different without his hard, sardonic mask, but she still wasn't sure which face — if either — revealed the true man. For now, though, she felt secure with him. More so than she had with Jan, earlier.

He leaned forward and kissed her deeply, and she returned it, feeling that, at least for the moment, she could put aside the fear that had been simmering inside for days now. When he released her, he rose from the bed and turned off the studio light, casting the room into near-pitch darkness. A sliver of moonlight pierced the window and glanced off the oily surface of a nearby painting.

The image highlighted there nearly caused her heart to stop. It was a pale, indistinct face, roughly skull-shaped, with deep, empty eye sockets, its features crisscrossed by what appeared to be the shadows of intricate latticework — as if the thing were staring in through a window in the canvas.

She sat upright and leaned closer to the painting, as curious as she was unsettled, and as she examined the image more carefully, she discovered that the moonlight had fooled her eyes. In reality, the "face" was a stylized depiction of the moon itself, floating above a swirling cloudbank that smothered a landscape studded by the same burnt-looking trees from the portrait of Jan.

As David slid back into the bed with her, she felt his eyes studying her intently. "What's the matter?" he asked.

She shook her head. "Nothing. Just…I think I might need glasses."

"It is a bit dark in here for reading," he said with a chuckle. Then he took her hands in his. "And tonight, all you need to see with is *these.*"

"So he does have a sense of humor — however lame."

His arms encircled her and drew her to him. "I'll show you lame."

Their lips met again, and now she lost herself in his kiss, her body growing warm as his hands roved up and down her body, slowly and tenderly, so unlike the way he had touched her the night before. The icy fingers that had seized her melted and became a hazy memory, and she surrendered to his caresses, which he lavished on her with gentleness and genuine affection.

It was wonderful, revitalizing. Perhaps, she thought, *this* was at least a glimpse of the real man.

Somehow, though, she suspected that his more cruel performance the previous night represented his true, governing nature. To her own shamed surprise, she found herself beginning to hunger for that darker, harder side. She *wanted* him to take pleasure in dominating her, in using her as nothing more than an object, because maybe, for all her sins, she deserved nothing better.

At least, that was how every man she had ever known intimately saw things.

#

At 3:00 AM, she woke feeling terribly cold, and after a few groggy moments, she realized that David was no longer in bed with her. She sat up slowly, wondering why the room felt so frigid, and she remembered that, ever since she had come here, she so often felt chilly, even though autumn was still a few weeks away. A low rumble rose and fell somewhere beyond the walls, accompanied by intermittent groans and shudders, and she realized that a strong wind was pummeling the creaky old house. Darkness, unbroken except for the dimly illuminated rectangle of the window, filled David's studio, and her eyes automatically sought the painting of the moon she had previously seen. The fact that it was now invisible to her felt somehow comforting.

Outside the window, the moon had passed beyond her line of sight, but its pale light still shone on the nearby tree branches, which were dancing and bowing beneath the force of the gale. She was halfway thirsty and her bladder desired relief, but she didn't particularly want to get out of bed — mainly because she was afraid she wouldn't be able to find the door to the hall without tripping and breaking her neck.

Where had David gone, she wondered — and why? The bathroom? The kitchen? If so, wouldn't he have left the door open, and perhaps a light on in the hall?

She lay back down and pulled the covers tightly around her body, listening intently for the sound of footsteps or other movement beyond the door, a little disconcerted by his absence and the ominous rush of the wind outside. Maybe she had been sleeping restlessly, and he had gone back to his bedroom for a reprieve. That sometimes had happened with Frank, particularly when she was under stress, and he would end up going to the living room to sleep on the couch. The idea that she might have driven David out of bed on their second night together did not thrill her.

Which meant she must anticipate more nights to come.

"Let's not jump the gun," she grumbled and turned her eyes to the window, half-fancying that a shadow had passed just beyond the glass — something other than the swaying tree branches. She suddenly felt very alone and vulnerable here. It should have seemed silly, being nervous about the dark, but in light of recent events, certain old, juvenile fears hardly seemed so outlandish.

At least Aunt Martha had forgone her nocturnal yowling session, at least so far, and at this hour, it seemed unlikely that she would start.

The image of Hank Surber hanging from a broken, jagged tree branch formed in her mind, and a cold lump rose in her stomach. Like Jan, she wouldn't consciously wish such a horrible death on anyone; yet somehow, deep inside, she felt a certain, perverse satisfaction that the little freak bastard had gotten what was coming to him.

No. She couldn't think like that.

These grim thoughts were reeling through her mind now, and she *really* wished David would come back.

She heard a shuffling, creaking sound somewhere outside the room, which brought with it little rush of relief, for it *had* to be David returning. He had probably just gone to the bathroom, and he would be back in bed to warm her up any moment. She waited expectantly for him to slip back inside, but it didn't happen. Again, the floor creaked, nearer this time. Then all went silent except for the moaning wind.

Dammit. That hadn't been just the house settling. If not David, then Jan, perhaps. Surely not Aunt Martha, for she had her own bathroom upstairs, and she wouldn't even pass the studio door if she were on her way to or from the main floor.

The pressure in her bladder increased; she *really* needed to get up and relieve herself. The hard part would be getting from the bed to the door without colliding with David's easel or knocking paintings off the wall. Drawing a deep breath to bolster her determination, she slid her feet out of bed and carefully rose, holding onto the headboard to steady herself. She was wearing only her underwear, but under the circumstances, propriety was hardly her foremost concern. In the hazy moonlight, she could make out one leg of David's easel, and she carefully maneuvered around it, gritting her teeth against the crash that would result if she misjudged its position. Once clear of it, she extended her hands and, very slowly, one shuffling step at a time, crept toward the door, praying that no other obstacles lurked in her path.

She was halfway there when a rustling sound and a long creak rose out of the darkness — very distinctly inside the room with her. She froze, but one outstretched hand struck a hanging painting and sent it swinging back and forth on its wire, the wooden stretcher scraping the wall with the sound of an old woman's laugh. Thankfully, the piece didn't fall. But now, an all-too-familiar, cold dread had begun to spread through her body, binding her muscles like taut cords, and she remained stock still, listening for any suggestion of sound. For uncountable seconds, she heard nothing. Then a creak, only a few feet away.

"Who's there?" she whispered. "David?"

"Not David," came a low, raspy voice, and a claw like cold steel encircled one of her wrists. She tried to pull away, but the vise-like grip refused to yield. "Be still! Do you hear me?"

She braced herself and tugged her arm as hard as she could, but to her disbelief, the old woman's strength more than matched hers. She realized she could either attempt to scuffle with Martha in the dark or submit, at least for the moment, and find out what the creature wanted.

She relaxed a tad, but set her legs in a ready stance in case she needed to defend herself against some physical assault. "What do you want? Where's David?"

"Don't worry about David," the woman said, her voice like an angry cat's. "Worry about yourself."

"Why?"

"Because you have reason to." In the dull moonlight, Courtney saw two gleaming eyes. "Tell me, girl. Do you believe in God?"

Incredibly, the vise around her wrist tightened even more painfully. "I think so. I — I believe I do."

"You *think* so. Just what I might have expected. A girl who doesn't know her own mind."

"It's not so simple a question."

"Oh? Either God exists or he doesn't, and you either believe or you don't. Nothing complicated there."

"Why are you asking me this? Let go of my arm."

"I ask because I'm curious."

"Let go of me."

"Why don't you try to free yourself?"

"I might hurt you."

Martha cackled harshly. "Go on. Try."

For a second or two, she nearly gave in to the urge to simply use her weight to overpower the old woman, but something — fear or better judgment — stopped her. She shook her head at the darkness. "I won't be responsible for injuring you."

"I'm touched by your concern. Now, let me ask you another question, Miss Maybe-I-Believe. Has he made you pregnant?"

"What?"

"Answer."

"What business is it —?"

A second claw gripped her other wrist, and Courtney felt herself being pulled forward. She felt rather than saw the old woman's face an inch from hers, and the growling voice came again.

"David. Has. He. Made. You. Pregnant?"

"No."

"You're certain?"

"Pretty certain. Now you tell me," she said, trying to force confidence she did not feel into her voice. "Why are you asking me this?"

"So I might know what to do with you."

"What does that mean?"

A long silence followed. "I have a vested interest in these children," Martha finally said. "I wonder if I have any interest in you."

"Are you threatening me?"

Martha exhaled a chuckle. "I don't need to threaten you. Or make promises. I just do what must be done."

"You had no business coming in here."

"And you had business coming into my room? You forget where you are, girl. I come and go where I please, any time I please." Martha's voice lowered. "You've seen something… unusual… around this house, haven't you? But you doubt your senses. I have some advice for you. Do not doubt."

Courtney shuddered under the old woman's invisible glare. "I haven't seen anything," she whispered weakly.

"Fool yourself if you wish. That's not good for you, though. Not good at all. I asked about your belief in God because, if you have any issues to take up with him, now might be a good time."

"Explain yourself," she said, her dread melting as her old friend rage began to simmer. "If you're going to threaten me, you'd better speak plainly."

Martha cackled again. "I've said what I came to say." The steel claws released her wrists. "Now, good night."

"Wait."

She heard a few creaks and groans, and then the door opened and closed quickly, never revealing a glimmer of light in the hall. Only the sound of the rushing wind outside now filled the chamber.

"Damn it."

She stood there for a few terrible minutes, her heart pounding, her head aching with fury and frustration. My God, how could that old woman have so easily immobilized her, in the dark and with just her bare hands?

Shortly, she again heard a creaking outside, and a few seconds later, the door opened to reveal the hallway — now illuminated by the overhead lights — and David's framed silhouette. As he stepped inside, he caught sight of her in the encroaching light, and he flipped a switch beside the door. The studio lamp above his easel flared to life, scorching her sensitive eyes.

"Courtney? What's the matter?"

"I had to go to the bathroom," she said, disappointed to find her voice quavering. "But your aunt came into the room."

"Martha? In here?"

She nodded. "She seemed to be interested in whether you've made me pregnant."

David raised an eyebrow. "Nosy old biddy, isn't she?"

"Much more than that. Where did you go?"

"I wasn't sleeping well, so I went to get a drink. I didn't want to disturb you."

"*You* didn't."

He came to her and slipped an arm around her shoulders. "You're upset. I'm sorry."

"You didn't know she would come in here — did you?"

"She's never done anything like that before." He glanced at the ceiling. "I've got to take her into town in the morning for some things from the drug store. I'll straighten her out then."

"David, what's wrong with her?"

"I take it you don't mean physically."

She shook her head. "It's much more than just dementia."

"What do you mean?"

"That woman is dangerous. And you know it as well as I do."

His eyes narrowed. "Why don't you tell me what's on your mind?"

"First, I am going to go pee. Then I'll do exactly that."

#

Chapter 11

After breakfast, David left for the drugstore in his BMW with Martha, whose expression suggested more than disgust that she might be subject to any ordinary human frailties. From the living room window, Courtney watched the car turn out of the driveway, doubting that David would so much as mention the previous night's incident to Martha, much less "straighten her out." Then, as soon as the car passed beyond the trees, Courtney turned and hurried up the stairs, past the second floor, up to the third, too resolute now to feel nervous, only hoping that Jan would stay in her room for the next few minutes and not come looking for her.

However, once she stood alone in the silent gloom of Martha's secretive domain, a cold sense of foreboding swept over her, and her thudding pulse became a hammer against her eardrums. She crept toward the closed bedroom door, wary of the floorboards groaning and alerting Jan to the fact that she was up here. Testing the doorknob, she found it locked — as she expected — so, from her jeans pocket, she drew the skeleton key she had taken from David's door and slipped it into the keyhole, praying that it worked on both the upstairs and downstairs locks. She took a bracing breath and carefully turned the key.

With a gratifying click, the lock yielded, and she pushed the door open, releasing a noxious mélange of mothballs and disinfectant. Leaving the door open in case she needed to make a hasty retreat, she stepped into Martha's inner sanctum.

The first thing she noticed was that the soft drink cans were gone and the furniture had been dusted. In fact, in the morning sunlight, the tidied room bore an almost cheerful glow. The old witch must have grown weary of living in squalor, she thought. Apart from the rather morbid-looking grandfather clock and the peculiar, rope-framed bed, the sheer ordinariness of the woman's room seemed at odds with Courtney's expectations, and for a terrible few seconds, she felt her resolve wavering. But the moment was fleeting, and she went straight to the huge dresser and began opening drawers.

Nothing but Martha's undergarments, sweaters, and a few scarves. A cardboard box filled with toiletries. A sewing kit and a few loose spools of thread. A couple of small jewelry boxes, both empty.

How could she possibly expect to discover what Martha was up to when she had no idea what she was looking for? But something pressed her to believe that she would know it when she found it. Heaving a sigh of frustration, she went to the closet — where she learned what had happened to the soft drink cans.

As she opened the door, a dozen or so cans came clattering out to roll across the hardwood floor, and as reflexes sent her stumbling back from the avalanche, she nearly lost her balance, maintaining her footing only by grabbing one of the tall bedposts — which budged the heavy bed just enough for its feet to scrape the floor with sound of a bear growling.

Jesus! That tore it. Jan would be up to investigate any second now, and there was no earthly way she could explain her presence here a second time. Undoubtedly, Martha had rigged the cans as an alarm — just to ensure that Courtney would be caught should she be audacious enough to repeat her original, ill-fated stunt.

Bravo, you clever shrew.

Well, if anything were to be found here, it must be in the closet. And if she could no longer hope to escape discovery, she might as well go all the way. Galvanized by adrenaline, she began rifling through the hanging dresses, the blouses, the fine satin nightgowns, the blankets and bed sheets folded on the end shelves. In here, the odor of mothballs was almost unbearable. She found a ton of old clothing piled in the corners — probably garments that should have been disposed of but that Martha had saved, for whatever reason. There were blouses, slacks, skirts, jackets, even shoes, and nothing looked less than thirty years old. At least a dozen shoeboxes, a few handbags, and a large hatbox occupied the upper shelves.

Her heart fell, for surely, Jan would even now be on her way up to investigate; Courtney was going to get caught snooping — again — and for what? Confirming that Martha was a hopeless packrat?

She stood and listened for a few seconds, expecting to hear Jan's footsteps on the stairs. So far, nothing. She could hardly breathe any easier, but she welcomed every remaining second before she had to answer for her actions. She was just about to abandon the closet when something at the corner of her eye caught her attention, and she turned to identify it. There, behind the pile of clothes at one end — a familiar pattern. Too familiar.

She pulled it free and held it up. A black, white, and mocha striped sweater, obviously newer than the other clothes in the pile.

And very obviously Courtney's.

Something fell to the hardwood floor, and she looked down to see a small brown paper packet, which she picked up and opened without hesitation. A pair of silver, sapphire-studded earrings fell into her palm.

Also hers.

"Why, you crafty old…"

"Courtney? Fancy finding you here."

It wasn't Jan but Arlene standing in the doorway, regarding her with narrow, suspicious eyes. Courtney's heart sank, for she had appeared the fool once already to the kindly housekeeper. Regardless, at the moment, her ire had the upper hand. She held up her sweater and earrings. "I thought I might retrieve these. They belong to me."

"Do they?" Arlene's gaze turned doubtful.

"Yes, they do. Dear Aunt Martha isn't only demented, she's apparently a kleptomaniac."

Arlene reached out and touched the sweater. "Where did you find them?"

She pointed to the closet. "In there. That was the racket you heard. Martha piled cans up so they'd fall if anyone opened the doors."

"How did you know Martha took them?"

She hesitated. "I didn't, actually."

"So…you weren't in here looking for these specifically?"

"No."

"I didn't think you were going to do anything like this again, Courtney."

"Neither did I." So far, Arlene had shown herself to be compassionate, so she decided to stick with honesty. "Look, I don't know if you know anything about what's going on, but Martha threatened me last night."

"Threatened you?"

"She came down in the middle of the night and basically suggested I should make my peace with God."

"I see." Arlene stared deeply into her eyes. "And you believed her?"

She shrugged. "At the time, it seemed like a good idea to take her seriously."

"So you reckon that's grounds to come up here and start poking around — again?"

"Arlene, that old woman is scheming something. It apparently involves me, and I want to know what it is." She held up her sweater and earrings. "Why do you suppose she would take these?"

"I don't have the first idea." Arlene shook her head in annoyance, but after a long look at Courtney, her expression turned sad. She sighed heavily. "I have to tell you, I don't imagine it was for anything good. Did she mention the Monarch again?"

"Not directly. But she suggested that I accept it as real. That I should believe in the things I've seen and heard."

Arlene now stood close to her and said in a soft voice, "Courtney, I'm going to tell you something. Now, I don't know if the Monarch is real. My head tells me there can't be any such thing. But that old woman. She can sure make things happen, one way or another. And if she's threatening you, it's not something to take lightly."

"That," she said with a hard swallow, "is why I'm here now."

"I understand. But this isn't the right thing to do."

"What do you think she could 'make happen'?"

"Let's just say she gets her way. She *always* gets her way. That's the most I can tell you."

Courtney sighed in frustration. "Is there no such thing as a straight answer around here?"

"Courtney. You understand I'm risking my livelihood talking to you right now. You know that?"

She gave Arlene a long, remorseful look. "I'm sorry. The last thing I want to do is put you in an awkward situation."

"Girl, you've already done that." She looked around at the scattered cans and scowled. "Well, let's get this mess cleaned up. This time, and this time only, I won't say a word to a soul."

"Why are you helping me?"

"Because I believe you're a good person at heart. And you're Jan's friend." She knelt to gather up a few of the cans.

"I appreciate your kindness," Courtney said.

"That girl does think the world of you."

"Where is she?"

"Out in the garage, cleaning out her car. I gathered y'all supposed to go to the beach this morning."

"First I've heard of it. So she doesn't know I'm up here?"

"No."

"That's a relief. You know, you don't have to stay here and help me, if it makes you uncomfortable."

Arlene chuckled. "I'm a lot more uncomfortable leaving you here alone."

"I didn't mean to drag you into this."

"We'd better hurry," Arlene said, placing another armload of cans back in the closet. "Unless you want to have to explain this over again to Jan."

"I suppose I should tell her, shouldn't I?"

The older woman gave her a stern glance. "I don't think you should say a word about it. Not to her, not to David, not to anybody. You don't want it getting back to the old woman — assuming she doesn't figure it out on her own."

Courtney felt a little chill. "You're frightened of her, aren't you?"

Arlene shook her head. "Girl, I'm too old to be frightened of her. No, ma'am, I *dread* that woman."

#

The afternoon at the beach with Jan was excruciating. They exchanged perhaps three meaningful words on the hour-long drive there, three more while catching the few rays that occasionally slipped through the gaps in the clouds, and a final three on the way home. Jan did carry on aplenty, but it was all chitchat — mostly fond reminiscences about their times together in college and people and places they had known over the years. Several times, Courtney wanted to break down and confess what she had done, or at least lay out her fears and try again to extract some answers; however, each time she even started to mention Aunt Martha's name, Jan tensed up and either fell completely silent or moved on to topics such as drinking games and attracting the opposite sex.

Clearly, Jan was suffering from shock and denial. The events of the past few days had been traumatic, certainly, but it was something more than that. Her parents' and fiancé's deaths, perhaps. Whatever her outward face, Jan still had not come to terms with them. Maybe these recent events had dragged her pain, which she had tried so hard to bury, back to the forefront of her consciousness.

Somehow, Courtney thought, she had to get away from Fearing. No more idle days lounging at the beach or sipping wine with Jan. Beginning tomorrow, she must redouble her efforts to find a job, a new place to live, and become independent again. Having all her needs provided for, at least in this environment, no longer held the slightest appeal.

She had racked her brain trying to think of somewhere else to go, someone she might stay with until she found her feet again. But Frank had been so possessive, so jealous of anyone else in her life, that any close friends she'd ever had, except for Jan, had long since drifted away. Seeking help from her parents was out of the question. After the things her own father had done, she had vowed never to speak to him again, and her decrepit, alcoholic mother could barely sustain herself, much less help her.

Truly, she was on her own.

She had been apprehensive about returning to the Blackburn house, uncertain whether Martha might have learned about her latest round of trespassing, but something told her that Arlene had seen to covering her tracks. Eventually, Martha would discover the sweater and earrings missing, but by then, hopefully, Courtney would be gone for good and beyond worrying about the demented old witch ever again. She could still scarcely believe Martha had stolen her things — the senselessness of it! — and she wondered how the old thief would take finding that she had been robbed of her prizes. Courtney had half-expected Arlene to suggest she return her things to the closet to allay any suspicion, but that was something she would never do. If Martha were to discover the theft immediately, it just might draw her out and reveal her motives. The idea was almost enticing, but for the inevitable consequence of having to face the crone's fury.

Jan was her only company at dinner, and it was as grim as the afternoon at the beach. Arlene had made a fine meal of ham, potatoes au gratin, and fresh green beans, but Courtney barely ate any of it, and afterward, she retired to her room and logged onto the Internet to do some job hunting. She posted her résumé at a few promising-looking sites, but she didn't find herself feeling very hopeful. After an hour or so, a knock came at her door, and her heart stuttered. Summoning her courage, she called, "Come in," only to feel a warm wave of relief, broken by a sharp stab of anxiety, when David, rather than an irate Martha, stepped inside.

"How about a run?" he asked, looking infuriatingly cheerful.

"It's dark outside."

"Best time for it, don't you think? It's getting cooler, and there's less chance of anyone seeing you."

"You think someone might be out there watching for me?"

"No. You do."

She gazed coolly at him. "How do you know there isn't a murderer lurking nearby?"

"I don't consider that our problem."

"No? And why not?"

"Because whoever had it in for Hank Surber took care of his business, and I expect that's that."

"You're very confident."

"No reason not to be."

For several moments, she studied his carefree posture, his earnest expression. Why *should* he be so certain they would be safe?

"I could stand to get out of here for a little while," she said slowly, unsure she liked where her mind was going.

He smiled warmly. "Then how about we both change, and I'll meet you here in ten minutes?"

She felt her face burning, but he didn't seem to notice. "All right. In ten."

"Good."

If she felt safe with anyone here, it was David. He had already proven he would protect her against physical threat. *But he had all but brutalized her, sexually.* What was really happening behind those luminous, sapphire blue eyes that appeared so adoring of her?

She changed into her T-shirt and running shorts, only then realizing that the air felt quite chilly again. There was no air conditioning in her suite. Why did it so often feel cold here, in late summer, in the Great Dismal Swamp? If she believed in unnatural things, she might think it was exactly that. Well, when she considered the thing she had glimpsed, and that Aunt Martha *wanted* her to believe in, she couldn't be sure that her definition of "natural" was quite what it used to be. So far, she had dealt with the chaos in her mind by accepting that, somehow, her senses had been fooled.

But they hadn't been fooled. If anything, manipulated.

When David reappeared, dressed in white gym shorts and a gray T-shirt bearing the logo of Beckham College, she couldn't help but admire his well-toned arms and legs, his slim waist, his tanned skin. Her heart pounded a little, just as it had when she had first seen him — how many days ago was it? Even now, after having spent two nights with him, each time they came together, he seemed more complex, more fascinating.

More perilous.

"I distinctly recall you saying you didn't like to run."

"I like being with you. Which trumps my aversion to running."

"I see."

"Shall we?"

She shrugged and followed him out the door, into the humid but distinctly cool evening air, taking a few long, deep breaths to prepare herself. As she started around the corner of the house after him, she glanced up and noticed in the illuminated upstairs window a dark, hunched silhouette, its head slowly swiveling as its unseen eyes tracked them across the lawn. She tried to ignore the image, to banish the notion that Martha was something other than an eccentric old curmudgeon who delighted in making mischief, but the very sight of the woman dropped a cold stone into her stomach.

A crescent moon hovered in the hazy sky, turning the landscape a dull silver-gray, so she could see far enough ahead to avoid any hazards. At the bottom of the driveway, somewhat to her surprise, David turned right, away from town and toward the darker reaches of the Dismal Swamp. At first, her mind rebelled at the idea of venturing into unknown territory in the dark, and she nearly halted to voice her protest. But David's point that she would be camouflaged against prying eyes was well-taken, and she forced herself to trust his judgment. She let him set the pace, a comfortable jog she could sustain for a couple of miles or more, and once they rounded a curve and left the hulking old house behind, she began to relax a little.

Still, the memory of that *other* thing lurked undimmed in the back of her mind, all the more so since Martha had seen them leave. Though her mind might accept the possibility that her perceptions had been distorted, her heart certainly didn't. David's presence reassured and steadied her, so she ran with confidence, yet she knew that if he were not here right now, her self-control wouldn't hold up any better than a matchstick tower in the wind.

They ran without speaking to each other, which suited her fine. For one thing, she didn't care to waste her breath while working out her body, and for another, the silent night clearly disapproved of any sound louder than the syncopated thumping of their shoes on the asphalt. Tonight, there was no wind, and the lonely calls of night birds and crickets crept out of the close-pressing trees only sporadically and from a distance.

Her eyes continually darted into the dark thickets, her senses alert for any movement or other sign of someone or something shadowing them. Once, she heard something crunching through the nearby brush, seemingly keeping pace with them, but her roving eyes failed to spot anything. David ran on, oblivious to the noise, though she knew damn well that he must hear it too.

For God's sake, it's just an animal. There are "normal" animals in the woods, you know.

By running, she had hoped to find relief from the stifling atmosphere of the Blackburns' ancient keep, but inside or out, it no longer mattered. For her, Fearing held only gloom, and despite his impenetrable veneer, David seemed the only fixture firm enough to cling to.

The road threaded its way deeper into the abyss, and they passed only one farmhouse, a vaguely sinister-looking thing with a single light burning in an upstairs window. As she glanced at it, a dark silhouette appeared briefly in the window, bringing to mind the image of old Martha watching from her aerie. Even after the figure disappeared, the eyes of the night seemed to have awakened to her presence and now regarded her with icy disapproval.

Something crunched heavily in the woods off to the right, and she nearly slammed to a halt. David kept going, though, his eyes set firmly ahead, evidently oblivious to the noises. The trees now hid the moon, and she feared finding loose gravel or a hidden pothole that might send her stumbling. She slowed down, hoping it would signal David to do the same, but he maintained his pace, unfazed by the diminished visibility.

"Hey," she finally called softly. "Hold up, will you?"

"Tired?" he called back.

"No, I can't see."

She heard his footfalls winding down, and she closed the distance between them, barely able to make out his faint, silver-limned figure against the featureless black backdrop. "The road's straight," he said. "Nothing to worry about."

"We should have gone the other way. At least we'd have the moon."

"I like the dark," he said, his teeth flashing as he grinned. "And the privacy back here."

"I've always preferred to see what I was getting into."

Their pace had dwindled to a fast walk, which suited Courtney fine. Only the faintest gleam revealed David's eyes. "You're not afraid, are you?"

"Just a little worried about myself, for following you so willingly."

"Yes, in your position, I'd worry too."

She didn't laugh. "So where *does* this road go?"

"About half mile on, there are a couple of forks that lead a ways into the river basin before they just peter out. Years ago, there were a few plantations out this way, but the swamp just swallowed them up. That land's no good for anything now. Arlene grew up back there, you know."

"Really?"

He nodded. "Her family pretty much came apart at the seams when their farm failed. My grandparents — Dad's parents – basically rescued her from destitution, and she's been loyal to the family ever since."

"I see."

She gazed at his hidden face. "I'm going to ask you the same question I asked Jan. What keeps you tied to this place? With all the trouble you've had, haven't you considered moving somewhere else?"

He didn't answer for a moment, and she could feel his stare. "You never had a home place that your family occupied for generations. A place where you grew up that you loved."

"No."

"Then I wouldn't expect you to understand. For all its troubles, I've always loved it here. So has Jan. We'd do anything to protect our home. This is our heritage."

"Basically the same as Jan's answer. I guess it's a matter of perspective."

"I'd say it's a shame you've never really had a place to call your own. This place has made us who we are. I mean, we've both been out in the world, spent time in other places, but we've always known that *this* is waiting for us. That it's where we ultimately belong."

She tried to focus on him in the darkness. "I've always felt it was better not to get attached to something you will eventually lose. Nothing lasts forever, David."

"No, but many things will outlast you and me. My family's legacy, for instance. It's worth working to preserve."

"What about children?" she asked. "Do you want to have kids — to preserve your legacy?"

"Well, I'd say I want to have children," he said with a little chuckle. "I'm just not sure I want to be a father. Not anytime soon, anyway."

Something heavy crashed in the darkness to the right. Then a splash, like a boulder dropping into a shallow body of water. They froze.

The sound of wood cracking.

Another crash.

"What the…?" Courtney said, her eyes burning holes in the darkness. "What the hell is that?"

One of David's hands slid around her shoulder and gripped her bicep fiercely. He said nothing, but she could sense his eyes intently scanning the dense woods.

"What is that?"

"I don't know."

The crunching-splashing sounds continued for a moment, drawing nearer, and then stopped.

Something in Courtney's field of vision moved: an indistinct shape, pale and huge, some indeterminate distance into the trees. To her horror, David let go of her arm and began moving forward slowly.

"David!" she whispered, her nerves rapidly unraveling now. *What in God's name did he think he was doing?* "David, stop!"

He didn't answer and continued creeping toward the woods until his figure dissolved, wraithlike, into the darkness, though she could still hear the sound of his footsteps. The pale thing in the trees shifted slightly, and she heard a low, heavy rumble — the sound of breathing, like a big cat, or a bear. *But this was neither.*

David's footsteps died at the edge of the road. Even though he was much closer to the thing, she felt vulnerable, alone. She took a few steps forward, her eyes trying to trace the contours of the amorphous shape just beyond the tree line. She thought she saw a huge, oval skull with a pair of deep, black sockets, within which something twinkled, but then the thing moved and became a formless blob of mist.

It was watching them. *Her.*

This was the instrument of Hank Surber's death. Aunt Martha's Monarch. No flawed perceptions, no imaginary concoction of shadows and light here.

She felt David's presence nearby, but when his hand closed on her wrist, she nearly yelped. "Don't move," he whispered. "And maybe it'll leave us alone."

He had no sooner spoken than the misty shape began to undulate like a huge glowworm; then it swirled into motion and vanished. A moment later, something splashed, and the sledgehammer pounding in the mud followed, punctuated by the staccato cracking of tree limbs. Gradually, the sounds receded into silence.

She stood there for several ages, contemplating the consequences of moving a muscle. She could hear David's breathing, at first rapid and shallow, finally softening to a regular, deep rhythm.

Overhead, she heard a rapid beating sound, like great wings, and she looked up quickly but saw nothing.

Just a big bird. A buzzard, perhaps. Frightened by the thing in the woods.

"That was odd," David finally said.

She shot him a surprised glance, but said nothing for a time. Finally, she asked, "Is it gone?"

"Yeah, it's gone."

"That," she said, "was what came to my window the other night. *That* was your Aunt Martha's Monarch."

#

Once reasonably certain the thing had retreated beyond the possibility of returning, they had broken into a sprint, heedless of obstacles that might lie in their path, never pausing to look back, stopping only when they reached the relative safety of the driveway. Before they made it halfway to the house, Courtney's legs buckled and she collapsed, less from the exertion than delayed shock. David knelt next to her and offered his hand, but she waved him away.

"Just give me a minute. I'll be all right."

"I know."

She gazed at him, panting. "'Odd.' You called that thing 'odd.'"

"It was."

"It was a fucking horror. Don't you have any idea what this means? Don't you know what that thing did?"

"You're certain you know what it was?"

"What else could it have been?"

"Well, it was damn big. Wild dog, maybe."

She stared at him in amazement. "You're as demented as the old woman. A *dog?"*

He shrugged. "Well, it was too pale to be a bear, and it certainly wasn't a horse."

"Didn't you see it? That thing was twice the size of a horse."

"How could you tell in the dark? You don't know how far away from you it was."

She dragged herself to her feet and faced him defiantly. "It wasn't so dark that I would mistake a damn dog."

"Dark enough," he said, glancing toward the road. "What say we get back inside?"

"You think it might come back this way?"

"Who knows? Look. Humor me, and let's assume it was a dog. It could still be very dangerous."

She said nothing but began walking, her muscles on fire, her eyes fixed on the shadowed hulk of the Blackburn house, her mind beyond caring whether David remained with her. How could a man be so blind?

No, not blind.

Complicit.

He must be. To think she was just coming to trust him, and now this. The sting surpassed her fear.

She found herself shivering as she walked and realized the air was frigid, like wintertime.

As she went around the house toward the back door, David trailing several steps behind, her footsteps crunched too loudly in the gravel, and she stepped more gingerly, her ears sensitized to any sound in the trees. She paused at the door, for she could hear, far in the distance, the vaguest whisper of wind beginning again, and for a second or two, what sounded like a heavy, rhythmic thumping.

David opened the door and started inside. "Are you coming?"

"I'll be there in a minute."

"You sure you want to stay out here alone?"

"Go."

He complied with a wry shrug, leaving her gazing into the wall of darkness, her head cocked slightly as she listened, trying to decide whether the distant, nearly indiscernible sounds indicated something approaching. After a full two minutes, when the wind was all she could hear, she went inside, locked the door, and stood at the window for yet another minute, numb to the idea that she might actually be in danger.

How, she wondered, could anyone even hope to convince her that she had seen anything so mundane as a wild dog — or that she couldn't tell the difference between the sound of a four-legged animal running and a two-legged one?

#

Chapter 12

Even after standing beneath a near-scalding shower for ten minutes, she felt as if she had bathed in ice water.

She dried her hair, luxuriating in the warm breath of her blow dryer, and then went to her dresser to pick out some fresh clothes. Opening the top drawer, the first thing she noticed was the sweater she had retrieved from Martha's closet. For one wild moment, adrenaline spiked in her veins, and she wondered whether she was prepared for a nasty confrontation, after having hoped, just this afternoon, that the old woman would not discover what she had done until she had left this place permanently.

Trembling, she pulled on her sweater, and then went to her jewelry case and slipped on the earrings Martha had stolen.

Hell, chances were, she wouldn't even encounter the hag tonight. What she desired most was a stiff drink and some time to determine how she was going to escape from this madhouse in which she had unwittingly imprisoned herself.

Confronting David was pointless. If he were already aware of the true nature of the thing in the woods — which he surely was — then he had his reasons for withholding it from her, and nothing she could say would make any difference.

She made her way to the great room, headed straight for the bar, and began rummaging through the bottles on the various shelves, taking stock of the plentiful spirits. One interesting-looking bottle proved to be a half-full fifth of Woodford Reserve, so she took a tall tumbler from the overhead rack, dropped in a few ice cubes from the mini freezer, and filled the glass to the brim with the fine bourbon.

Then she sat down on a barstool, sipped the strong, smooth whiskey, and waited.

"Hey, sweetie."

Jan sat down next to her, already holding a glass of wine, her pupils dilated. She looked Courtney up and down and frowned. "Are you cold?"

She nodded. "I suppose you're not."

"No, it's quite warm."

"I'd like to borrow your car tomorrow, if it's all right. I've got more job hunting to do."

Jan shook her head. “As it turns out, I need to go in to hospice tomorrow. They’re short a person.”

Courtney’s heart sank a little, but this turn seemed almost inevitable. “All right.”

“Tell you what. You could ride in with me and then take the car for the day. I have to be there at eight, so you’d need to get up early.”

“I usually do.”

“Oh, that’s right.” Jan stared into space. “I hear you went running tonight.”

“Yes.”

“Had a bit of a scare?”

“A wild dog. Apparently.”

“You don’t think that’s what it was?”

“It was whatever David said it was.”

Jan’s already bright eyes sparkled with unkind humor. “So…you’ve come around to trusting him.”

“I don’t really have any choice, do I?”

“What do you mean?”

“I mean that instead of the truth, all I get from either of you is the standard Blackburn family line — that my perceptions have gone haywire. That I ‘don’t understand.’ Well, I understand enough to know that I made a mistake coming here.”

“Courtney…”

“It’s true. There’s something very wrong about this place, and I don’t want any part of it anymore. I need to find somewhere else to go.”

“And where might that be?”

“I don’t know. Yet.”

“You’re being rash. Come on. This is me, you know.”

Courtney glared at Jan, her stomach twisting in knots, the ice in her glass tinkling as her hand began to tremble. Torn between the overwhelming desires to lash out at her friend and humbly beg for honesty, her voice failed her.

Jan downed her remaining wine and gazed at Courtney for a long moment before turning her eyes away. “Why don’t you just accept how things are with us and be happy?” she said. “You don’t want for anything here. You have everything you need. You’ve even got David…if you want him.”

“Yes. But I don’t have all the answers.”

“So what? A wise person knows which questions to ask and which ones not to. Maybe you need to learn to differentiate between the two.”

“Your secrets affect my life. How can I ‘be happy’ without trust between us? Here I’ve entrusted my life to you, but evidently, you don’t trust me. None of you do. I can't keep living like this."

"Given your personal situation," Jan said coldly, "you really don't have any choice." She placed her empty glass on the bar and turned toward the door. "I'll see you early in the morning."

Courtney didn't bother to watch Jan leave. She looked down at her drink through a tapestry of crystal tears, lifted the glass to her lips for a long swallow, and then wiped the water from her eyes. There could be no feeling sorry for herself. She had to remain in control, to *think,* to determine what to do next.

Tomorrow, she thought, she would have access to Jan's car.

Whether she would return it, she didn't yet know.

She heard a heavy *thunk* and, thinking Jan must have re-entered the room and let the door handle strike the wall, didn't bother to turn around. But when she realized she was still alone, she slowly swiveled her head, and as her gaze fell on the window that faced the woods, an icy, iron fist slammed into her, dumping her from her stool onto the floor. Her drink sloshed and the glass rattled as it spun on the bar, thought it didn't tip over. A few drops fell onto her outstretched hand, but her blood was so cold she didn't feel them.

Pressed against the windowpane was a tall oblong of pale bone, with deep hollows for eyes, within which something glittered icy blue, and a gaping mouth rimmed by crooked battlements of ivory. Before she could open her mouth to cry out, it vanished.

She struggled to her knees, desperate to keep fear from immobilizing her. Grasping the barstool with one hand, she shakily pulled herself to her feet, wavering like a willow in a gale, breathing deeply to try to steady her nerves. Her first impulse was to call out for someone — for David — but she fought it back, some small, rational part of her mind insisting that it would be pointless now. She would only look the fool to him. Again.

The thing was toying with her.

Or perhaps *it* wasn't.

Aware of a new presence in the room, Courtney turned and saw, standing in the doorway, the stooped, withered figure of the witch from the attic, her eyes shining like globes of polished glass. Beneath a drab gray nightgown, Martha's legs appeared motionless as the wiry body began gliding toward her, the too-bright eyes never blinking.

As Martha drew nearer, Courtney detected a faint whiff of an acrid, chemical odor.

"Oh, my," the old woman croaked, eyeing her sweater. "You've been messing where you're not supposed to be messing, haven't you?"

"I could say the same about you," Courtney managed.

Martha's eyes roved up and down her body, her expression unreadable. Crooked fingers came forward to caress her shoulder, to stroke the rib-knit fabric of her sweater. Finally, Martha's lips spread into a grin so wide that the ancient skin of her cheeks looked as if it would split, and she began to chuckle.

"Yes, you would be cold, wouldn't you? Very cold."

"What?"

"Naughty girl, I should be cross with you. But it's all right. I don't need those anymore. It already has your scent!"

Then, with shocking vigor, the crone whirled and glided out of the great room, her laughter ringing through the hall like an ecstatic crow calling to the wind.

"It doesn't matter anymore! It doesn't matter anymore!"

#

Instead of retreating to her room, Courtney went straight up the stairs to David's studio, where she knew she would find him. He was standing at his easel, dressed in old, paint-streaked jeans and a tattered T-shirt, a palette knife in hand. Mellow electronic music, almost eerie, wafted from speakers somewhere behind him. His eyes flickered toward her as she stood in the doorway.

"Did I hear Aunt Martha yowling?"

"Yes."

"At you?"

"You might say that."

"You're very pale. Do I need to go deal with her again?"

"Can you commit her to an asylum?"

"Someday, maybe. Are you cold?"

"Yes."

"Odd. It's warm in here."

"So I'm told."

He set down his palette knife and looked into her eyes. "What's wrong?"

She gazed accusingly at him. "Oh, I suppose I'm just paranoid. What with that old woman fussing and a wild dog lurking outside."

He raised an eyebrow. "You're still upset about that?"

"I'm upset with your willful blindness."

"Meaning what?"

Her voice barely above a whisper, she said, "That was no wild dog out there. And you know it."

He sighed. "We're back to that, are we? Okay, Courtney. Maybe I was wrong. Why don't you tell me what it was?"

"I want to hear it from you."

"I hate to disappoint you."

She didn't want to tell him. She didn't want to appear to him a frightened, deluded creature whose nerves and will had been broken. But she wanted to melt the ice in his gaze. She needed the eyes that had gazed adoringly at her the night before.

"It was at the great room window. That thing. I saw it."

"When?"

"A few minutes ago. Just before your aunt came in and started on me."

"Okay. Tell me what you saw."

"A huge face. All bony, like a skull. But…different…from a human's."

"Different?"

"Misshapen. The proportions are wrong. David, I want to get out of here."

"Where to?"

"I don't know. Anywhere. I can't take this anymore."

"I don't know what to tell you, Courtney. I don't know who or what else there is for you."

"There's no one," she said softly, holding back the emotions that threatened to cascade over her. "There's no one."

"Come here." He raised his arms to her, and she shuffled forward, helpless to do anything else. She fell into his embrace with some relief, but his eyes had yet to lose their chill. Here she was in the arms of a man who was lying to her. No better than Frank, she thought. Men knew nothing other than to lie to her.

Still, she wrapped her arms around him, for his warm, strong body was an anchor, and without one, the maelstrom in her mind would bear her into an inescapable abyss. She pressed her head against his shoulder to keep from having to meet his cynical gaze again. She hated seeing it.

Most of all, she hated being the one responsible for it.

You fool. If you believe you're responsible, then he's played you so well that you're already beyond hope.

She felt him maneuvering her toward the bed in the corner.

Of course. Why not? Only natural for a man to use her vulnerability to his advantage.

Instead of lowering her to the bed, he turned her body so that her back was against the cold, hard wall. His hands pressed against her shoulders, pinning her there, and he stepped back to make her look into his eyes.

Deep blue seas. Alluring, but still icy.

He leaned forward and pressed his lips to hers, and they were hot, and she *needed* his heat, so she responded fervently. One of his hands lowered, fluttered briefly over her breasts, and then moved to encircle her hip. He drew her body into his, then pressed forward, grinding her back against the wall before pulling away again. His hand slid back around her waist and moved to unbutton and then unzip her jeans. She moved her hips to work them over her thighs, and his hand assisted them on their way down.

He pulled her toward the bed, roughly, and then said, in a hard voice, "Get on your knees."

She complied without saying a word. And she understood exactly why she was doing it, which nearly brought tears back to her eyes. But they didn't come.

She didn't think she would ever weep again. Not ever.

#

Chapter 13

By Jan's almost-ebullient mood on the drive to Elizabeth City, Courtney might have thought there had never been a tense moment between them.

As soon as they left Fearing, the merciless chill loosened its hold on her, and her spirit rejoiced at the prospect of escaping the bonds of the Blackburn house. Rather than engage Jan in an uncomfortable and pointless discussion about the horror of the previous night, she focused only on the promise of the future and her resolve to become self-sufficient again. During her online forays, she had found a couple of office jobs that looked more than half-promising, so after dropping Jan off at the hospice on Cedar Street, she set her sights on at least making a few interview appointments.

Jan got off at noon, so she had four hours to make her ultimate decision.

She drove several blocks along a picturesque, the tree-lined avenue, where the houses were very old and very large — and beyond all thought of ever owning, even if she secured gainful employment. They were for people like the Blackburns, and who knew what secrets might hide within *these* ancient mansions? Whatever. Right now, her foremost concern was getting out of Fearing permanently. If she could just nail down some job, anything that could get her halfway on her feet, she wouldn't hesitate to accept Jan's offer — if it were still good — to help with paying for an apartment.

According to her directions, the first of her targets — a lawyer's office — was on Colonial Avenue, down near the waterfront.

It was an hour's drive to Norfolk. A couple of more to Richmond. Maybe five to DC. How far could she get on the small amount of cash she had with her and a worthless bank account – in a stolen car?

In the grip of last night's terror, fleeing had seemed her only choice. Now, the idea of venturing solo into the world seemed more daunting than facing Aunt Martha's Monarch. At least at in Fearing, she wasn't alone.

Alone.

It was a damned ridiculous fear, but one that had ruled her since the day she left home. And a horrible, shameful reason for having married Frank.

She found the lawyer's office in a non-descript brick building a few doors down from the municipal plaza. She parked on the street a short distance away, gave herself a once-over in the rearview mirror, and got out of the car, only to freeze, her heart jumping to her throat, when a rusty, red pickup truck came rumbling by, moving at a snail's pace.

An old farmer, who glanced at her and smiled toothlessly as the truck chugged past.

"Dammit," she muttered, one fist clenching. She steadied herself with a hand on the roof of the Jaguar until her heart stopped pounding. Then she smoothed her skirt, tugged the bottom of her lightweight linen blazer to straighten it, and headed for the office door, still feeling ill at ease and a little frumpy in clothes two seasons old.

For Christ's sake. Who in this town would even notice?

Drawing herself up and dragging forth the confident businesswoman who seemed to have taken an unwelcome leave, she pushed open the office doors, went down a short hall to a door that bore the sign "Bowman, Cooper, & Kidd, LLP," and entered a small reception area furnished with several uncomfortable-looking wooden chairs; an incongruous, antique chaise lounge, upholstered in a hideous fuchsia; and a huge wooden desk, presumably the receptionist's, presently vacant. Several spidery ficus plants congregated in the corners, and above the chaise lounge hung an ancient, Rockwell-esque painting of an Elizabeth City street corner that would have made David gag. The room smelled of hardwood floor varnish, flowery perfume, and an old man's hair tonic.

After a long minute, a rotund, fifty-ish woman with battleship gray hair and glistening, oily skin waddled in through a swinging door and settled herself behind the desk with the grace of an arthritic bulldog. Only after she had taken a few relieved breaths and given her short, dull fingernails a thorough examination did her topaz eyes peer over the top of her 1960s-vintage horn-rimmed glasses and acknowledge Courtney's presence. "May I help you?" Her voice was the croak of a longtime smoker.

"Hi. I've come about the office manager's position. I submitted my resume online, but I thought I'd stop by in person and see if I could set up an interview."

The woman's eyes retreated behind the thick lenses so they could scan a couple of stacks of paper on the corner of her desk. She picked up a sheet, stared at it as if uncertain whether it was quite the ticket, and finally handed it to Courtney. "I'll let you fill out an application. Which one are you, anyway?"

"Edmiston. Courtney Edmiston." She took the application form, which had questions front and back, set in type smaller than an IRS tax form's. The woman flipped through a number of papers, found the one she wanted, read over it, and then peered back over the top of her glasses. "You the one from Fearing?"

"Yes." She felt obliged to add, "But only temporarily."

"Wait here a second." With a groan to emphasize how inconvenient she found all this, the woman rose again from her seat and disappeared through the door, which obviously led to the offices in the rear. Courtney sat down in one of the hard-backed chairs and began filling in her information. She had completed half the front page when the receptionist shambled back in and held up her hand like a teacher looking to nab her students' attention.

"Never mind. The job's been filled."

"What?"

"Might as well not bother with that. I didn't realize we'd already hired someone."

"Oh," Courtney said, unable to conceal a grimace of dismay.

"Sorry."

She nodded and rose from her chair. Spying a metal trashcan beside the desk, she wadded up the application form and, with complete disregard for decorum, tossed it across the room. It dropped into the can with a rattle. She felt herself scowling at the woman with too-obvious contempt but did nothing to soften it. "You should update your web site."

"Mr. Kidd manages it in his spare time. I guess he's been busy."

"Apparently."

"I'm sorry."

Without another word, Courtney turned and left the office, her face burning with a rage that had no business surfacing so easily.

Calm down. It's nothing more than unfortunate timing.

But it wasn't. Surely, the receptionist would have known from the start whether the position had already been filled. It was learning of Courtney's current residence that had prompted the woman — or her superiors — to terminate the application.

At any other time in her life, she would have dismissed such a notion as paranoid. Now, it was difficult not to believe that some insidious hand was manipulating circumstances against her.

Outside, the air had turned chilly again, or so it seemed to her. She started back toward the car, trying to remember the address of her next target — an insurance office, somewhere on Water Street, not far away. As she walked, though, the library building just beyond the municipal plaza caught her eye, and on a whim, she veered toward it and went in through the main doors. The distinctive smell of pulp and glue sent her mind back a dozen years, to happier days when she frequented the library at Duke — which was probably the last time she had set foot in one.

Two women stood at the main counter, though Courtney saw only a handful of patrons. Putting on her most confident smile, she strode toward the nearest of the women, a tall, pleasant-looking redhead in her mid-forties, conservatively dressed. The woman smiled in return. “Hi. May I help you?”

“Hello,” Courtney said, making a mental note to create some business cards on Jan’s computer so she’d have something to hand out besides a copy of her resume. “I’m new to the area, and I’m wondering if the library is doing in any hiring.”

The woman glanced at her partner, a younger, rather pudgy blonde, who smiled but shrugged with evident regret. “I don’t think we are right now. We were looking for a purchasing agent a while back, but we‘ve already hired someone. What kind of work are you looking for?”

“I’d really like to get into an administrative position. I have extensive customer service, accounting, and bookkeeping experience.”

“You’re probably overqualified for anything we might have, even if we were hiring. You’d need to talk to our director, Mr. Hobbs, but he’s not in today.”

The dreaded “overqualified.” She despised hearing the word. “Could I leave a resume? I’d be happy to fill out an application, too.”

“Goodness, I don’t know if we have any up here. I’ll have to look.”

The blonde woman gave her a sympathetic smile. “You say you’ve just moved here?”

“Well, I’m in Fearing right now. I expect to be moving very soon, though.”

The red-haired librarian, who had bent to search a shelf under the counter abruptly straightened, her warm eyes cooling. “I don’t have any forms here just now. I’d recommend you come back another time and ask for Mr. Hobbs.”

Courtney could feel the crestfallen mask sliding down over her face. She held up a copy of her resume and asked, “May I leave this with you?”

“If you like, but you’d be better off giving a copy to Mr. Hobbs directly.”

“Please.” She thrust the sheet of paper toward the woman, who took it reluctantly, her expression indicating she didn’t particularly care to touch it. Courtney realized that it was unlikely her resume would ever reach Mr. Hobbs’s hands.

Forcing herself to hold her temper, she stepped back from the counter and looked around at the bookshelves lining the aisles. Something occurred to her then, and she wondered why she hadn’t thought of it before.

“You have computers with internet access, right?”

The librarian’s smile returned and she pointed to a glass-walled partition to the right. “Yes, ma’am. Right in there. I’ll need you to sign in here, please.”

Courtney scribbled her name, affirming that she would abide by the library's usage policy, and then went to one of the desks with a free computer. She opened the Google search page and entered "Blackburn, Fearing, NC" into the search field.

The top entries came from the Fearing Weekly Observer, the only newspaper published in the town. The first entry linked to the newspaper's online archives, and from there, she found a number of articles concerning the family that had taken her in. She began reading, starting with the most recent and working her way into the past.

#

Elizabeth City Man Killed in Accident in Fearing

Phillip Trull, an Elizabeth City native, was killed Saturday when his Buick Regal left the road and flipped several times. According to Fearing Police Chief Roger Flythe, Trull was traveling on Owen Swamp Road at about 11:00 PM when the accident occurred. Chief Flythe has not indicated whether alcohol was involved in the crash.

A witness, Martha Blackburn, told police that Trull was driving erratically, at a high rate of speed. "As if something were chasing him," the witness stated.

According to Ms. Blackburn, Trull had been visiting her niece, Jan Blackburn, prior to the accident. Ironically, less than a month earlier, Herbert and Patricia Blackburn, parents of Jan, were killed in wreck in virtually the same spot. Martha Blackburn was also involved in that accident but suffered no serious injuries.

Trull, 31, was the former owner of T & B Sporting Goods in Elizabeth City, which had gone out of business only a few weeks prior to his death. He is survived by his parents, Roland and Wanda Trull, of Edenton, and two sisters, Mrs. Sharon Trull Murphy and Mrs. Lori Trull Wilson, both of Greenville.

#

Leading Fearing Businessman and Wife Killed in Auto Accident

Moratok County's wealthiest and most controversial entrepreneur, Herbert Blackburn, 66, and his wife, Patricia, 61, were killed Friday when the vehicle in which they were traveling left the road and struck a tree in the nearby woods.

The accident occurred on Owen Swamp Road about 10:30 PM, said Fearing Police Chief Roger Flythe.

Herbert Blackburn's aunt, Martha Blackburn, also in the vehicle, survived without serious injury. She was treated at Albemarle Hospital in Elizabeth City and released.

Ms. Blackburn, also of Fearing, stated that a tire must have blown on the Cadillac DTS, causing the car to swerve out of control and crash into a large tree. The two victims were thrown through the windshield and probably killed on impact, Flythe said.

Herbert Blackburn was well known as the founder of numerous Fearing enterprises over a forty-year period. During the 1970s, Blackburn Farms, Inc., became Moratok County's largest employer, though it was troubled by years of controversy over the legitimacy of certain of the Blackburn family's agricultural holdings.

Mr. and Mrs. Blackburn are survived by their son, David, and daughter, Jan, also of Fearing.

#

Worker Killed in Accident at Blackburn Farms

Clayton Surber, 64, of Fearing, was killed Monday in an accident at Blackburn Farms, Inc., where he was employed. Witnesses indicated that Surber ran into the path of a corn harvester, which struck and fatally injured him, about 6:15 PM. He was pronounced dead at Albemarle Hospital in Elizabeth City at 7:00 PM.

The victim's son, Dwayne, and grandson, Henry, were also working at the site when the accident occurred. Dwayne Surber witnessed the accident from another harvester and rushed to his father's aid. However, the victim was already in shock from severe trauma and could not be revived.

"A number of people saw the accident happen, but no one knows what prompted Mr. Surber to run into the path of the harvester," said Herbert Blackburn, owner and CEO of Blackburn Farms, Inc. Blackburn indicated that Surber had been employed by the company for 18 years and was due to retire in less than a month.

Two witnesses who asked to remain anonymous stated that there had been friction between Surber and Blackburn for some time, though neither suggested that foul play was involved.

"We have no reason to believe this was anything other than a tragic accident," Moratok County Sheriff Donald Eaton said. According to Eaton, the Occupational Safety and Health Administration is investigating the accident.

"Of course, the victim's family is very upset, particularly Dwayne, who saw it happen," Eaton said.

The work site, just west of Fearing, was closed for the rest of the day following the accident.

"It's a terrible tragedy, and I feel for the family," Herbert Blackburn told reporters. "However, this will have no impact on our production schedule, which we are committed to upholding."

#

Courtney realized she was staring vacantly at the computer screen only when her eyes began to blur and burn. The ordinary silence of the library had become an overwhelming void, and she tapped her fingernails on the tabletop, just to make sure her ears were still working properly.

So Martha had been in the car with Jan's mom and dad, yet she had survived the wreck with barely a scratch.

And she had witnessed Phillip Trull's death.

Courtney could envision the old woman telling the police that Trull thought something was chasing him, gleefully aware that no one would even think of taking her at her word.

Suddenly, she wanted to see exactly where these accidents had occurred. She didn't know where Owen Swamp Road was, but there was obviously a connection to Arlene's original family.

She went to the Google map site and entered Fearing, NC, into the search field. When the map appeared, she zoomed in on the town and quickly located Owen Swamp Road. It looked to be a tiny lane that connected Winfall Road, where the Blackburns lived, to the western arm of old U.S. Highway 17. Conceivably, someone driving between the Blackburns' house and Elizabeth City might use it as a shortcut. Now she remembered where the road was; she had passed it each time she had traveled to or from the Blackburns' house.

What in God's name would Martha have been doing out there in the middle of the night?

She navigated back to the story about Clayton Surber's death. It had happened three years ago, with witnesses again intimating that something had chased him to his final fate.

No doubt, that incident had something to do with the current trouble between the Surbers and the Blackburns. For all she knew, it might have started the whole sorry business. But no; the article mentioned several years of friction between the Blackburns and the Surbers.

Some "tragic accident," she thought. If the Surber family had been extorting money from the Blackburns even then, David and Jan's parents certainly had a motive for murder. If Martha were loyal to them, then she might have taken matters into her own hands and performed whatever unimaginable tricks she did to affect people's minds.

Had Jan and David's parents also been fleeing from something when they died? That didn't seem to make sense — especially if Martha were with them at the time.

Or did it?

On a whim, she returned to the Google search page and entered "Fearing, Monarch," just to see if any relevant articles turned up. Nothing, at least amid the first few pages of hits, most of which were stories with Biblical references. For good measure, she added "Blackburn" to the search string, and this time when the results appeared, one entry a few pages deep caught her eye.

It was a brief article from the Greenville, NC, *Daily Reflector* — part of a retrospective of odd headlines from years past, dated July 14, 1971.

#

East Carolina Professor Killed in Bizarre Accident

Fearing, NC. John "J. D." Lees, a professor at East Carolina State University, was killed when he drove his car into Owen Swamp, just outside of Fearing, NC. According to Moratok County Sheriff Donald Eaton, Lees was apparently traveling at high speed and lost control of his Ford Mustang, which left the road and plowed some fifty yards into the swampland before sinking in over ten feet of water.

Sheriff Eaton indicated that Lees had been a guest of Miss Martha Blackburn at her family's home in Fearing. "Miss Blackburn has been questioned, but could offer no insight into the accident," Eaton said.

Lees survived the crash itself and is presumed to have died from drowning, following grave trauma. Evidently, prior to his death, Lees wrote on the trunk of a tree, in his own blood, "MONARCH," followed by an illegible scrawl.

"We'll continue to investigate, but at this time, we're operating under the assumption that the victim may not have been of sound mind," Sheriff Eaton said.

An autopsy is scheduled to determine the exact cause of Dr. Lees' death. He is survived by two sons, Andrew V. Lees and Todd T. Lees, both of Greenville; and a brother, Brett H. Lees, of Milwaukee, Wisconsin.

#

Courtney could find no further references to that incident or the Fearing Monarch. To her original search string, she added various modifiers — "Folklore," "Monster," "Surber," "Accident," and others — but all came up empty.

Before she knew it, most of the morning had slipped away, and she realized that getting to the insurance office she had intended to visit before picking up Jan was out of the question.

As was making a break in Jan's car. How could she have even thought of fleeing? By nightfall, she would be caught and sitting in a jail somewhere, not only destitute but friendless.

No. She had no choice but to confront whatever fate might await her back in Fearing, even if it meant discovering that her mind was coming unhinged.

There was no Monarch. Only a mad woman accomplished at playing mind tricks on others, at manipulating people to suit her whim.

Sufficiently to drive them to their own deaths?

Why? She had been made to wander into the woods in the middle of the night — she knew this — and for no healthy reason.

Arlene, Courtney thought. She would go see Arlene. Of all the people in the Blackburn household, Arlene was the only one who had been forthright with her, and surely, having known Martha for many years, she must have some insight into the old woman's inexplicable — perhaps even preternatural — abilities.

The question was whether Arlene would willingly reveal more to her than she already had. It was up to Courtney to persuade her.

She closed the browser and stood up, her legs numb from sitting, bemused by how insidiously the minutes had turned into hours. She glanced back and saw the red-haired librarian watching her with a sour expression, the fingers of one hand drumming the countertop as if she had been counting the minutes. Giving the woman a saccharine smile, she made her way out of the library, into the late-morning sunshine, and walked back to the car, irritated at having spent so much time gathering only a thimbleful of information.

But what a thimbleful. Hints that Martha hid more secrets than she could have imagined. Suggestions of murder. A cryptic but powerful reference to the Monarch. Still, it only opened up more cans of worms and provided no solid answers. She could always try digging for more information using Jan's computer, though doing it at the Blackburn house somehow seemed foolhardy — like playing with fire beneath a dragon's nose.

As she got into the car and started the engine, her eyes lingering on the library building, a little voice whispered in her ear that she would find no work anywhere in this town.

She pulled out into traffic and headed back toward the hospice, disgusted that her job search had ended up a total wash. This wasn't just paranoia. The staff at both places *had* turned cold shoulders to her when she revealed she was staying in Fearing. Had the Blackburns' negative influence spread all the way here, or was it something about the town itself? Or were the two simply interchangeable?

What choice did she have now but to move on — to find some new location altogether and eke out an existence with nothing to her name but the contents of a few suitcases?

When she pulled up in front of the hospice building, Jan was just coming out the front doors, and her face lit up with a smile when she saw Courtney waiting for her. But as she headed for the car, her eyes shifted toward the street, and a shadow fell over her features. She picked up her pace until she was almost running.

Courtney glanced in the rearview mirror and saw a vehicle turning from the side street to pull up behind her.

A familiar, rusty red pickup truck.

This time, there was no mistaking the identity of the driver.

#

Chapter 14

"Drive," Jan said, falling into the passenger seat and throwing a bright-eyed glance back at the approaching truck. "Don't speed, just drive."

Courtney shoved the car into gear and stamped on the accelerator, just as a young man carrying a satchel began to cross the street in front of her. She jerked the wheel to the left, and her heart skipped a beat as the man leaped back to the safety of the curb, avoiding a crushing impact by inches. His satchel, though, thudded over the hood and struck the windshield before falling away, and she saw him in the mirror, stomping after the car and yelling, "Stupid bitch!"

"Sorry," she said under her breath, but then sighed in relief, for the young man's unwitting intervention had forced Ben Surber to brake and wait for the other to get clear. She went through a couple of intersections on the treacherously narrow lane; at Main Street, she turned right, found no obstacles, and smashed the accelerator to the floor, her eyes glued to the rearview mirror. So far, the red truck had not reached the intersection.

"Where the hell did they come from?" Courtney asked. "Do they know you work at the hospice?"

Jan shook her head. "I wouldn't have thought so."

"They must have found out."

"Here they come."

"What do I do?"

"Turn right up here," she said, indicating a narrow side street. "These roads are a checkerboard. We can try to lose them."

"Maybe we should go back toward the police station."

"That's too far to backtrack."

She grimly agreed and followed Jan's directions, making several turns, first going north, then east. But a couple of more turns put her back on Main Street, again heading west, toward the main highway — hopefully, ahead of the Surbers.

But at the stoplight at U.S. 17, which would lead them back to Fearing, she saw the truck coming up fast in the rearview mirror.

"Damn it, there they are."

She could see Ben Surber glaring at her through the windshield. She did not recognize the passenger.

“I thought the Surbers were all bluster.” She gave her friend an accusing glare.

Jan winced. “I guess you just never know.”

“Who’s that with him?”

“George Tillery. He was Hank’s best friend.”

“Oh. Good.”

When the light changed, she floored it again, and the Jaguar roared away. Traffic wasn’t very heavy, and Courtney weaved around car after car, caring little whether the police might pull her over. The more she thought about it, the more she wished she had insisted on going back to the station. The Elizabeth City police would have no connection to their corrupt neighbors in Fearing, and even if they couldn’t actually arrest Ben Surber, they would be in a position to intervene if the worst happened. Running was a terrible idea.

“I don’t see them,” Jan said, keeping watch out the back.

“Stoplight coming up.”

“Run it.”

“No way,” Courtney said, pressing the brake pedal hard. “Too much traffic.”

“Damn it,” Jan whispered, her eyes wildly searching for a way around the stopped cars ahead. No good. It was a major shopping center, and all they could do was wait for the light to change. She thumped the dashboard impatiently. “Come on.”

“We should have gone to the police,” Courtney said.

“Just keep going,” Jan said, as the light finally changed to green. The cars ahead crept forward, oblivious to their need.

At the first opening, Courtney punched the accelerator and whisked past several of the slow-moving vehicles.

“Maybe they got hung up at the last light,” Jan said, her expression showing a little relief. “Just keep moving.”

“They know exactly where we’re going, you know.”

“This Jag will outrun that beater of theirs. You can handle it, can’t you?”

Courtney sighed. “I can handle it. Sit tight.”

Jan reached into her purse and retrieved her phone. “I’ll call David. Maybe he can come out this way to meet us.” She dialed her brother’s number, listened for a few moments, and then tried another. Again, no luck. “Damn,” she said. “Wouldn’t you know it.”

By the time the four-lane avenue turned to open highway, Courtney was already doing ninety, the Jaguar’s engine purring happily. She held it at that speed, her eyes watching the mirror for either the red pickup truck or blue flashing lights. When nothing appeared after five minutes, she began to breathe easier.

"I think we've lost them," Jan said. "But don't slow down."

The wide, green fields to either side of the highway slid past in a blur, and the occasional car Courtney whipped around quickly became a dwindling dot in the rearview mirror. After a few minutes, she inched back to seventy, figuring that if they had escaped the most immediate danger, getting stopped by the highway patrol would be pointless. Jan didn't protest, but kept her head turned to the rear glass.

"Good God," she said. "We're not even safe in Elizabeth City. We've got to do *something*. I can't let them disrupt my whole life."

"And what do you suggest?"

Jan glanced at her. "David will figure something out."

"Or maybe you could go to the county sheriff. The state police. The SBI. Just because the Fearing cops are corrupt, it doesn't mean there's no remedy. Those men are dangerous. And they're stalking us, for Christ's sake."

"I know." Jan's eyes gleamed with desperation, but after a minute, she seemed to relax a little. "We'll figure something out. We will."

"I hope so."

"How about you? Did you have any luck?"

She shook her head. "Nope."

"I'm sorry."

"I ended up spending time at the library I hadn't counted on."

"The library?"

"You never mentioned your Aunt Martha witnessed your fiancé's death. How would that happen to be?"

"How did you—?"

"Just a little research."

Jan grimaced and heaved a sigh. "Well, as you've probably figured, Martha tends to get out and wander a lot. That's what happened that night. And she ended up on the road where Phillip was driving."

"Owen Swamp Road."

Jan nodded.

"In the article, she said that Phillip was driving like 'something was chasing him.' You wouldn't know anything about that something, would you?"

Jan gave her a cold stare. "What would you expect from that crazy old bat? Why would you even give her that much credibility?"

"Um, maybe a few experiences I've had at your place?"

"You don't get it, do you?"

"Get what?"

Jan sighed again. "Courtney, Martha was out in the road in the middle of the night. Phillip came up on her and crashed trying to keep from hitting her."

The blow to Courtney's gut felt like an iron fist. She gave her friend a doubting look. "Is that the official version?"

"It's what happened."

"I didn't see anything like that in the archive."

"Then your 'research' wasn't very complete."

Jan's statement shouldn't have stunned her, but for several minutes, she couldn't gather her wits enough to speak. Finally, she managed, "There were other things. It also said Martha was in the car when your parents were killed. But she came out without a scratch."

"What can I say? She was buckled in the back seat. Mom and Dad were in front and went through the windshield when the car hit a tree. The airbags failed. It happens."

"And Dwayne Surber's father. He was killed at your dad's farm. Is that why they despise your family so much?"

"I don't know, Courtney. Probably. That was years ago. I never knew much about it. Still don't."

"I guess you've got an answer for everything."

"I thought you wanted answers. Or do you just want answers that fit your particular view, however based in fantasy?"

"You know that's not so."

"Oh? I'm not so sure anymore."

Courtney fell silent, fighting back her rising anger, knowing that arguing with Jan would only sever their friendship's already unraveling ties. So she held her tongue and drove, half-certain Jan was lying to her, but only half-trusting her own convictions. The road behind them was empty. She sped up to eighty, just for good measure, until she reached the Fearing turnoff. From here, she thought, they could get back safely to the Blackburn house. What they might do once they arrived, she didn't know. Best prepare for unwelcome company, she guessed.

Just before town, a little S-shaped bridge crossed the Moratok River. A number of elderly men stood on the pedestrian walkway with their fishing rods, and a few turned their faces, all sullen and resentful, to regard the Jaguar. More than one pair of eyes glared at Courtney with unconcealed contempt.

She *had* to get out of this place. No matter what it took.

Just past the bridge, Winfall Road branched off to the right. She made the turn onto the last leg of the trip home and picked up speed, just because the Jaguar wanted to. Finally reining in her ire and swallowing her pride, she decided to offer Jan an olive branch, if only to keep the peace. "Sorry, Jan. I'm frustrated and still a little scared. I don't mean to take it out on you."

"I know, hon."

"I suppose it's too early for a drink."

"Not necessarily."

She could have kicked herself for bringing up the idea, but a couple of drinks would at least mellow her out and make Jan sociable. It wasn't just to drown her woes. "David needs to know what happened," she said.

Jan raised an eyebrow. "So you do trust him to take care of things?"

"I know he won't take this lying down."

"No. But if you think —"

Courtney saw the old Cutlass in the middle of the road at the same time as Jan. She slammed on the brakes, realizing that the other car was fully blocking the highway just beyond the intersection of a small road to the right. She spun the wheel to make the turn; the tires screamed, and her body slammed against the door as the Jag fishtailed and swerved precariously back and forth before straightening out and picking up speed. She found herself shivering, less from the shock of the near-collision than from having glimpsed the name on street sign as the car slid into the turn: Owen Swamp Road.

Her first impulse was to stop the car and go find out whether the other driver needed help or a piece of her mind. But Jan reached over, clutched her knee, and said, "That was Ray Surber. Don't go back."

"Jesus!"

Jan looked back to see whether the other vehicle was following them. At least for the moment, there was no sign of it. "This road goes back out to old 17, which joins with the main highway north of town," she said, her mental gears whirring. "He diverted us this way on purpose."

"This is the road where your parents were killed," Courtney said, giving her an anxious glance. "Phillip, too."

"Yeah."

"How far are we from your place?"

"Maybe a mile, as the crow flies." She nodded to herself. "There's an old utility road up ahead somewhere that leads back to our property. Goes right through the damn swamp, though. Haven't been on it in years."

"You don't know if it's usable?"

Jan shook her head. "We could end up stuck. I'd hate to risk it unless we have to."

"What do I do? Keep going?"

"Yeah, for the moment."

The trees pressed close to the narrow road on both sides, forming a gloomy tunnel of foliage, and she could see stagnant pools, like inky black moats, around the bases of the trunks. A dank, fishy odor, tinged with sulfur, wormed its way into the car, assailing her nostrils with every inhalation.

A sick feeling had begun to churn in her stomach even before she saw the pickup truck in the distance, heading toward them. Then, as clearly as if the plan had been drawn out on a chart before her, she realized that the Surbers had set a trap, and she and Jan had fallen into it. Ben, in the pickup truck, hadn't wanted to catch them on the highway; he needed only to trigger their flight and then race to Owen Swamp Road north of Fearing, while his uncle blocked their way home and herded them straight into the trap's jaws.

"God, that's them," Jan said, leaning forward with her jaw agape, equally aware of their predicament. Frantically, her eyes scanned the road ahead, looking for the turnoff that might offer them an escape. With no sign of it nearby, she shook her head in despair. "That utility road is still ahead. We have to get past Ben somehow."

Courtney shot a glance at the rearview mirror, and her heart went frigid. The Oldsmobile was racing up behind them now, taking up both lanes of the road.

"We're boxed in," Jan said.

"Get on the phone," Courtney said. "Try to get David again."

Jan reached for her phone, but she had no time to make the call. The Surbers' truck loomed larger as it raced toward them, and now Courtney could see Ben's homely features above the steering wheel. Behind them, Ray Surber closed the distance, and she realized that he, too, was carrying a passenger.

Four men against the two of them.

"When's the last time you played chicken?" Jan's voice was reedy thin.

"What? You're crazy."

"He'll turn. He's not out to get killed."

"Neither are we."

"It's our only chance!"

Courtney had three seconds to decide.

"Damn them," she whispered. Her foot shoved the accelerator forward.

She saw Ben's eyes become golf balls as the Jaguar leaped toward him, but he barreled onward, either dauntless or too dull to react. Courtney's heart hammered in her ears, her fingers vises on the wheel, her throat sandpaper dry as she realized the collision was inevitable.

At the last possible instant, by sheer reflex, her hands twisted the wheel to the right, and she saw Ben throw himself toward his passenger, pulling his own wheel with him. The Jaguar's left fender swiped the truck's with the sound of great claws scraping over metal, and the car lurched to the right, tires screaming. The Jag hurtled toward the shoulder, resisting her efforts to drag it back, and the tires slipped off the pavement, thudding and bumping over soft, rough earth, strengthening the wheel's pull.

"Hold it steady!" Jan cried. "Get back over. Get back over!"

A tree loomed ahead, its low-hanging branches reaching for the windshield like outstretched arms, the spongy loam stubbornly gripping the tires. Then the steering wheel bucked like a stallion, wrenched itself from Courtney's grip, and with a bone-numbing jolt, the Jaguar smashed into the thick tree trunk, airbags exploding around the passenger compartment. Her face pitched into a hot, yielding surface, and everything went black.

For several seconds she sat dazed, her forehead and cheeks numb from the airbag's impact. A bitter, burnt smell filled her nostrils, and when her vision swam back to normal, she saw through the cracked windshield a thin plume of smoke rising from the crumpled hood. A rapid, metallic ticking sound from the engine wound down to an occasional sharp clank. Then she heard Jan moan.

After a few seconds, she said, "Oh, God. We've got to get out of here."

For a few more seconds, Courtney remained blank. She couldn't remember why they had been running — until she heard a door slam somewhere behind the car. Then the searing image of Ben Surber's truck racing toward her head-on flashed before her eyes, and she jerked upright with a gasp of dread as awareness of their peril rushed back to her.

"Lock your door," Courtney said, checking hers. "Don't let them in."

"We're trapped," Jan said in a shrill voice. "We can't stay in here."

A figure materialized at Courtney's window, and she drew back as she saw Ben Surber glaring in at her, a rifle or shotgun tucked under one arm. With one hand, he grasped the door handle and tugged. "Open the door," he growled at her. "Open the door, right now."

Courtney shook her head. "Get the hell away from here!"

"I said open this goddamn door."

Another figure — the man she had seen in the car with Ray — appeared at Jan's window, and he pounded the glass with a fist. "Open up, you."

"Shit," Jan whispered. "Johnny Spencer. More bad news."

"We'll bust our way in, if we have to," Ben said in a chillingly calm voice. "You'd better open up. Right now."

"I said get away from here," Courtney said, trying to keep her own voice calm. "You're in trouble enough as it is."

Ben then lifted his gun, butt-first, drawing it back as if to smash the window. "You don't open that door, I'm gonna bust right through there. Don't think I won't."

Panic mounting, Courtney glanced around at the surrounding trees, the empty roadway, the pools of black water just to the right. Another man was approaching from behind the car, the one named George Tillery. Now she recognized him as one of the smart-mouthed men at Tall Ships the other night.

No hope of escape.

Courtney brought her hand down on the horn and held it. Its voice cried miserably in the silent afternoon, and she heard herself singing out in crude harmony, "Get the hell away from here!"

Ben sent her a long look of disgust. Then, dark resolve shadowing his face, his muscles tensed, and he brought the butt of his rifle down on the window. The sound of the blow nearly deafened her, and the glass cracked but did not break. He drew back again, and this time, the rifle butt came hurtling through, spraying Courtney with jewel-like fragments. She ducked, screaming, but retained enough presence of mind to reach for the hand that came scrabbling in and jam it down into the sharp wreckage of the window.

Ben bellowed but did not retreat. Instead, he thrust the rifle stock through the window and smashed it into her shoulder, forcing her back and keeping her from grasping his arm as he reached for the door lock. Crying out in pain, she tried to bat at the encroaching hand but landed only a couple of glancing blows. She watched in horror as he unlocked the door, tugged it open, and leaned down to give her a look of cold triumph. Then he reached in, deftly unbuckled her seatbelt, and dragged her out of her seat with one quick, powerful tug. She landed in soft, dank earth, only to find herself being hauled to her feet by George Tillery. He clutched the back of her neck and her right bicep in taut iron claws, forcing her to watch as Johnny Spencer tore open the passenger door and extracted Jan, screaming and flailing, with barely an effort.

Ben glanced at Tillery and then pointed to Courtney. "That one in Ray's car. The other one in my truck. Let's get 'em moving."

Tillery shoved her forward, throwing her off-balance, but his grip on her neck held her upright. She moved forward mechanically, her voice frozen by terror, her heart pounding so fiercely it felt ready to burst. Somehow the idea of dying on the spot, leaving her captors in an unexpected bind, struck her as rather funny.

Assuming they didn't intend to kill her anyway.

As Tillery forced her toward the waiting Cutlass, she saw the driver, Ray Surber, standing nonchalantly beside the open door, eyeing her thoughtfully, one arm thrown carelessly across the roof of the car. He was tall, with coarse, graying hair and a scrubby beard. Lewd tattoos covered both of his bare arms, and his deep blue eyes looked both intelligent and cruel. He couldn't be any younger than forty, Courtney guessed.

He bore little, if any resemblance to his brother's sons.

"Your choice of friends could be better," he said to her in an unexpectedly smooth, urbane voice. "Damn shame." Then, to Tillery, he said, "Put her in the trunk," and tossed him the keys.

"Wait," she said, digging her heels into the ground, vainly trying to impede her captor's progress. "Come on, don't do this."

The response was a sudden tug on her arm that nearly sent her sprawling. Tillery then shoved her down to her knees while he opened the trunk. He tossed the keys back to Ray and then, without a word, grabbed her around the waist, effortlessly hefted her up, and dropped her into the well, her head painfully striking its metal edge. Before she could even shift her position, the trunk door came slamming down, closing her in total darkness.

The sound echoed through her skull until the bone felt as if it would crack. She was lying awkwardly on one arm, and she struggled to shift her weight off it, barely able to move in the cramped compartment. The air reeked of gasoline and oil, quickly becoming suffocating. She knew beating on the top of the trunk was pointless, but she did it anyway and unleashed one long cry of white-hot rage.

Two doors slammed and the engine started, followed by a numbing jolt as the car began to move. She braced herself by lying on her side and tucking her body against the forward wall, pressing her feet against the end of the well. After a minute, the worst of the jostling passed, and she could feel the car picking up speed, evidently back on the paved road. She assumed they were driving back toward town, but even if she could estimate how far they went and how many turns the car made, she didn't know the local roads well enough to guess their destination.

She had never been claustrophobic, but the close darkness and the knowledge that this might be the last ride of her life quickly overwhelmed her. The petroleum odor crawled like a cold worm into her throat and lungs until she feared she might gag. But the intolerable idea of vomiting on herself prompted her to regulate her breathing as best she could, and after a time, the acrid stench lost its edge.

On and on they went, and she didn't even know if their captors were even taking Jan and her to the same place. She felt around, searching for a tire iron or some other instrument she could use as a weapon, but Ray Surber had apparently emptied the trunk specifically to accommodate her. The idea that someone had actually orchestrated her abduction and prepared some unknown fate for her sent her stomach lurching again. Somehow, she had a feeling that Dwayne Surber must also have had a hand in all this. Close-knit the family might be, but Hank had been Dwayne's son.

The last few minutes, the ride was bumpy and evidently slow. When the car finally made a sharp turn and came to a stop, she guessed they'd been traveling for at least fifteen minutes. She shifted into a facedown position, drawing up her right leg and putting her weight on her knee so that when the trunk opened, she might have enough leverage to spring out and surprise the bastard coming to get her. But the compartment was too tight, and when the trunk did pop open, she didn't even succeed at heaving herself upright, much less out of the well itself.

An ocean of light swallowed her, blinding her temporarily, and a rough pair of hands again grabbed her, hauled her bodily out of the trunk, and set her on her feet, gripping her upper arms to keep her from falling.

"Steady," came Ray Surber's low voice. "Just do what you're told and you'll be all right. You got me?"

She glared at the older man without answering. The rage that came from helplessness, like that which had boiled up when Hank Surber had a knife at her throat, was burning in every muscle, and it wouldn't take much to send her into a frenzied attack, without regard for her own life — or her friend's. She forced herself to remain outwardly docile, if not for her sake, then for Jan's.

The pickup truck had parked behind the Cutlass, and Ben Surber and George Tillery were manhandling a bound Jan out of the cramped rear seat of the cab. The vehicles were parked in front of a crumbling wooden cabin surrounded by towering trees, whose branches formed a thick green canopy over the sharply angled roof. Pools of black water and clusters of reeds painted a dark mosaic around the bases of the trunks, and the raucous calls of birds Courtney had never heard before rang like eerie sirens from the depths of the swamp.

Ben had hefted Jan over his shoulder and was carrying her toward the cabin door. Tillery followed close behind, holding a battered brown briefcase in one hand and a revolver in the other. Ray's friend Johnny Spencer, a lanky, weathered-looking man of about thirty, had already gone up to the porch and was unlocking the door. Ray gave Courtney a shove.

"Move."

Something splashed off to the right, and she heard a heavy, sledgehammer thump. Then another. And another.

Tillery paused for a moment, his tiny, marble-like eyes peering into the darkness beneath the trees. "Whatzat?"

"Nothing," Ben said, stepping up onto the rickety front porch. "Let's get 'em inside."

Ray had also paused and was staring into the trees in the direction of the sound. Courtney caught a glimpse of something tall and pale moving against the dark foliage far in the distance.

"Oh, God, no," she whispered, her heart nearly bursting. "Not that."

"You see something?" Tillery said to Ray, standing on the short flight of stairs to the porch.

Ray continued to stare, one hand crushing her neck. Finally, he shook his head and said, "No." Then he started forward, this time dragging her with him, and one of her mud-splattered pumps slipped from her foot. He clumped up the stairs, followed Tillery into the house, pulling Courtney with him, and then turned and pushed the door shut.

They were inside a small, sparsely furnished room, its walls peeling, the ceiling stained and cracking. Grimy windows faced the front and one side of the house, and a crooked archway led to another room filled with dark shadows. Without hesitating or bothering to turn on any lights, Ben carried Jan into the next room, and Courtney heard a heavy thump as he dropped his burden to the floor.

Ray followed, keeping a tight grip on Courtney's neck and arm, his hands seemingly strong enough to snap her neck with little effort. She saw Jan lying on her side, her feet bound together, hands tied behind her back, and a bandana stuffed cruelly into her mouth. She sent Courtney a pleading look and moaned softly behind the gag. Ben stood over her, a satisfied grin pasted on his ugly face.

The room might have been a dining room at one time. Now, only a single wooden chair occupied the center of the room. A ratty brown carpet covered the sagging floor, and thick curtains blocked what little light might have stolen through the single window. A narrow door opened to another pit of shadows, and Ray began dragging Courtney toward it.

"I'm not going to gag you," he said to her. "The first sound you make, I'm going to kick the shit out of you and then sew your lips together. If you think I'm joking, think again. My friend Johnny's got some interesting tools in that briefcase of his." His eyes burned into hers. "Do you understand?"

She nodded, her throat too dry to speak.

He turned her to face a blank wall and released her. "Don't move," he said. "If you do, I'll hurt you."

She heard him fumbling with something, and a few moments later, one of the strong hands grabbed her right arm, and she felt a length of coarse rope looping around her wrist. He pulled her other arm back and deftly tied her wrists together so that there was no play, but not so tight as to cut off her circulation.

He must have experience with this, she thought. Her heart's pounding still nearly deafened her.

"You just keep still," he said, his tone gentle. "I really don't want to have to hurt you."

Next thing she knew, her remaining shoe came off and another length of rope was encircling her ankles. Ray drew it around several times and then knotted it securely, just shy of painful. He then took hold of her shoulders and gently pushed her down, forcing her knees to bend, until she was seated on her haunches. She noticed a long tear in the front of her skirt.

"Didn't want you to fall," he said. "Now, I'm going to leave you in here. Like I said, you keep quiet, and everything will be okay. Our problem isn't with you. That doesn't mean I won't do what I have to if you get out of hand. You clear on that, Ms. Edmiston?"

Unable to do otherwise, she nodded.

"All right," he said, pointing into her face. "Not one word out of you. If I hear you speak, I'll have Johnny hold you down, and I'll do a little stitchery on your face."

She nodded again, and Ray lowered his finger, apparently satisfied. He turned and left the room, and a second later, she heard a bolt sliding home on the other side.

Her pent-up rage could not sustain itself indefinitely, and now that they had left her alone, it began to wane a little. She sat in a tiny room — a closet, perhaps — with no windows, the only light coming from beneath the door and a narrow split in the wall near the ceiling. They were somewhere out in the middle of the damned swamp, God knew how far from help, even if they could escape.

And that thing. The Monarch. It was out there, as real as life.

What was it going to do? Burst in and kill them all? Watch and wait?

What in the living hell was it?

She half-expected to hear the heavy, pounding footsteps outside the cabin, but for countless ages, she heard nothing — from either the outdoors or the other room. The longer the silence inside the house, the more it overshadowed her fear of the nebulous thing she had seen in the swamp.

The Surbers must own the cabin, she thought. It looked to have been unused for years, though they had obviously prepared it for whatever they intended to do now. She carefully shifted her position, to see if she could slip her arms under her rear end and pull her feet up between her bound wrists, so her hands would at least be in front of her. No — not enough play in the rope. So she rolled onto her side so that her weight wasn't on her hands, and she tried to relax. Chances were good she would be here a long time.

A couple of low voices — masculine — rumbled from the other side of the door. She shifted closer to it, hoping to make out what they were saying, but the only thing she could discern was Ben Surber's voice saying "…remove your gag."

A few seconds later, there came a scuffling sound, followed by Jan's long, agonized scream.

#

Chapter 15

Horror rushed over and through her like an icy torrent, but taking Ray at his word for what would happen to her, she bit her lip to keep from calling her friend's name. Any one of these men might commit brutal murder, and together, they formed a single, rabid, conscienceless animal. Tears scalded her eyes, but she could not wipe them away.

More muffled voices trickled beneath the door, which must be heavier than it looked, she thought. Another dull thump, like the weight of a body falling to the floor.

Another scream from Jan, this time cut short.

Courtney felt her gorge rising again, and she turned her focus to the growing pain in her wrists and ankles, the throbbing in her head, anything other than her fluttering stomach and the threat of retching.

More banging from the other room. A harsh voice growling, "Fucking bitch."

Then a voice — Tillery's, she thought — came through clearly. "I want the other one."

"Not yet." Ray's voice.

Right now, the elder Surber seemed loath to harm her, yet of all of them, he struck her as the most dangerous. His more refined demeanor and evident intelligence suggested that he might be capable of far worse than his cruder, more volatile companions.

And still, she could not escape the feeling that his brother Dwayne might be the brains behind this abduction, and Ray acting as his capable executive.

For a time, little sound came from beyond the door — just an occasional groan or soft whimper — and somehow this seemed even worse because she could only guess what was happening. But then a shrill scream exploded from Jan's lungs, which sent Courtney cowering into a corner, pulling her knees up to her chest, silent, bitter sobs racking her body.

Finally, such a long silence followed that she feared Jan might be dead. Not even a whisper or mutter from any of the men.

A distant door slammed, probably from the front of the house. A few seconds later, the sound of a car door closing, followed by an engine grinding to life. Ben's truck, she thought.

Was it Ben leaving, or one of the others?

Another long silence, and she realized that her senses were becoming dull, her eyes getting heavier. Through the crack near the ceiling, the sunlight appeared to be waning.

How the hell long had she been here? She had lost all track of time. It might be three in the afternoon or seven in the evening. Her arms and legs had gone completely numb, her nose itched, and dried tears had turned her cheeks brittle. She shifted her position and shook her legs to try to restore the circulation. The pins and needles that gradually began to stab her feet were actually a relief. She could do very little to help her arms except roll her shoulders back and forth.

The next time she looked up, it was almost completely dark outside. She finally heard a faint moan on the other side of the door, and then the distinct sound of movement.

Someone began fumbling at the door. She sat upright, all her senses once again alert.

The door groaned open, revealing only dim light from the other side. Then Ray Surber stepped into view and gave her a long, pensive stare, as if unsure what to do with her. Finally, he stepped inside, and she saw he was carrying a metal cup, evidently from an army mess kit. He lowered it to her lips, and she sipped fresh water, its coolness a balm to her burning throat. When she finished drinking, she leaned away from the cup and nodded. "Thank you," she said, her voice a hoarse croak.

He set the cup aside, and a second later, a long hunting knife appeared in his hand. Reflexes caused her to draw away from him, but he shook his head, grasped her upper arms, and turned her back to him. She felt the blade sawing through the rope around her wrists, and a moment later, her hands were free. The blood that rushed through her arms and into her hands felt like molten lava. He shifted her so he could cut the bonds around her ankles.

When she was free and rubbing her aching legs, she looked up at him as a feather of rage tickled her brain. "I couldn't get out of here," she said. "Why did you tie me up?"

"To protect you."

"Protect me?"

"Yep. If you'd been free, you'd have tried to help your girlfriend. You'd have yelled and hammered on the door. Then I'd have had to hurt you."

"You didn't gag me and I didn't yell."

"No. With you partly immobile, you were more prone to believing what I told you. And you did. Good girl."

"I believe you'd kill me."

“Yep.”

“You still might.”

“Yep.”

She lowered her head, his words barely sinking in. “What did you do to Jan?”

“Personally, not a thing.”

She heard a rustling sound, and a moment later, Ben appeared, dragging an unconscious, naked Jan with him. He pulled her into the room and dropped her on the floor next to Courtney.

Livid bruises covered her body, and she was bleeding from between her legs.

“Bitch,” Ben muttered, glaring at Courtney. Then he backed out of the room, his lustful eyes never leaving her figure.

A large leather-bound book appeared in Ray’s hand, and he tossed it onto the floor beside the unconscious young woman. “You’re entitled to know why you’re here,” he said. “If you don’t understand what’s in it, just ask your friend when she wakes up.”

“It’s dark,” Courtney said, her voice cracking. “I can’t see it.”

“You will,” came Ben’s voice. A second later, he reappeared, carrying a small, battery-powered lantern. He placed it next to the book. “You two got a lot to talk about,” he said. “Till later. Then we start up again — on you.”

“I hope it won’t come to that,” Ray said. “I know you didn’t have any part of what they’ve done. But then sometimes life just isn’t fair.”

“She had a part in what they done to Hank,” Ben growled. “I wanna fix her myself. George can go fuck himself.”

“We’ll see,” Ray said, his tone like a stern father’s. He leaned down to gaze into her eyes. “You take a good look at what’s in that book. Personally, I think you might be the one who can reason with young Mr. Surber and we can avoid any further unpleasantness. But we’ll just have to see about that.”

“Isn’t it you who’s gone beyond reasonable?”

“Ask your friend.”

With that, Ray and Ben left the little room, bolting the door again behind them. A few moments later, doors slammed, and Ray’s car engine started.

Now, Courtney turned her attention to Jan, who lay so still she might have been dead. Courtney couldn’t even see her breathing, though when she leaned close, she could hear a very faint inhaling and exhaling. She pulled the lantern over so she could examine Jan’s wounds — most of which appeared to be from blows to her arms, legs, and head. But the blood that ran down her legs was deep red.

When she touched Jan's forehead, it was clammy and cold. A moment later, though, Jan groaned and her eyes flickered open. They searched for focus for several seconds before falling on Courtney. A faint expression of relief lit Jan's face.

"Courtney," she whispered. "What's happened?"

"You're hurt. I don't know how bad."

Jan's eyes turned inward, and her features registered horror as her memory began to return. "Oh, Christ. There were three of them."

"I know."

"I can't feel anything."

"You're in shock. I don't have anything to give you. I'm sorry."

Jan nodded slowly. "Ray. He just watched while the others did it. He wouldn't help me. The bastard wouldn't help me."

"They're sick. They're all sick."

Jan's eyes went to the ceiling. "They're going to die. They're going to die like Hank."

Courtney leaned closer to her. "You know who killed Hank?"

Her eyes shifted in Courtney's direction. "At first, I thought it was David. But…"

"But it wasn't."

She shook her head. "Not David. Martha."

"Martha killed Hank?"

"Had it done."

Her heart skipped a beat. Then she nodded to herself. "Martha. She controls the thing."

"Don't know what she does. She calls it somehow."

"Her 'singing.'"

Jan nodded.

She glanced at the book on the floor and lifted it. The thing weighed a ton, and when she opened it, she saw that it was a handwritten ledger — page after page containing names, Social Security numbers, dates, dollar amounts, transaction numbers. There was no corporate or individual's name to identify its source, but she knew immediately that it had belonged to Jan's father.

"What does this mean, Jan?"

"The real books."

"Real?"

"Not cooked."

"What are you telling me?"

Jan flexed her muscles and pulled herself up on her elbows, grimacing in pain. But she managed to sit upright, propping her back against the wall. For a long time, she stared vacantly at the ledger, her jaw working slowly back and forth. Courtney said nothing, but let Jan try to compose herself.

Finally, Jan's eyes turned to hers. "Dad…he withheld tax payments… altered loan amounts…fixed land deals. The official company records don't show any of it."

"He swindled the people that worked for him?"

Jan nodded. "That's why the Surbers — and others — they took Dad to court, time after time. But he owned the judges."

"Jesus," Courtney whispered. "So they're taking their revenge on you."

"Not just that. Before he died, Dad changed. Was going to make good on everything. He made deals to repay what he owed. But then, the accident…"

"So the Surbers — they weren't actually looking to extort money from your family?"

Jan shook her head, her expression bitter. "Just wanted what they had coming to them."

"Why haven't you given it to them?"

"David. He was going to, until he realized we would be wiped out. Completely wiped out."

"He went back on his father's word."

Jan nodded. "He tried to bargain with the others, so they'd take less. A few did. But the Surbers wouldn't budge."

"Why should they?"

"You don't understand," Jan said, tears rolling down her cheeks. "We'd be wiped out. Everything gone."

"What you have was built on lies."

"But it's *all* we have."

"No. You could always start over. Somewhere else, if necessary."

"Wouldn't work."

"Yes, it could, Jan."

She shook her head. "You still don't understand."

"That's for later," Courtney said, sighing. "Look, I want to see how bad you're hurt."

Jan laughed harshly. "You're no doctor."

"I just want to see if you're still bleeding."

Jan reached down between her legs and wiped at the blood. "It's let up, I think."

Courtney took the lantern, swallowed hard, and gently spread Jan's thighs. A thin stream of red still leaked from her raw-looking vagina. Large splotches of purple and blue discolored her inner thighs, and a streak of feces ran down the back of one leg.

"Oh, God," Courtney said, tears beginning to well again.

"After they..." Jan shook her head. "They used something big on me," Jan said, her voice barely audible. "A nightstick, I think."

"I need to get you cleaned up somehow." She looked down at her clothes. She was wearing a slip beneath her skirt, so she stood up, tugged it down, and began wiping Jan's legs with the silky fabric. Jan began to weep like a child.

"You'll be okay," Courtney said. "We're going to get out of this."

Jan shook her head. "Oh, honey," she whispered. "They're going to do this to you, too. They almost got into a fight over who gets you first."

She barely held onto her makeshift towel. Stabbing pains began in her chest and gradually moved toward her stomach.

I will not throw up.

"What are they doing now? Do you know?"

"Going to David. For half a million dollars, they'll let us go."

"Can he get that kind of money?"

"Not quickly. But it doesn't matter. I think they're going to kill us anyway."

"Why?"

"David will never pay."

"He must!"

"She won't let him."

"Who? Martha?"

Jan shrugged. Then Courtney detected a vibration — an engine — and after another few seconds, a door closed.

"They're coming back."

Jan's hand closed on Courtney's wrist. "You can't let them do this to you. Whatever you have to do, don't let them do it."

She looked around the little room. There was nothing to use against the men. Just the ledger and the lantern. The little thing was made of plastic. Hardly a viable weapon, but she had nothing else except her hands and feet. She shut off the light, stood up, and positioned herself next to the door, giving herself room to raise the lantern and smash it into the face of anyone who came inside.

The front door creaked open, and she heard slow footsteps in the other room. Only one of them, she thought. But which one?

The footsteps paused outside the door, and the bolt slid back. She lifted the lantern and prepared to strike, her hands shaking so badly she could barely hold the weapon.

Slowly, with a baritone sigh, the door swung inward. Courtney held her breath, knowing she had to time the blow perfectly or the opportunity was gone. As soon as the bastard took a step forward…

Move, you son of a bitch!

She did not expect a flashlight to flare abruptly to life, its beam burning straight into her eyes, blinding her. Knowing it was futile now, she swung the lantern toward a spot where she hoped the man's head would be.

All she succeeded in doing was throwing herself off-balance. A strong hand caught her arm, forcing her to drop the lantern, which struck the floor with a crash. A deep voice rumbled, "Damn you!" Then the hand shoved Courtney backward, and her back slammed into the wall with enough force to drive the air from her lungs.

She recognized the man standing at the door as Ray's brother Dwayne. The one she had first met at Tall Ships.

Hank and Ben's father.

"You goddamned twit," Dwayne said, glaring at her with contempt. But when his gaze turned to Jan's figure propped against the wall, her watery eyes boiling with hatred, his face turned ashen. "What the hell is this?"

Dazed, Courtney gaped stupidly at him for a moment. "You don't know?"

"Ben did this, didn't he?" he said, dropping to one knee to inspect Jan's bruises. "That fucking jackass."

"Not just Ben," Courtney said. "Ray and two others."

Dwayne swiveled his head, his small, dark eyes brimming with contempt. "My brother Ray?"

She nodded. "George Tillery and Johnny Spencer were the other two."

"Son of a bitch!" His voice thundered in the confined space. He rose and drew himself up in front of Courtney, his face so full of fury she thought he might flatten her with one of his huge paws. "Ray and Ben. And those two lame pricks. They did this?"

"Yes."

"What if I say you're lying?"

"She's not lying," Jan said, trying to pull herself upright, getting only as far as her knees before sinking back against the wall.

"I knew that little bastard was up to something when he drove off," Dwayne muttered, mostly to himself. "But Ray. I never thought he'd do anything like this."

"Ray orchestrated the whole thing," Courtney said, unable to resist shoving the knife in deeper. "I'm sure of it."

Dwayne spun and aimed his finger at her face, just as his brother had.

"You shut the hell up. And keep it shut. I gotta think."

"How about just letting us out of here? If you're not involved in this, you don't want to be."

The back of his hand swatted her hard across her cheek, and she saw stars. "Do you listen? Shut. The fuck. Up."

Defeated, she nodded, but now she felt an ounce of hope that they might yet get out of this alive. Apparently, her suspicions about Dwayne Surber had been wrong.

The big man looked down at Jan, and something akin to sympathy glinted in his eyes. With a woeful shake of his head, he sighed. "Damn. They hurt you pretty bad." To Courtney, he said, "They do anything to you?"

"Not like that."

"They plan to come back for her," Jan said.

He looked back at Jan. "I reckon Ben being tore up about his brother might make him do crazy things. I got a hard time believing this about Ray, though."

"It's true," Jan said, her voice nearly gone. "And they could be back anytime."

"Well, it's over, far as they're concerned. We got our own issues, Jan, and we're gonna deal with them yet. But not like this."

"Can you just get us out of here?" Courtney said, drawing back from him a little.

He glared at her. "Yeah. We're getting out of here."

"Thank you."

He knelt next to Jan and slipped a muscular arm behind her head. "I'm gonna lift you up. Can you stand on your own?"

"I don't know. I'll try."

He gently drew her to her feet, and she wobbled for a moment before finding her balance. "You'll have to help me," she said, her voice quavering with shame.

Dwayne nodded, took hold of her biceps, and began guiding her out of the room. "Where'd they put your clothes?" he asked.

"In there somewhere."

"I'll look," Courtney said, and slipped past him to search the dark room. She found them in a bundle in a corner, and there was blood and feces on the floor near them. Jan's blouse was in shreds, but her jeans appeared intact. No sign of her underwear or shoes. "Let me help her into these," she said to Dwayne.

He nodded. "I got an old jacket in the car she can put on. I'll go get it." He eased Jan into a once-plush chair near the front door and left her in Courtney's care.

She carefully lifted Jan's legs and slid them into her pants. Jan managed to pull them all the way on and fasten them. "Thanks," she said. "God, I'm starting to feel it."

"We've got to get you to the hospital. Where is it?"

"There's an urgent care center out on the highway. The nearest emergency room is in Elizabeth City."

"Jesus. That's a haul, but I say we take you there. I don't like these jack-in-the-box doctors."

"The urgent care will do. I know a couple of the doctors there."

"Whatever. As long as we can get help for you."

Dwayne came back through the door carrying a camouflaged hunting jacket, which he slipped over Jan's shoulders. He threw a nervous glance back through the open front door. "I think somebody's out there."

Courtney froze. "Somebody?"

"Sounded like footsteps in the woods. Heavy ones."

Icy fingers again crawled up and down her spine.

Could she reveal her fear of the Monarch to Dwayne? Good God — he'd think she was so crazy he'd probably tie her up himself. But now, her every instinct assured her that their lives depended on getting out of here as quickly as possible.

"We've got to go," she said, and with all her strength pulled Jan to her feet. "Come on. Let's get to Dwayne's car."

He eyed her curiously but did not protest or question her. Together they supported Jan and half-dragged her out to Dwayne's vehicle — an old, weathered Land Rover. "She can lie in the backseat," he said. "You ride up front."

"I should stay with her."

"Up front."

There was no point in arguing, so once they had Jan settled in the back, Courtney climbed into the passenger seat beside Dwayne. Her eyes automatically scanned the dark trees around the cabin. She felt Dwayne's gaze boring into her.

"What are you looking for?"

She shrugged. "Whoever — or whatever — you heard."

"Maybe it was nothing."

"Maybe."

"You're look mighty spooked for nothing."

She gave him a hard stare. "You'd be mighty spooked too, after what we've been through."

He nodded, unconvinced, but much to her relief, he started the engine and began to turn the Land Rover around to drive away from the cabin.

"What is this place?" she asked.

He jerked a thumb back at Jan. "Matter of fact, it once belonged to her black woman's family."

"Arlene?"

"Yeah."

"So what brought you out here — if you didn't know anything about what was going on?"

He grimaced and said nothing for a time as he drove down a narrow, rutted track through a tunnel of towering trees. The Land Rover bounced and splashed its way through darkness so thick the headlights barely penetrated it. At last, he said, "I got a call from somebody. Don't know who. Said Ben was up to something out here, something bad. I know he uses this place to do drug deals and such. I almost didn't come, but something told me I'd better. That stupid little bastard."

"He's your son."

He gave her a stern look. "Listen. Both him and Hank have gone out of their way to be trouble to everybody in this town for a long time now. You think it don't break my heart what's happened to Hank? Well, it does, but I knew that boy was gonna come to a bad end. And Ben's going down that same road." He glanced in the mirror to look at Jan. "And now he's done it."

"Why would your brother be involved?"

He sighed, his temper rising. "He's been supplying Ben with crack for a long while. The boy's too stupid to come up with a plan on his own, so he must've told Ray what he wanted to do. I reckon Ray just took the reins from him, figuring he'd cash in. Still, I'd never thought he'd pull anything like this."

"Looks like you were —" Courtney's voice failed as a gray shape flashed in front of the windshield and the vehicle slammed into something solid. Her head flew forward and struck the dashboard, and then she was hurled back in her seat as Dwayne spun the wheel wildly, trying to keep the vehicle from careening into the trees. Something heavy rammed the driver's side, and the Land Rover slid sideways across the road, coming to a halt only when the passenger side smashed into a massive beech tree, blocking the doors. The engine sputtered, clanked a few times, and died with a whimper. Then the headlights went out.

"What the fuck?" Dwayne's voice rang out of the near-total darkness. "What the fuck was that?"

In the backseat, Jan moaned and slowly sat up, leaning toward the front.

"What did we hit?"

"Look," Courtney said, pointing through the windshield as something began to materialize a few yards ahead.

A pale, spindly shape, almost like a giant spider, seemed to be unfolding in the darkness, and she saw one long, jointed appendage spring forward and slam down into the mud with the sound of a huge sledgehammer. A tall, skull-like shape, its features indistinct, slowly swam toward them like a bizarre fish in an ocean of black ink. Its half-seen, hollow eyes regarded them for several moments, and Courtney could feel a scream building deep in her lungs.

"Oh, Jesus!" Dwayne whispered, his eyes bulging half out of their sockets. Finally, he turned to Jan in the backseat. "There's a shotgun back behind the seat. I need you to grab it for me."

Jan twisted around to search for the gun, but something like a cannon round smashed into the left front fender, pitching her into the floor behind the front seat. The driver's window imploded, and something that looked like a giant pitchfork burst inside, its tines slowly closing over Dwayne's head. He thrashed wildly for only a moment, and then the ghastly arm jerked his body through the window as if he weighed no more than a child.

The scream in Courtney's lungs now erupted as a fountain of blood sprayed in through the window to paint her face and clothes.

In the back, Jan pulled herself up onto the seat, looked at Courtney with wild, bulging eyes, and then began to laugh like an insane banshee.

#

Chapter 16

The thing was gone.

Courtney's lungs were empty and her chest felt ready to collapse, but she could not draw a breath. Behind her, Jan's mad wailing had given way to a soft cooing, and soon it dwindled to silence. Courtney could move only her eyes, so she turned them to the mirror and saw Jan sitting rigid in the backseat, her face frozen in a mindless grin. The pain in her chest grew until, finally, her muscles reacted, and with a yelping sound, she gulped a lungful of air. The paralysis left her, and she brought her hands to her face to wipe away Dwayne's cooling blood. Some dribbled onto her lip.

"The Monarch won't get me, I've been good," Jan said in a singsong voice. "The Monarch won't get me, I've been good."

With excruciating caution, Courtney slid over to the driver's seat, brushing glass out of the way with a glistening red hand. Trembling with electric terror, she reached for the key in the ignition, grasped it in two slick fingers, and twisted it.

A click and silence.

The Land Rover, as dead as its owner. They sat there for a time, buried in near-pitch darkness, probably miles deep in the place called Owen Swamp.

During their run, David had pointed out the general area where Arlene's family had lived. If this rutted track led back to Winfall Road, she might be able to get her bearings. But there was no telling how far they were from the Blackburn house.

Where the hell was the Monarch now? Why hadn't it finished the job?

"Jan," she said. "Do you know this road?"

"The Monarch won't get me."

"Do you know where this road leads? Does it go back to Winfall?"

In the mirror, Jan's eyes, bright with hysteria, rolled to meet hers. After a time, they dulled slowly to lucidity. Her breathing became labored as her mind struggled to grasp their situation.

"What?" she whispered. "What are you asking?"

"This road. Where does it go?"

"Where are we?"

Damn it. Jan was still in shock, and with the physical abuse she had suffered, her chances of getting out of here on foot were slim, at best. But if they remained here, either the last two Surbers or the Monarch were bound to return and finish them. No matter how bleak the outlook, they had no choice but to try to make their way out of this dismal pit.

"Jan, can you walk? I need you to be able to walk."

"I can walk."

Courtney looked down at her own shoeless feet, her ruined skirt, her torn hose, and the idea of having to trek through pitch-dark swampland nearly sent her swooning. What if they did wait here for Ray and Ben to return? How much worse could that be?

In Dwayne's wrecked truck, a spray of blood being all that remained of him?

She shoved open the driver's door and lowered herself to the ground, her feet squishing into cool mud, her hand automatically holding onto her skirt to keep it from pulling up, which ultimately struck her as silly. She tugged open the back door and leaned in to appraise Jan's condition, hoping to God she could somehow get her on her feet and keep her that way, at least until they could reach a real road.

"The ledger," Jan said in a low, distressed voice. "The ledger's back at the cabin."

"Forget the damned thing."

"How did Ray get it? It was locked away in Dad's old office."

"Who knows? Don't worry about it now. Come on, we have to get out of here."

Jan grasped her shoulder, and Courtney held her hand as she eased herself through the door and onto the ground. She wobbled a little, but managed to remain upright. She waved away Courtney's hand and nodded to indicate she was coming back to herself. "I can make it. Hurts like hell, but I can make it."

"Do you know where we are?"

"Sort of. I think this road comes out at the end of Winfall. Then it's about two miles back home."

"Long way."

"No choice."

"No."

Jan gazed into the dark woods. The calls of night birds rang eerily from its depths. "No lights anywhere. Not even any haze from town. That doesn't help."

Courtney clambered back inside the Land Rover and opened the glove compartment, where she found a high-powered flashlight and a box of 12-gauge shotgun shells. Then she got into the back and reached behind the seat for Dwayne's shotgun. She found it and lifted the heavy weapon awkwardly, wondering if she could possibly load and use the thing.

"Can you handle that?" Jan asked.

"I'm going to have to."

"Better let me. At least I know how to shoot." She took the shotgun and ammo from Courtney, the gun's weight nearly dragging her to the ground, but she managed to steady herself. It was an expensive-looking Remington, and she pumped it assuredly. "You mind the light, I'll mind the gun."

Courtney nodded, leery of entrusting such a weapon to her, but she knew that Jan's experience with guns gave her an advantage. She shone the flashlight beam up and down the road, dreading what she might see, but only gnarled trees and thick clusters of reeds and underbrush eyed them from either side of the rutted road.

Then she looked up.

Just beyond the truck, a pair of legs dangled out of the darkness, black blood still dripping from one of them.

"God!" she cried, turning away from the obscene sight, fixing her eyes on the road leading away from the wrecked truck.

Jan didn't even bother to look back.

At first, they moved quickly, anxious to escape the scene of death. Jan wobbled a bit on her feet, but she was holding up better than Courtney would have expected, especially after having been in such deep shock only a short time before. Her eyes and the flashlight beam roved constantly, searching every shadowy pool, every dark thicket. Her neck began to ache from her head's constant swiveling as she kept watch behind them for an inhuman pursuer.

"The Surbers could come back anytime," she said. "We've got to be prepared to get off the road and hide in the trees."

Jan's eyes turned to steel. "If they come back, I'm going to kill them."

A stab of fear made Courtney falter because she knew Jan meant it. She also knew that Jan would dismiss any suggestion of showing restraint.

And, she had to admit to herself, no matter how badly Jan's family had wronged the Surbers, as far as she was concerned, anyone who would do what they had done to Jan deserved nothing less than death.

Of them all, Dwayne had been the only one who *didn't* deserve such an awful fate.

They pressed onward, the cold, muddy earth constantly sucking at their feet, wearing them down with seemingly deliberate glee. Occasionally, broken twigs or thorny vines would cut into their flesh, and once Courtney stepped on something slick that wriggled away, which nearly sent her into a panicked frenzy. The virtually nonexistent road seemed to go on and on, and she could see Jan beginning to droop from exertion. Despite the terrible secret her friend had been hiding, Courtney found herself feeling increasingly sympathetic toward her, even admiring her resolve, which was keeping her going in spite of her acute pain.

After a time, Jan drew up short. "I saw something," she said. "Turn off the light, will you?"

She did, and after her eyes adjusted to the sudden fall of darkness, she could see a pinpoint of light somewhere far ahead through the trees. It vanished and reappeared a couple of times, but she couldn't tell whether it was actually moving.

"Is that a car?"

"Can't tell," Jan said. "I don't hear anything."

Courtney stood still for ages, holding her breath, her ears keen for any sound, but finally the light vanished and no vehicle approached. She began to breathe a little easier, though now she was reluctant to turn the flashlight back on, fearing that questing, hostile eyes might see it. However, attempting to navigate the overbearing darkness without it was an invitation to serious injury or worse, so she switched it back on, both blessing and cursing its hot, piercing beam.

"Could that light have been from a house?" she asked.

"Looks like we'd still see it. Maybe, though. The trees are so dense."

"Who would live out this far?"

"There are still some old-timers who've been here forever and probably won't ever move."

"How you holding up?"

"Barely."

"It must still be a long way. No end in sight."

No sooner had she spoken than they came to a fork in the road, the right one branching into what appeared to be even deeper woods, the left one leading into an ocean of tall reeds, with few trees visible nearby.

"Great," Jan said. "I don't know this place."

"What do you think?"

She gazed at the sky through the break in the trees. "We're heading roughly south. Left, I guess."

"But you're not sure?"

"No."

"Oh." By now, fatigue had begun to overpower her fear, and she felt the early twinges of rekindling anger. She wasn't far from hoping the Surbers *would* return soon and that Jan was an excellent shot. "You want to rest a little before we go on?"

Jan nodded. "Yeah. Just give me a couple of minutes."

Courtney sagged to the ground, the tear in her skirt widening. Her feet ached from pounding the uneven ground, and her legs stung from the underbrush's lashings. She breathed slowly and deeply for a time, trying to replenish oxygen and energy. It wouldn't do to stay down very long, though, or she might not be able to pull herself back to her feet.

"I'm surprised they haven't come back by now," Courtney said. "I doubt they intended to leave us out there forever."

"If they delivered the news to David personally, he probably gave them some trouble."

"What do you think he'd do?"

Jan's eyes shone in the darkness. "He'd be inclined to kill them. But not knowing where we are, maybe he won't go that far."

Courtney was silent for a few minutes, trying to work up the nerve to ask. Finally, she said, "Jan, you've denied the Monarch's existence from the start. But it's out there. You've known all along it's out there. Tell me what the hell it is."

She shook her head. "I don't know what the damn thing is. You know who knows? Martha. She's the only one."

"But you were aware of it."

Jan sighed. "No. I never thought it was anything more than some crazy tale of hers. You know, I really believed David had killed Hank Surber. Why do you think I've been so upset? He's got it in him to do that, you know."

"So do you. Now."

"If only they'd taken David's original offer. None of this would have happened."

"I guess." She swallowed hard. "Jan, tell me. Did the Monarch kill your fiancé?"

"Why would you think that?"

"Because Martha was there."

"Doesn't mean anything."

"She was there when your parents died, too."

Jan said nothing, but shook her head. One of her fists began to clench and unclench. After a couple of minutes, she gave Courtney a cool stare. "We'd better get going."

Courtney nodded, and when she rose, her calves and thighs felt as if hot steel spikes had been driven into them. She could only imagine Jan's agony, but her friend dug the butt of the shotgun into the ground and pulled herself up by its barrel.

"Well. I guess we go left."

"To the left."

They emerged from the trees under a waning crescent moon. The rutted road went into the vast expanse of reeds and low brush, edged by the deep woods some distance to the left. If the Surbers came back this way, there wasn't much place to hide. Which left them only one option.

They walked on beneath a cloudless, starry sky, a soft breeze blowing in their faces, carrying the rank, dead fish odor to their nostrils. Courtney kept a sharp eye out for any lights, but saw none. She could only wonder about the one they had glimpsed earlier. *Had* it been a car on a road, somewhere not so far away?

As they went deeper and deeper into the broad marsh, Courtney realized her arms and legs were cold. That terrible, inner chill she had been feeling virtually since her arrival in Fearing.

Then she heard it — the distinct sound of a rough-running motor, very slowly gaining in volume.

A minute or so later, the headlights appeared, perhaps a quarter mile ahead, some distance to the right, but closing steadily.

They both stopped in their tracks. And Jan raised the shotgun, her body and her aim rock-steady.

#

Chapter 17

"Is it them?" Courtney asked, moving off the road into the tall reeds. Her feet sank in six inches of muck.

"It's a pickup truck."

Somehow, after all they had been through, only now did the prospect of death, miserable and ignominious, begin to seem real to her. There could be as many as four men, and any or all of them might be armed. Could Jan take them all out before one cut her down? If a single one managed to gain an advantage, the end would not be long coming.

For a few seconds, she thought about how Sheila, her little girl, must have felt in those last moments, when her own father came to end her young life.

My God, such horror.

She looked around for something she might use as a weapon. Rocks. A sharp stick. Anything. But the reeds and deep mud offered nothing of value. She should have searched Dwayne's vehicle more thoroughly, she thought. There might have been a handgun or a hunting knife tucked away somewhere. Too late to rue their haste now.

"If we can get out of sight, they'll pass us by," she said, giving Jan a hopeful look. "It'd buy us some time."

"So we have to face them again when they come back — after they've found Dwayne? They'll really be out for blood then."

She knew Jan was right. Not much for her but to lay low near Jan and be ready to take up the shotgun if the worst happened. She knelt down in the clinging ooze, trying not to think about its cool, organic grip, like something alive trying to pull her to its bosom. She realized her pale blue blouse would stand out in the truck's headlights, so she gritted her teeth and began slapping dark mud over her torso, limbs, and finally her face, camouflaging herself with the swamp's own lifeblood.

The headlights had closed to about a hundred yards, and the engine sound rumbled toward them like the growling of a huge animal. Jan stood fast in the middle of the road, the gun's muzzle tracking the vehicle without wavering. They'd see her any second now. The truck was moving slowly, its driver obviously unhurried, the occupants hardly suspecting that circumstances had changed drastically since their leaving the cabin this afternoon.

Fifty yards, and the headlights were shining right in Courtney's face.

They *must* see Jan now! Indeed, for the brakes groaned, and the truck lurched, throwing up a spray of mud that briefly dimmed the headlights. Then the shotgun roared, glass shattered, and someone was screaming. The cab doors flew open, and she saw a figure dive into the reeds to the right. Jan fired again, and mud and foliage exploded where the man had just vanished. A male voice yelled something, and another figure appeared next to the truck, this one moving to the left. The shotgun bellowed a third time, and a headlight went out. Somewhere nearby, something went *boom,* which Courtney at first thought was another gunshot. But it came again, and again, and then she realized what was coming.

In the glare of the truck's remaining headlight, an array of writhing shadows, a tangled mass of insubstantial serpents, melded into something gigantic: a towering figure that stood on two trunk-like legs, its upper portion blending into the deep darkness above. One huge, hoof-like foot lifted, cascading mud, and crashed down only a few feet from Courtney's face, the vibrations crawling over her skin like a horde of ants. Like a monstrous blackbird, an arm of shadow soared over her head, and with a resounding crash, the remaining headlight vanished, leaving her blind inside a living, pulsating dome of darkness.

Jan's voice rang out in an indecipherable cry, only to be stifled a second later, and something wet — Courtney prayed it was mud — rained down on her back. A deafening, metallic smashing sound followed, then another and another. A male voice rose in a shrill scream, only to die with a thick, wet gurgle. She buried herself in the mud, covering her head with her arms, wishing herself invisible, praying the Monarch would not see her and pluck her from her hiding place.

But the thing had her scent.

She shuddered at the memory of Martha's words, knowing full well that if the thing wanted to take her, there was no place in the world she could hide.

Several seconds crept by before she realized that the thing was walking again, the thudding footsteps receding rapidly in the distance. Muddy water dribbled maddeningly into her ears and eyes, tempting her to lift her head and wipe it away, but she could still feel the vibrations in the ground, and she didn't dare; not while the thing was still close enough for any movement to attract its attention.

Eventually, when all was quiet again, she rose up, propped herself on her elbows, and dared to wipe the mud from her eyes, mostly just smearing it around because her hands were slick with the vile stuff. Once she could almost see, she found the darkness unbroken except for a the glimmering stars overhead. A dim gleam a few yards away might have been the grille of the old truck. Not a sound drifted out of the night; not a breath of wind, not the nervous call of a single bird or insect.

Her hand reached out, seeking solid earth, and her fingers fell on hot metal — the barrel of the shotgun. She pulled it toward her, only to find the barrel bent and the stock splintered into fragments.

"Oh, God," she whispered. Jan had been firing the weapon even as the thing fell upon her.

Something splashed not far away.

She froze and listened, holding her breath, trying to catch any sound beyond the pounding of her heart. Something that might have been a soft, human moan came from the direction of the truck.

Taking a bracing breath, she dug her fingers into the earth and dragged herself from the pit of mud, until she lay fully exposed beneath the stars. She had lost her ruined skirt, and now she tore off the shredded remains of her hose. She grabbed the mangled shotgun and heaved herself to her feet, thinking that the barrel might at least make a suitable club. She scanned every shadow for a sign of her friend, even though she knew it was futile. The Monarch had taken her, and she couldn't bear to think about whether Jan might be alive or dead — not after having seen that horrible, talon-like hand pluck Dwayne Surber from the truck like a doll to tear him limb from limb.

She nearly leaped into the air when, as if God had thrown a switch, the night exploded with sound: chirping, cawing, trilling, from near and far, nervous and raw.

She fought down her shock and crept toward the truck, pausing after every aching step, wary of finding broken glass or hunks of metal with her bare feet, until she could get a clearer view of the damage. The sight of it sent a fluttering through her groin. The hood was completely smashed in, as if a boulder had fallen on it. Only a few jagged fragments remained of the windshield, and both doors hung open, one dangling by a single hinge. The chassis looked as if a giant had attempted to twist it into the shape of a corkscrew, the bed and rear axle bent so that one rear tire hung three feet above the ground.

Someone was still inside, in the passenger seat.

She glanced around either side of the wreckage, searching for any sign that the other men might be hiding nearby. Nothing. She thought at least one of Jan's shots had been true, so one or more of the men probably lay dead or dying in the mud and reeds. Satisfied that no one would leap out of the darkness and grab her, she made her way to the passenger window and peered inside, keeping a firm grip on the shotgun barrel in case she needed to fend off an attack.

It was George Tillery, his legs pinned by the crushed dashboard. Both his arms hung immobile at his sides, and blood pooled in the folds of his shirt at his waist. His anguished eyes turned to meet hers, and she saw tears rolling down one cheek.

"I can't move," he said in a thin, wavering voice. "I think my back's broke."

For any human being in such condition, she would ordinarily feel only compassion; yet this man had yearned to see her tortured and probably killed. He had specifically wanted *her.* Remembering that, and seeing him here this way, she expected that old, familiar rage to come rushing back and take her over. It did not.

"I can't help you," she said in flat voice.

"Please. Get me out of here."

"I won't."

"Look, I'm sorry for what I done. Okay? I'm sorry."

"Yeah."

"I mean it."

"Who came here with you? The same three as before?"

He tried to nod, but could only grimace in pain. "She shot Johnny. I think he's dead."

"Good."

She started to turn away, but he called to her. "Hey, wait. What was that thing? What the hell was that?"

She stared into his terror-bright eyes. "What do you think it was?"

"I dunno. I never saw it. Just something big."

"Then that's what it was," she said, turning away from him. "Something big."

"Hey, wait. You gotta get help for me. Please, get help for me."

She ignored his pleas and went around to the driver's side, her eyes scanning the mud and foliage for Johnny Spencer's body. She saw it a moment later, amid a cluster of tangled reeds. Just a leg and booted foot, protruding like a bent branch from the thick, black soup. The body lay face down, obviously lifeless.

At least two of the four were out of commission.

She leaned back to the open door. "Where are the others?"

Tillery could only shift his eyes in her direction. "How would I know? I don't know."

"Is there another gun in there?"

"No."

She tried to find something other than contempt for the trapped, wretched creature, but there was nothing. "How far is it back to the main road?"

"I dunno, maybe a mile. You're gonna get help for me, right?"

"Doubt it. Good-bye."

"Wait," he called, his voice turning shrill. "I said I was sorry. All right? All right?"

She walked around the truck, minding where she stepped. After twenty feet, when she looked back, the truck was just a silhouette in the darkness, its edges barely limned by the sinking sliver of moon. If Tillery was right, she still had a long way to go just to reach a paved road, and then who knew how far back to the Blackburn house. Already, her feet felt as if they were encased in ice and yet on fire. She might not even be aware of stepping on anything sharp.

The Monarch was gone, at least for the time being, but if Ray and Ben Surber were still alive, they could be anywhere. They might have fled in the other direction, or they might be trying to return to the main road, just as she was. Her one advantage was that they would not know whether she was still alive, and whichever way they had gone, they would probably be moving faster than she could.

"Just let me get back," she whispered to the night. "Just let me get back home."

She had walked for a full minute before she realized that she had no home, and that the refuge she sought was the very haven of the witch who had unleashed the impossible horror.

To the left, she could make out the pitch-black tree line, perhaps a hundred yards away; to the right, the nearby reeds disappeared into a gulf as empty as outer space. The road stretched on ahead, narrow but straight, leading toward what appeared to be another extensive stand of trees. Surely, she thought, this must be the last before she reached pavement.

She walked slowly, hugging the side of the road, the fire in her legs spreading to her hips and back. Pavement would hurt even worse, but at least her feet wouldn't sink into mud that tried to pull her backward with every step. She knew she must look like a black ghost lurching through the darkness, her clothes gone except for her mud-covered blouse and underwear. The mud she had smeared over her body had cooled and was hardening in places, making walking all the more uncomfortable. But it was either keep going or fall down to die. So she kept going.

Trees closed over her again, and though it was nearly pitch black, she felt less exposed. The road became firmer beneath her feet, and now and again, she stepped on rocks that felt like nails piercing her soles and driving into the bone. After this, she thought, she might not be able to walk for days. But that was a small price to pay if she could get out of this with her life.

The road curved in the darkness, and she left it several times, stumbling amid rocks and tangled foliage. Once, she fell and dropped the bent shotgun, and when she tried to find it again, she couldn't. But now she saw something gray and shimmering ahead — a paved road, surely! — and she knew the woods were ending. With a sigh of exultation, which was all she could coax from her lungs, she pulled herself up and finally stepped onto asphalt, which to her feet felt like jagged glass and a soft swatch of heaven, all at the same time.

The dying moon peeked over the trees in the west, and a few thin clouds rolled past a blazing star field, their shadows undulating like vast worms along the road. Here, the trees soared into the sky like towering parapets, and a cacophonous insect song pealed shrilly from the dark hollows beneath them. Still, like a refreshing wave, the realization that her destination might actually be attainable came washing over her, and she picked up her pace, casting out all pain by force of will alone. At the same time, however, fear, like an old, unwelcome acquaintance, re-emerged from its hiding place and began to creep just as boldly forward.

She hadn't walked a hundred yards when a coarse voice called out of the darkness, "Well, well. At least one of them made it out of there. Evenin', sweetheart."

#

Chapter 18

She froze, trying to determine from which direction Ray Surber's voice had come, even as she realized that it didn't matter. Two seconds later, she heard rapid footfalls behind her, and for an instant, she ached for the bent hunk of metal she had carried so far and then lost. But as she turned to watch Ray and Ben Surber bearing down on her from out of the trees, she realized that, even if she still had the weapon, she didn't have the strength to wield it. Her muscles were near-useless sheaves of tissue, her bones spent kindling. As the men strode up to her, their eyes shining dangerously, she simply sat down on the pavement, ready to accept whatever variety of death they had come to deliver.

The pair paused in front of her, regarding her warily, perhaps uncertain whether she had any surprises for them remaining. Then they began to circle like cagey dogs, occasionally glancing back into the trees.

They were as afraid as she was.

Ray stopped in front of her and glanced over his shoulder again before kneeling down and glaring at her, trying to wrest her gaze from the ground. Finally, he said, "Okay, what was it?"

She lifted her head and met his stare. "What was what?"

The back of one rough hand landed a blow to her cheek. She heard Ben coming up behind her. "The thing that hit us," Ray said. "What the fuck was that?"

Did she dare?

"The same thing that killed your brother."

Ray stiffened, and he raised his arms before him, resembling a grotesque praying mantis. Behind her, Ben released an explosive breath, and in a flash, he appeared next to his uncle, his face contorted with hatred.

"What are you saying about my dad?"

"I said he's dead," she said, without inflection. "The thing killed him."

Like the mantis reaching for its prey, Ray's hand shot forth and clutched her throat. He slowly rose to his feet, pulling her with him, sealing her breath inside her lungs.

"You don't know what you're talking about. You don't know anything about my brother."

"This is bullshit," Ben said, his voice a shrill whine. "Let's just finish her."

"No," Ray said, pressing his face close to hers. "I want to know what she thinks she knows. Or if she's trying to pull something smart."

His fingers opened and she collapsed onto her backside, her legs no longer able to support her weight. After managing to draw a couple of deep breaths, she said, "I'm not trying to pull anything. Your brother Dwayne is back at the cabin — hanging from a tree. You can go check it out. I'm sure he's still there."

Ray could not stop Ben from shoving past him and pushing Courtney onto her back. "You're a liar." His breath came out hot sulfur. "My dad wouldn't have come back here. He didn't have no reason to."

"He found out what you were doing. He aimed to stop you."

"Bitch." He slapped her cheek, already numb from Ray's blow. "He wouldn't have had no way of knowing where we were. None of us told him."

"Someone did," she said weakly.

"This is bullshit, Ray. She's trying to throw us off. Let's just finish her."

The older man shook his head, his eyes narrowing as he stared at her. "No," he said, his voice low and pensive. "No, I think she does know something."

"Like I said, go check it out."

"She wants us to go back in those woods," Ben said. "That thing must still be back in there. She wants us to go back in there."

"Not gonna happen." Ray folded his hands in front of his. "Okay, little girl. Where's your friend?"

"I don't know. That thing took her."

"Dead? Alive?"

"I don't know."

"Okay, sweetheart. If Dwayne really did come out here, who called him?"

She shook her head. "I don't know."

"How do you even know someone called him out here?"

"He told me."

"Oh, yeah? And why would he do that?"

"He said you'd gone too far. All of you. So he let us go."

Ray looked around to glare at his nephew. "You didn't say anything to him, did you?"

"Shit, no," Ben said with an explosive snort. "Neither did Johnny or George. That would've blown everything. You know that."

Ray turned back to her. "What about the other two? The ones who were with us."

She looked him straight in the eye. "Dead."

"Shit." He huffed in frustration. "I've lived here all my life, and I never seen or heard of anything like that out here."

"You're wrong," she said, barely able to draw a breath now. "It's been here a long, long time. Your father was Clayton Surber, right? It killed him too."

Ray's eyes turned to red coals, and he leaned forward to clutch her throat again. "Okay. You seem to know just enough to get yourself in trouble, don't you?" He looked back at Ben. "I guess we're gonna have to cut the answers out of her."

Ben produced a long hunting knife — the same one he had threatened her with in the parking lot of Woodard's — and now his face began to beam with pleasure.

Ray tore open her mud-coated blouse and held up an open hand, like a cruel surgeon, into which Ben slapped the haft of his knife. Then Ben knelt, grasped her wrists, and effortlessly pulled her arms above her head, pinioning them with his strong hands. She heard a dull popping sound in her left shoulder and pain flared through her upper body.

Ray now put his mouth close to her ear and said, "You think you can play games with us? Whatever you know, you're going tell me. Because I'm going to start asking you questions, and every time you give me a wrong answer, I'm going to slice off a little piece of you." He ran the flat edge of the knife blade over her stomach. Its cool touch, the anticipation of what was to come, brought terror bursting from its hidden compartment. He pressed the pointed tip hard into the flesh of her solar plexus, until a tiny bead of blood appeared.

"Don't," she whispered, trying to keep her voice from pleading. "Let's just talk. All right? We'll just talk."

"Yeah, that's it," Ray said, giving her a little smile. "We'll just talk. Now. I want you to tell me. Where's my brother?"

She gazed at him for a time, not wanting to answer, but the pressure of the blade against her flesh ensured that she could not remain silent. So she spoke the truth. "In the woods. Dead."

Fire blazed in her abdomen, and she realized the knife had laid open her flesh, just below her breastbone. Her body tried to jerk forward, but Ben's grip on her wrists kept her prone. She glimpsed a thin, red line running horizontally across her abdomen, six inches across. Just deep enough to be excruciating.

"I'm not lying," she said, gasping in pain and shock. "I told you what happened."

"What was it that attacked us?"

"Something…something called the Monarch."

Vague recognition flashed in his eyes, and he glanced at Ben, who shrugged and shook his head. "And what is the Monarch?"

"I don't know exactly," she said, her voice barely audible. "Something Martha Blackburn called up. Something horrible."

"Something Martha Blackburn called up?"

She nodded.

Icy fire shot through her abdomen again as Ray drew the knife vertically down her stomach, crossing the first cut. This time, she couldn't hold back a cry of pain.

"What do you mean something she called up? She talk to it on the telephone?" Ben spat a harsh laugh.

She shook her head. "I don't know how she did it."

Ray stared at her for a time, and Ben gave him a quizzical look. "Something rang a bell there. You heard of this Monarch before?"

He scratched his chin. "Seems like Dad talked about a Monarch, back when we were kids. A crazy story about a thing that lived in the swamp." He leaned toward her again. "By the way, Miz Edmiston, your friends, the Blackburns, they claimed my dad died in an accident. Now, I've always known it wasn't any accident. Are you trying to tell me that this Monarch thing, that's what killed him?"

She hesitated to answer, afraid of the blade's bite. But he brought the knife up toward her face and let it hover before her eyes, and she nodded. "That's what I think. I saw the newspaper story."

"Up in Elizabeth City, right? You were there looking for information about my family?"

"Not your family. The Blackburns. I just happened on the article."

"Cut off her ears, Ray," Ben said, excitement bubbling in his voice.

"Hush up a minute." He lowered the blade so that it rested on her cheek. "Like I told you, Miz Edmiston, your choice of friends leaves something to be desired. You must know that the Blackburns cheated my family for years. Not just us. Lots of families."

"Yes. I know."

"The fact my dad got killed while he was trying to do something about it, well, that was no coincidence, was it?"

"No. But I had nothing to do with any of this. You know that."

"Don't tell me what I know," he said, his temper close to boiling over. "If something really happened to my brother, I'm betting you know a lot more than you've let on."

"It's bullshit," Ben said. "Dad ain't dead. I'm telling you, she's just saying that to try to get us to go back in there."

Ray turned to glare at his nephew. "You shut up already. Just shut the hell up. I've a good mind to send you out to the cabin to look for him."

"Like hell! Not with that thing still running around! Come on, Ray, you know she's lying."

"Suppose she's not?"

Ben leaned down so Courtney could see his face, which appeared to register for the first time that she might be telling the truth. After a moment, he said, "If Dad's really dead, she's going to wish she was."

"Well, Miz Edmiston?"

She could feel warm blood running down her side. "I've told you everything I know. I've told you."

"Where is David Blackburn?"

"Home."

"No, he's not. Where do you think we went all that time?"

"I haven't seen him since last night."

"How much does he know about the Monarch?"

"He doesn't even believe in it."

"No?"

"I tried to tell him…I'd seen it in the woods around the house. He wouldn't believe me."

"Then you have seen it before."

"Just a glimpse."

"Come on, Ray. Just cut her up."

He ignored his nephew. "What about old Martha? You say she called the thing up. What's that mean, exactly?"

"She sang into the woods at night. It answered her." Her voice softened to a weak whisper as her energy ebbed.

"This is the biggest load of shit I ever heard," Ben said. "That was a bear or something that hit us. A fucking bear."

"It wasn't a bear," Ray said, impatience blazing in his eyes and voice. "Was it, sweetheart?"

She shook her head, barely able to move any longer. A brutal hand grabbed her hair and pulled her head forward.

"No passing out allowed." He patted her cheek a few times to bring her around. She groaned but felt her pain growing more distant. Then, with a look of resignation, Ray took hold of her underpants, sliced through the cotton fabric, and with a quick jerk, tore them away. She felt a sudden coldness on her inner thigh, which drew her back to full awareness. He had slipped the knife between her legs and was slowly moving it upward.

Ben began to laugh. "Yeah, Ray. Do it."

Again, the older man leaned close to her. "Okay. Unless I get some real answers from you, this thing is going to get to know you intimately."

"I've told you the truth," she whispered.

"I think you can do better."

"It's everything I know. I swear it."

"We'll see. Now. I want you to tell me again. What happened to your friend? After she stopped shooting."

Courtney swallowed hard. She felt the blade beginning to press hard against her tender flesh. "Didn't see. The thing must have taken her. I looked up, and she was gone."

"Where's my brother Dwayne?"

"I'm sorry," she said. "He is dead."

"That's it," Ben said, his voice a buzz saw. "Fuck her with it, Ray."

Again, hot agony shot through her body, and she jerked forward, but all her remaining strength was useless against Ben's unbreakable grip. The keen edge of the blade had sliced the skin of her left inner thigh right up to the swell of her vulva. She felt the knife's pointed tip glide slowly forward, and she knew Ray was going to impale her. No answer she could give him would be sufficient to change his mind.

"You're very sure?" Ray asked.

She couldn't nod her head, couldn't speak, couldn't even force her mouth to open. This, then, was going to be her end: humiliating, painful, useless, her body destined to be discarded in the swamp. Police Chief Flythe wouldn't even investigate, and no one outside this little town would miss her. Her mother might grieve for a time, if she received the news at a sober moment.

She would be lucky if an accounting of her disappearance ended up as a sidebar in the small town's weekly newspaper.

"Answer me."

She forced her eyes to meet Ray's, rage burning deep inside her, but impotently, her body beyond even its motivation. At last, aware that it might be her final act of volition, she managed a weak nod.

She felt Ray's muscles tensing. Hovering above her like a huge, grinning bat, Ben said, "Say good-bye, bitch."

Around them, the night was an endless void, as if the deadly tableau in its midst had confounded the universe. The touch of cold steel had overwhelmed her senses, but now she became keenly aware of the vastness around her, which seemed to be waiting to swallow her soul the moment it departed her body, that moment now only seconds away.

It was into this overbearing silence that a sharp, raspy croaking rang out, like the continuous cracking of timber, modulated into a semblance of speech, but in a language that did not exist. It only took a second for Courtney to realize she had heard this awful sound in the night once before.

Fear vaporized, and in its place came a pulsing, electric current of dark hope. The Monarch had her scent, and it was coming for her. Somehow, a quick death wrought by such an exotic horror struck her as preferable to suffering prolonged torture at the hands of these human cockroaches.

She found some solace in the knowledge that her tormenters were unlikely to escape the impending onslaught.

Rage filled the air, as tangible as the smoke from a funeral pyre. Then she felt the cold clutch of dread, but it was not hers.

"What's that?" Ray said, his eyes searching the tree line. Something slammed into his body, knocking him backward, and the knife fell with a clatter to the road between her legs. Then Ben uttered a shocked cry, something between a growl and a chirp, and his hands flew from her wrists as an unseen force jerked him into the darkness.

Ray shot to his feet, his jaw agape, his curiosity turning to blank-faced terror. He froze there, his face angled upward, his eyes locked on the sky.

Courtney craned her head back, until she saw, inverted, the thing that had turned Ray to mesmerized stone.

At first, she thought it was Ben, thrashing and dangling from the limb of a spindly tree. Then she realized that the young man was hanging in the grip of a pitchfork-like hand, the tines folded obscenely over his head and shoulders. The Monarch stood over a dozen feet high, its long, cylindrical body supported by two stalk-like legs, giving it the appearance of a four-legged animal that had learned to walk upright. Its bony head was a monstrous parody of a human skull, perhaps a yard tall and half as broad, with a pair of pronged, antler-like stalks protruding from its temples. The eyes — deep, asymmetrical hollows within which she could see cold, sapphire sparkles — appeared fixed on Ray. A wrinkled mantle of gray and black hung from its back, which she thought might actually be wings. A dripping coat of black and brown slime covered its obscene-looking torso and limbs, giving off a stench like swamp gas.

An abomination; that was the word that sprang into her mind. A travesty of ordinary terrestrial life that sent tremors of utter revulsion rippling through her body — the physical reaction she might have to a huge, venomous spider, only amplified countless times.

Suddenly, the idea of the thing laying its sharp, tine-like fingers on her seemed far worse than Ray Surber gutting her with his knife.

The huge head swung downward, and the glowing blue hollows appeared to focus on her, their bizarre gaze boring into her brain. The aching cold she had known for days now spread through her body like frigid worms crawling through her veins.

With a deft twist that made a nauseating cracking noise, the thing broke Ben Surber's back, and let the body hang like a marionette from one huge, pitchfork hand. Then, its spine bending grotesquely in the middle, the thing leaned forward to peer at her more closely.

Its tooth-studded jaw dropped open, and from deep within its black gullet, a series of bass syllables rumbled forth — what sounded like *"Gah-nakh, ick-ick eeyah vew-lock gah-nah."*

Then it swiveled stiffly on its stalk-like legs and, with the sound of pounding kettledrums, disappeared into the darkness, carrying its gruesome prize with it.

#

Chapter 19

The remnants of Courtney's rational mind screamed at her to stay motionless, for fear the thing might come back for her if she so much as shifted. Her muscles, however, seemed determined to move, and she found herself rising to her knees, one hand moving to cover the fiery cuts in her abdomen. She retained the presence of mind to pick up the fallen knife. A dull ache had seized her shoulder, and pain throbbed in her legs with every heartbeat, but she gritted her teeth against the agony and dragged herself to her feet.

Several yards away, she could see Ray's silhouette, a half-crumbled statue peering sightlessly into the too-silent woods. After a time, he turned around, his eyes gleaming faintly, but if he saw her at all, he gave no indication.

In the dark, he looked small and withered, a thin shell of his former self. She could almost hear his heart pounding across the space between them. Anyone else she might have pitied. His shell-shocked eyes peered past her, at nothing, and she almost laughed bitterly, for here she was, tortured and worn — so much at his hands — but still alive and lucid. At least for the moment.

She turned from him and took a single, painful step in the direction she thought would lead back to the Blackburn house. Her feet shuffled forward again, and then she was walking. She felt a scratching at the back of her neck and realized that it was renewed terror driving her on. Whatever was happening had only begun. It would not do to remain here.

Why, she wondered, had the thing not taken her as it had taken Jan? For that matter, why had it killed Ben but left Ray alive? She knew too well that, before this night was over, she might yet end up hanging from a tree like the rest of its victims; no better, no worse than the vilest or most virtuous of those it had destroyed during its unimaginable existence. She clutched the knife with all her remaining strength, for when her time did come, regardless of how futile, she would go neither resigned nor dread-stricken, but with a defiant sting. The rage she had lived with for so long, so jealous and consuming, demanded no less.

She heard the footsteps behind her but could not turn in time to avoid the powerful hand that closed around the back of her neck. The other hand seized her right forearm, preventing her from bringing the knife to bear, and began to twist it behind her back, sending bolts of pain through her arm and upper body, triggering a feeble cry of both protest and dull resignation.

“You’re not going anywhere,” Ray said, his voice a hoarse rasp. “Not with what you know.”

She tried to move her left hand so she could drop the knife into it, but his body pressed too close to hers. Her voice was spent, and she couldn’t even shake her head.

“Enough is enough,” he said, applying crushing pressure to her neck and forcing her down to her knees. “You can say good-bye now, bitch. Just say good-bye.”

His fingers moved like a spider to the front of her throat and pressed into her windpipe, cutting off her air, the shock causing her to jerk backward, her left hand thrashing to find purchase on his arm. Even when her fingers closed over his wrist, his strength far outmatched hers, and she could not dislodge the crushing claw.

Maybe this was better. Her pain and humiliation complete, even her rage flagging, continuing to struggle seemed pointless. She had faced impossible odds, come this far the best she could, and now it was time to rest. It could not be so bad, for her precious Sheila would be waiting for her. But not Frank. He would be somewhere else. Not with them.

Her field of vision turned red, then violet, and then blue, and her body felt at once as if it were slipping away into a cool, deep pool of water and soaring into the sky, vibrant and alive. Her lungs ached for air, yet her pain began to ebb, first tentatively, then with welcome haste, bringing with it a sense of tranquility that could only mean the end. The deep thudding of her pulse in her ears became a low, rhythmic rumble, like a faraway train receding in the distance.

No more bitterness or rage. This was everything she could have ever hoped for.

Then, a dagger of noise, cutting through death’s soft whispers: a harsh, crow-like cackle.

The distinctive sound of an old woman’s laughter.

The pressure at her throat subsided, and pain and alertness came rushing back, piercing and unwelcome, and the dark colors of night returned to affront her senses. Oxygen was a drug, overwhelming her for a few seconds, nearly sending her plummeting to the earth; then she could feel Ray’s fingers, now lax around her neck, and she realized that she still clutched the haft of the knife. Tranquility interrupted, sparks of rage reactivated her nerves, and, driven by renewed vigor, her right arm swung up, around her left shoulder, and jammed to a halt as the blade drove deep into Ray’s bicep.

He cried out in pain and astonishment, and his fingers pulled away from her neck as if her flesh were molten iron. He staggered backward, clutching the wound, from which black blood pumped like oil from a ruptured line, leaving the dripping knife still in her hand. Her muscles again dominated by a dark will — she did not want to think it hers — she plunged after him, saw his eyes widen when he recognized the purpose in hers, and shoved the blade into the flesh below his collarbone, the impact hurling him onto the asphalt on his back.

The dark will not yet satiated, she dropped to her knees and pulled the blade free, this time with difficulty, and raised it again to deliver the blow that would fulfill her rage's demand. From a blood-spattered face, Ray's eyes blazed with dread and full awareness of the force that propelled her, but his mouth still opened to utter a half-hearted "No, please," which sounded to her like a full confession of his sins against her.

For a second or so, she thought he was Frank.

Some fragment of her old identity — the gentle, idealistic one; the one before the rage — slowed her hand, but did not turn it. In that brief moment, she realized that white light now surrounded them like a hot shroud, turning the dripping, oil-black metal in her grip to alizarin, and she heard a slam, like a car door, though she knew that was impossible. Then her hand came down, and the blade disappeared into Ray's abdomen, just below the sternum. His eyes bulged nearly out of their sockets, and his jaw gaped so wide that the skin of his cheeks stretched paper thin, and air came hissing from his throat like gas from a broken pipe. The hiss deepened to a gurgle, and she saw blood welling in the back of his mouth, which soon spilled over and ran down the side of his face. The eyes rolled slowly upward, and the sounds from his body fell silent.

"Don't move!" came a horrible, grating voice that barely sounded human. "Drop the knife. Drop it now."

If she didn't, she thought, perhaps the policeman's gun would send her again to that place where rage meant nothing and the light was cool and comfortable. The temptation to find out prompted her to clutch the knife a few seconds longer, but in the end, she felt strangely unprepared to venture back into that territory so soon. Her fingers opened, and the blade fell to the pavement with a clank.

"Stand up slowly. Slowly, now."

Her legs protested, but she rose with something akin to assurance, her body reinvigorated now that rage's hold had at least partly relented. She turned to face Chief Flythe, lifting one hand to shield her eyes against the headlight's vicious glare.

The son of a bitch. He had to be in on the whole thing. It was the only reason he would be out here now.

She felt the first faint vibrations in her soles several seconds before the awareness of what they meant settled upon her.

"Hands on top of your head," Flythe said, his .38 revolver aimed straight at her, his body backlit by the cruiser's headlights, his face a black void. He took a couple of steps toward her. "Easy, now. You're under arrest."

The pounding behind her became deafening, and just as it seemed the earth were about to shake itself apart, she saw Flythe freeze and lower his gun, his eyes shining like diamonds within the featureless black mask. He gawked at the thing standing over them for countless seconds, and then, finally, the gun rose again, but he appeared unable to coax his finger to pull the trigger.

Courtney felt something cold at her waist, and she looked down to see the huge, gray, pitchfork hand, its tines dripping swamp slime, closing around her from behind. It tightened uncomfortably, and she expected the pressure to become crushing, to snap her bones and end her existence, but the next thing she knew, she saw Chief Flythe's figure receding *beneath* her, and she realized the thing had whisked her into the air and was now turning to carry her into the swamp. The headlights' beam offered her a brief glimpse of the vast skull-face and the deep, hollow eyes, which fell briefly on her, but the thing that burned itself into her brain was the look on Chief Flythe's pale, shocked face as his mind fled in awed horror from the indisputable evidence of his eyes.

Then darkness overtook her body and her soul.

#

She had killed a man.

Oh, God. No, not me.

But an evil, horrible man. A man on the brink of taking her own life. She was alive only because Ray Surber was not.

Because his plot had been derailed by something beyond belief. The very same something that had seized her and was carrying her away even now.

She had no inkling where she was, other than somewhere in the deep swamp. The thing had tucked her body close to its huge, mud-slick chest and held her the way a human might hold an unruly child — firmly, its intent neither to injure nor allow escape. Dull daggers still burrowed through her shoulder and feet, and the monstrous arm around her midsection felt like a steel clamp, but she judged that she was in no immediate danger. The Monarch's long, rolling steps sent up eruptions of black mud that plastered her face and neck, and she constantly wiped clinging droplets from her eyes. Even then, she could see only spidery clusters of tree branches silhouetted against the star-speckled sky, and occasional wisps of ground fog that retreated as if in terror in front of the relentlessly advancing entity.

An occasional bird screamed in the distance, but apart from that and the slamming of hoof-like feet in deep mud, silence reigned in the night, and never in her life had she felt so isolated from the world of humankind — its sounds, its movement, its *lights*. Geographically, she must be only a few miles from town and the family that had claimed her, yet this was a vast, primeval, alien world, set apart in time, so removed from her experience that it might have been the darkest, most desolate corner of the globe.

She felt more lonely than afraid. Death had already touched her tonight, and it seemed a distant ally, a friend waiting to greet her at the end of an unexpected journey. Already, she had accepted that she would never see another dawn, and although anything resembling hope had long since fled, something within her lingered, sustaining her.

Knowledge. The knowledge that the Monarch could and would have destroyed her already if that had been its desire. It carried her with a purpose, and its fulfillment of that purpose might yet reveal the answers she still craved, regardless of her final fate.

That laughter she had heard. A cruel intimation of the truth behind the Monarch.

Had old Martha actually been present somewhere nearby, or had her voice traversed countless miles by some arcane channel? If not directly responsible, that frail, shrunken thing with her secrets and her cryptic talk was somehow in league with the entity. Of the two, though, which was the master and which was the servant? Or might such trite, human terms be altogether irrelevant?

The thing slowed its pace, which served to refocus her awareness on the signals from her body. Her feet still ached, but only dully, and her upper body had gone mostly numb. Her lungs drew only short, shallow breaths, and the back of her skull felt like a timpani occasionally struck by a hammer. Very slowly, she shifted her position in the crook of the thing's arm, trying to coax the circulation back into her limbs without reminding her captor of her presence. The sky seemed to have brightened a little, for the branches stood out in stark relief here, but she knew it could not yet be dawn. As the Monarch moved toward a clearing in the trees, she lifted her head to see better, straining her eyes in the darkness, and when she began to make out the shapes hanging from the trees at the boundaries of the hollow, her stomach lurched dangerously.

They were the bodies of men who might have been alive before the last sunset, impaled on spear-like limbs. Skeletons dangling like wind chimes from towering boughs. Blackened rags tangled in claw-like branches, the last evidence of corpses that had fallen back to earth. Some of the bones rattled like maracas as a low breeze whispered through the clearing.

To her right, one of the figures wore clothes she recognized. Ben Surber.

No way.

The Monarch had killed Ben and vanished into the swamp only minutes before reappearing to abduct her. It had taken many times that for the thing to bring her this far. How could it have carried Ben's body here and emerged again in such a brief time?

One of the other nearby figures, suspended from a gnarled, forked branch just above her head, also appeared familiar. George Tillery, whom she had left behind in Ben's demolished truck. Perhaps Johnny Spencer and even Dwayne Surber also hung like macabre monuments in this haven for the impossible.

Her mind must have snapped, she thought. If she were still sane, then the universe itself had come unglued and caught her up in its collapsing fragments.

The Monarch strode toward the center of the hollow, and in the dim, midnight blue light, she made out the twisted, charred-looking trunks of innumerable trees jutting like frozen snakes from shallow pools of black water, and the awful sensation of having been here before crept over her. At first, the vague impression made no sense — until she remembered having seen these very images in a number of David's paintings.

She should have known. He was a part of all this.

The monster shifted the arm that supported her, and she feared she was going to fall until the massive, talon-like fingers of its other hand closed around her torso again. This time, the pressure quickly became unbearable, cutting off her breath, and, as if she were a disembodied observer, she watched in helpless shock as the thing lifted her, held her up to its cold, alien eyes to study her for several seconds, and then released her. She felt herself flailing as she plummeted ten feet and splashed into a black, oily pool, which swallowed her as if it were a greedy, gaping mouth. Her feet bored into deep, yielding slime beneath the surface of the water, but the impact still sent her head snapping fiercely backward. The mud tried to pull her down into its embrace, but she kicked and clawed her way back up until her head broke free and she could suck in a lungful of air. As she wiped the viscous, foul-smelling water out of her face, she saw the abomination that had carried her here turning to stomp back into the endless darkness, leaving her alone again beneath a glowering, alien sky.

She half-paddled, half-staggered toward a bracken-ringed mound, where the ground appeared solid. She pulled herself onto an island of moist but relatively firm earth and collapsed on her back, exhausted, struggling to keep her mind from slipping into senselessness. Her body had taken all it could take. Every joint, every muscle blazed with pain. The skin of her back felt as if it had been flayed by metal hooks, and her ribs ached where the Monarch's arm had crushed her to its bony thorax. She lay there listening to the night's dead silence, wondering whether she cared in the least what might eventually happen to her.

Sometime later, a faint sound crept to her ears, and she sat up with a groan, scarcely daring to believe what she was hearing: the melodious ringing and grumbling of a distant train, barely audible, soon joined by the mournful wail of its whistle. Her eyes fell on a rampart of broken trees several yards away, and she saw beyond them only an endless curtain of impenetrable black. But the faint reminder that, somewhere, many miles away, life went on for others as it had for countless years sent of pang of longing burning in her heart, and she knew that, deep inside, she did still care.

A strange, rhythmic thudding noise above her head drew her attention to the tops of the trees surrounding the hollow. At first, she saw only the mocking stars above the spidery canopy, but then something big and dark passed overhead, briefly blocking the starlight. And she understood: the strange mantle on the Monarch's back *had* been a pair of wings, folded like a huge moth's.

That was how it had taken Ben Surber's body and returned for her so quickly.

Then the thing was gone. She felt a deep certainty it would not be returning; not soon, anyway. Another long silence followed, and her wracked consciousness was just beginning to fade when a new sound dragged her back to full alertness: a faint *crunch-splash,* repeated several times, somewhere in the distance. Impossible to tell which direction it came from — as if direction meant anything to her in the amphitheater-like hollow — but when the noise came again, it was distinctly nearer.

Footsteps.

Human.

Her heart beginning to race again, she rolled onto her stomach and lifted her head to peer in the direction of the sounds, for the first time considering that she was completely naked, her body covered head to toe in black mud.

The interloper might never even see her.

The longer she stared, the denser and more maddening the darkness became, as if she were peering through a series of lowering veils. She detected a hint of movement a short distance to her right, and she pressed herself close against the earth, hoping to make herself less visible to any searching eyes, certain that anyone entering this particular ring of hell could not possibly have her best interests in mind. The footsteps were steady and assured. Then they stopped, only a few yards away.

"I see you."

She had known it would be him. It *had* to be him. That he was here, and that he must surely know what she had been through tonight, struck her as unforgivable, horrible. Yet he was the only person in whom she felt she could still place an ounce of trust.

She slowly rose to face him.

In the darkness, she could just make out his face, a dozen feet away. He was smiling his inevitable wry smile, but his eyes were full of fear.

#

Chapter 20

Neither approached the other for a time. David stood at the edge of the mound, taking in the sight of her. He wore a denim shirt, mud-splattered jeans, and heavy work boots, now half-sunk in the mud.

"Did you come to help me or to finish me?" Courtney asked.

"If we don't get out of here, we're both finished."

"Martha?"

He nodded. "I think I convinced her not to have you killed. Which was easier than convincing her not to have Jan killed. No guarantees, though."

"Why would she do such a thing?"

"Jan displeased her. Long story."

"I think I've gotten a good portion of it. Where is Jan?"

"Elsewhere."

"She's alive?"

"Yes." He stared at the wounds on her abdomen for a moment, then took off his shirt and used it wipe away the dripping blood. She barely felt any pain from the gashes. The worst of the agony was in her feet. He wrapped the shirt around her midsection and tied the tails in back to make a crude bandage.

"Thank you," she said, her voice flat.

He looked around at the woods, eyes still nervous. "We should go."

"Where the hell are we?"

"Right in the middle of its territory." He held out a hand to her, and she took a tentative step toward him. Pain shot up her legs, and she stumbled.

"Damn it," she groaned. "I won't make it very far."

"We'll make do."

She took his hand, and he pulled her to him, the relief in his eyes so deep that she knew, whatever he had done, whatever he might be, she need have no fear of him. His arms encircled her body, his warmth helping dispel the chill in her bones. She must barely look human, she thought, covered in so much mud and tangled foliage.

His eyes scanned the clearing again, as well as the starry sky. She could detect no movement or other sign of the Monarch. "It left a while ago," she said. "Are you afraid of it?"

"Let's say I don't care to spend time in its favorite summer place."

"How far do we have to go?"

"Not as far as you've already come." He drew her left arm around his shoulders and wrapped his right arm around her waist, so that he could support most of her weight. "I can get us out easily enough — as long as nothing interferes."

"Why would it? Your aunt controls the thing, doesn't she?"

He snorted. "At best, she can influence it. If she didn't know how to raise barriers against it, that thing would just as happily tear her limb from limb. It's beyond any human being's control. Still, it comes when she calls it. And then it goes away."

"What in God's name is it?"

"Something very old. You see the charred trees? Martha says that, a long, long time ago, it came up from Hell, and left those in its wake. They've stood that way for hundreds of years. So I'm told."

He began leading her along a relatively dry path between the tall cedar and black gum trees, picking his footing carefully, his strong arms warding away any fear of falling. "Do you believe that?" she asked. "About Hell?"

"I wouldn't know. It's as likely from outer space. Or *other* space. But that's irrelevant. The thing exists."

She stared into the trees ahead. "Hell. What if there is such a place? Reserved for people who kill, maybe."

"You sound afraid."

"I killed Ray Surber."

He didn't break his stride, but he turned his head to look at her with questioning eyes. Then he gave her a nod of understanding. "There's killing and there's murder. They're not necessarily the same thing."

"I was defending myself. I had to defend myself." *No. She could have stopped short of butchering him. If not for the rage…*

"It wasn't murder," David said with assurance.

At the end, light had blazed all around her. A terrible, white light. The memory jolted her. "Chief Flythe. He was there. He saw the Monarch. He saw it."

"It's nothing for you to worry about."

"He saw what I did."

David squeezed her waist gently. "It's going to be all right."

"What are we going to do, David? What's going to happen to me? To us?"

His expression darkened. "She wants to see you."

"Martha? Martha, who would just as soon see me dead?"

"I told you. That's no longer a concern."

She stumbled, and David stopped, his arms keeping her upright. The trees were as thick as ever here, but she could see a faint golden glimmer to the left, which meant that dawn was near. They were walking roughly south-southeast. "I don't think I can go any farther," she said, holding onto his shoulder. Her soles felt as if she had been walking on broken glass, her ankles lacerated and swollen.

David cast a nervous glance backward. "We'll rest here for a couple of minutes. Then I'll carry you."

"Never happen," she said, sinking to her haunches and then to a sitting position, her back against a tree. "You'll fall and kill us both."

He sat down next to her. "It's not as far as you think. My car is near here."

"You drove in?"

"There's an old utility road off the rear of the property that goes out to Owen Swamp Road. Dad used to use it to get to one of the worksites. There's another spur that leads partway out here."

"Good God. That road must be the one Jan was looking for when the Surbers ran us down."

He nodded. "That's where I found her car. Not a hundred yards from the turn."

"You came out looking for us?"

"When you didn't come back home and I couldn't get Jan on the phone, I went driving out that way. It wasn't until later that I learned what Martha had been up to."

"What's her story? How does she do what she does? *Why?*"

"Why does anyone do anything? Power. She learned most of what she knows from Arlene's kin."

"Arlene!"

"I'm afraid we weren't exactly forthright with you about certain things. Arlene's not bound to us because of my parents. But because Martha's father owned her ancestors. Before the Civil War."

"Her father? That's not possible."

"How old would you say Martha is?"

"I don't know. Eighty-something, maybe?"

David chuckled darkly. "Double that and then some."

A cold blade sliced through the nerves in her back. "What?"

"It's true."

"It can't be. It can't."

"You say that even after all you've experienced tonight?"

For a time, she had no more words. Only hours earlier, she would have denied that anything that had happened tonight *could* ever happen. "What about Arlene?" she finally asked.

"She stays with us because Martha wills it. And I guess you'd say Arlene is the closest thing to a friend Martha has."

Courtney shook her head in dismay. "I would never have taken her to be Martha's friend. She seems so good-hearted."

"She is good-hearted. She likes you, too."

"She seems so genuine. But if she knows these things, these terrible secrets —"

"If she wasn't open with you, it was to protect you. Just like Jan and I tried to protect you."

"Is that what you call it?"

"We tried to divert you from learning what you shouldn't learn at every turn. But you'd have none of it. We didn't do it very well, I guess."

She glared at him. "I should hate you. I'm not sure I don't."

"Well, I'm sorry about that. I know all this is a lot to process. But I need you to trust me."

"Trust you?" She practically spat at him. "I didn't much trust anyone before I came here. And now…."

"Try." He glanced back the way they had come, rose to his feet, and held out a hand to her. "We'd better get moving."

She struggled upright and waved him away. "I will walk."

"I think you'd better let me —"

"I will walk."

He gave her a long, dubious look before nodding. "All right."

They had just started out, her legs and lower back again screaming at her in anger, when the first distant thumping sounds came creeping from the darkness.

"It's on its way back," he said, his eyes widening with apprehension.

"It brought me here for a reason," Courtney said. "Why should it harm us now?"

"Have you listened to what I've told you? If Aunt Martha's focus has wavered…if she's had to go piss and isn't paying attention to what she's doing…then that thing is going to seek out the first living soul it can find and take it back as a trophy. That's what it does. Its only *true* purpose is to destroy."

"Is it so easy for her to lose control?"

"Why do you think she loads herself up on sugar and caffeine? When she's made that thing active, she can't lose focus for a minute."

With renewed terror, she pressed on, unsure with each step whether her legs would buckle and she would fall headlong. But damned if she would have David carry her, not after having been carried by that *thing*. Her strength was almost gone, so she reluctantly allowed him to support her again, his arm around her waist, hers around his shoulder. For a full minute or so, the beating sounds in the air softened and died, but then they began again, somewhere behind them, clearly drawing nearer — and she felt certain the monstrous thing was going to overtake them, and that would be the end of everything. Then the sounds diminished again, and she wondered whether the thing intended to wait until they *believed* they had reached safety and then drop on them, like a cruel predator toying with its prey.

"How far?" she asked.

"Maybe a quarter mile."

"Jesus."

"Let's just keep up the pace, and we can do it in five minutes. Can you handle that?"

"We'll find out."

After only a few more steps, David was dragging her, and she no longer felt any pain in her feet and legs. Just numbness, and in the blossoming light she could see her feet leaving a trail of reddish-black, liquid worms that seeped quickly into the mud. Then, to her horror, David was sweeping her up in his arms, and she shook her head and whispered, "No, don't," but he was beyond hearing her.

Because now, behind them, the beating sounds had turned to a heavy pounding. Still distant, but the thing was on foot and on their trail.

If one of the Surbers remained alive and was pursuing them, she might not feel such deep, nauseating dread; one of them had offered her a taste of death, and it had not frightened her. Even in the Monarch's clutches, while the thing remained under Martha's dominance, her spirit had somehow endured. But now, almost certainly beyond the old woman's control, the beast offered only the promise of eternal torment, and the idea of that huge, pitchfork hand closing over her again sent her mind in panicked retreat to some dark corner so far away that her mouth could not voice her horror.

David began to run, his feet kicking up clumps of soggy earth, his hold on her still firm and assured, and she could see his eyes, desperate but determined. When she craned her head around, her heart nearly burst with relief, for in an area where the trees were thin, she could see pale, amber sunlight glinting on metal. After the initial rush of joy, however, she realized that their reprieve would be temporary, at best. She had already witnessed the disdain the Monarch held for such human devices, and if the thing were truly intent on taking them, the car offered no sanctuary.

The next thing she knew, David was dumping her unceremoniously into the passenger seat of his BMW, and she could see blood dripping from her soles as she drew her feet inside. Her body again felt pain, and she wondered if it was in anticipation of the rending talons that were about to descend upon them. He made sure she was securely inside, then slammed the door and hustled around to the driver's side, thrusting the key into the ignition before he was even behind the wheel. She wanted to tell him that all of this was for nothing, and in seconds, they would surely be dead, but her nerves and synapses had all disconnected, leaving her without voice. Even now, something akin to the acceptance she had experienced when Ray had strangled her was beginning to settle in, but beneath it, debilitating dread still seethed.

The engine roared, David spun the steering wheel, and the car bolted like an uncaged lion, the acceleration forcing her back in her seat like a blow from a huge fist. She saw trees rushing at the windshield at dizzying speed, but the sight failed to arouse either fear or relief; death from an impact at this speed would be quick and blissful. As the car slid around a curve, throwing up a fine, dark spray, she managed to lean around the seat and peer through the rear glass, now coated in slime.

Beyond the dark mosaic of branches and vines, she could see a pale shape standing like an immense marble sculpture, its misshapen head tilted so it could watch their retreat, one deep, glaring eyehole briefly visible to her.

David glanced back, realized their pursuer had halted, and eased off the accelerator a tad. His relief spread to her like a warm ocean wave, and only after her chest felt ready to burst did she realize she had been holding her breath. She released it and began to breathe more or less normally. A few seconds later, a brilliant beam of sunlight burst through the windshield.

The BMW burst like a charging bull out of the woods onto Owen Swamp Road, swerving perilously back and forth until David let off the gas and regained control of the bucking steering wheel. He slowed to a safe cruising speed, wiped his face with a sweaty, grimy hand, and drew himself up in his seat, his sardonic demeanor restoring itself almost as if his panic had been nothing more than a gaudy show.

He gave her a sidelong glance and with a little shake of his head, as if to expel any lingering fear, he said, "Well, if nothing else, I think it's safe to say the old bitch is awake."

#

Chapter 21

Her senses were too far gone for their arrival back at the Blackburn house to register as more than a vague impression of having reached a familiar place, if not actual safety. She felt as numb and dead as if her body had been drained of blood, and even when, as David helped her from the car, she glanced up and saw a dark silhouette watching her from the upstairs rear window, she felt nothing. When he took her in his arms to carry her through the back door to her suite, she had no voice left for protesting, even if she had desired it. With extreme gentleness, he laid her on her bed and then gave her a brief, heartfelt kiss on the lips.

He vanished immediately, and though consciousness came and went several times within a matter of seconds, she finally realized Arlene was in the room with her. The older woman had started a bath running and was standing at the edge of her bed, pouring a dark liquid into a metal basin. Her kind, wistful eyes shifted to Courtney's.

"Those are ugly wounds," she said in a soft voice. "I'm going to clean them for you. It's going to hurt, but you'll be better for it."

She felt herself nod, and when Arlene dipped a clean washcloth into the basin, squeezed it thoroughly, and touched it to her abdomen, Courtney thought another blade had sliced into her flesh. Her body jerked reflexively and her lungs unleashed their contents in a powerful explosion. The pain lasted only a short time, though, and as Arlene gently bathed the cuts and then blotted them with a dry cloth, she felt a sense of profound relief. When the older woman's fingers touched one of the wounds and came away with no blood on them, Courtney felt no pain at all.

"I'll be right back, honey."

She heard the bathwater stop running and then a sloshing sound as Arlene tested it with her hand. The pleasant sound of humming drifted from the other room, the melody bringing to mind a tune that her grandmother used to hum when she busied herself about the house — back in the days of childhood, when life was beautiful and exciting and the human beings she knew were not monstrous things that intended only to use and violate her. For a moment, she felt more content than she had in uncountable years.

"I'm going to do your feet now," came Arlene's voice. "I'm afraid it's going to hurt again."

This time, when the cloth touched her sensitive soles, the bolt of agony was even worse. The stabbing pain went all the way to her bones, causing her to cry out as her legs went into spasms and her back arched violently. Tears spilled from her eyes, and her fingers gripped and tugged the bed sheets until they tore. However, when the worst passed and the sting began to dull, the sensation of *healing* spread through her entire body, transforming her exhaustion and hurt to tranquil drowsiness. Arlene very tenderly patted the wounds, and again, she felt only the velvet touch of her caretaker's fingers. The terrible throbbing and burning was gone.

"Let me help you up," Arlene said, coming around the bed and leaning over her with eyes full of compassion. "We'll get you into the bath, and then you can sleep."

Courtney nodded, confident that, at least for the time being, she was safe. She sat up slowly, gauging the sensations in her body, hardly able to believe her pain had subsided so completely. She gave Arlene a wan but grateful smile.

"Think it's working," she managed to whisper.

Arlene smiled back. "Old family secret. Now, you just take my arm and we'll go slow. Okay?"

With Arlene's assistance, she made it to her feet and crept toward the bathroom, holding onto the housekeeper's arm to keep from stumbling. She still felt weak and a little dizzy, but she managed to step into the tub full of steaming water and settle into a sitting position without collapsing. She leaned back onto a comfortable, inflatable pillow, and luxuriated in the caress of the hot, sudsy water, her mind still so overwhelmed that nothing yet seemed quite real.

Arlene knelt beside the tub and produced another clean washcloth. "Just relax now," she said, "and I'll bathe you real good."

"Don't have to do that."

"It would be best," Arlene said, her voice edged with authority. "It will make you better."

She had no energy to argue, and, after the way Arlene had treated her injuries, she trusted that the older woman had only her best interests at heart. So, she nodded, closed her eyes, and laid her head back on the pillow, too weak and weary to feel an ounce of shame as Arlene's hands began to scrub and massage her body from top to bottom.

"Where is Jan?" she asked, after a few minutes.

"In her room. She's in a sorry state too — sorrier than you, even — but I expect she'll be all right."

She opened her eyes and watched Arlene work the washcloth up and down her legs, dissolving the casing of mud. Around her, the water had begun to turn black.

"Such a mess you are," Arlene said in a little singsong voice. "What a horrid time you must have had."

"How can you be Martha's friend?" she asked, staring at Arlene's impassive features.

Arlene's large, dark eyes turned to hers. "What makes you think I'm her friend?"

"I know about your family. And how old Martha is. David said you're the closest thing to a friend she has."

"That's as maybe," she said with a mirthless chuckle. "All that really means is that she hasn't seen fit to do away with me. She'd have a harder time for herself if she did, and she knows it."

"How's that?"

"Oh, I look after her things, her place. There's no one else who would, you know."

"I guess you told her about me going into her room?"

"No. I told you I wouldn't, and I didn't. I always keep my word, Courtney."

"Why do you help her?"

Arlene's hands ceased moving, and for a long moment, she stared at the wall. "Because I'd rather stay alive."

"So that's how it is?"

Arlene nodded.

"You weren't honest with me about the Monarch. You did know it was real."

"I still had hopes you'd never need to know the truth. Once you do know… well, Courtney, you're damned."

She turned her eyes to the ceiling, uncertain how to take Arlene's words. "That's what it feels like," she said, mostly to herself. "Damned."

"You stay in the bath for a few minutes, and I'll go change your sheets. You need sleep something fierce."

"What time is it?"

"Long about seven-thirty."

She nodded and lay in the black water for several minutes, finding that her consciousness kept drifting toward some dark territory that offered no comfort. When she closed her eyes, she saw Ray Surber's face looming before her and then felt the crushing, iron grip of the monster that had carried her. By rights, she should be quite mad now. Totally insane.

Arlene returned a few minutes later, helped her to her feet, which, to her surprise, did not protest, and wrapped a clean towel around her shoulders. As she stepped out of the tub, she examined the cuts just below her ribcage. They looked fiery and deep, but they caused her no pain and did not bleed.

"I'll tape those up for you," Arlene said. "Don't worry, they'll heal fine."

"Thank you," she said, somewhat relieved to know that Arlene expected her to survive beyond her pending appointment with Martha.

She allowed Arlene to towel-dry her body and tape some gauze pads over the cuts on her abdomen. Then she shuffled to her bed, now freshly made with clean sheets. She collapsed on top of it, and though her body ached to submit to obliviousness, the horrors that she knew would infiltrate her dreams had sparked a new undercurrent of fear.

"Here," Arlene said, tugging the sheets out from under her and covering her with them. "Let's get you fixed up. No one will disturb you for as long as you want to sleep." She studied Courtney's pale face for a moment and then nodded in understanding. "Ah, you're frightened, aren't you? Don't worry, honey. Nothing will harm you now."

"Bad dreams," Courtney said, her voice nearly gone again. "Going to have bad dreams."

"Well," Arlene said. "Let's do something about that." She went and pulled the old Boston rocker from one corner of the room next to the bed and sat down in it. Closing her eyes, she first began to hum a soft, slow melody, and then she started to sing.

"Go to sleep, go to sleep, little baby.
Mother will protect you and keep you from harm.
Go to sleep, go to sleep, darling girl.
I'll be with you always; my love is never far."

The sweet sound was like a warm blanket that smothered her apprehension, and consciousness quickly retreated, this time toward a secure, comforting place, where she knew nothing evil could trespass.

Just before sleep took her, she sensed Arlene leaning over her, and she heard the woman's voice whisper, "Sleep tight, child. I'll never let her do to you what she did to mine."

With that, a new darkness materialized and followed her into her dreams, but it was not dark enough to summon back all her terrors.

#

When Courtney awoke, long shadows filled her room, and she realized the sun was going down. Full consciousness returned slowly, and it was only when she felt a twinge of pain below her ribcage that the memory of all she had been through came rushing back. Rather to her surprise, disappointment at waking up still in the Blackburn house eclipsed any actual fear. The bedclothes felt warm and comfortable, and, as long as she lay still, pain remained at a tolerable distance. She moved her legs back and forth without undue difficulty and then sat up very slowly, hoping her body would not rebel with a sudden flare of agony. It did not. The cuts in her abdomen made for the worst of it, but the dull throbbing seemed merely an annoyance.

She placed her feet on the floor and then rose an inch at a time, until she discovered they could bear her weight more or less normally. She lifted her right foot and examined the sole — and was shocked to find only a few minor scratches and fading bruises. Same for her left foot. *Jesus*. Whatever the hell Arlene had used on her, it seemed to be working.

It wasn't natural. Any more than Martha being two centuries old and the Monarch coming from somewhere beyond the boundaries of known time and space was natural. The idea of accepting these premises as reality was enough to send anyone over the edge, she thought. But here she was, living in a veritable house of madness, and if her sanity had fled sometime earlier, she had no way of knowing it.

She took a few steps toward her dresser mirror and, feeling a little stab of fear at what she might actually see, regarded her naked, shadow-swathed body.

She looked normal.

Slightly dark circles under her eyes, hair in disarray, and a vague dark patch under her right breast — bruising from the Monarch's talons, no doubt — but otherwise it looked like the same young woman she always saw in the glass. She shrugged at her reflection, somehow having expected to see something *else*. Something she would not like.

But she found she was cold again. That damned, bone-chilling, unnatural cold that had gripped her practically from the moment she had stepped out of Jan's car onto Blackburn property.

After going to the bathroom, she got into a pair of fresh jeans and a sweater, brushed her hair and teeth, and pulled on a pair of flat sandals, wondering if she would ever be able to *feel* normal again. Glancing out the window at the dark woods, she found herself shivering with both the odd cold and some anxiety about the rapidly falling night. She had run through a lightless abyss for such a long, harrowing time, and now, having slept through the day, darkness was on its way to overtake her again, all too soon.

Knowing that the longer she waited, the worse the anticipation would be, she set off down the hall, measuring her pace in case the pain returned, determined not to falter. She could see a light burning in the kitchen, and as she reached the end of the hall, she found David and Jan standing together at the door to the dining room, facing her as if they had known she was coming. David smiled warmly at her, while Jan looked as if she might burst into tears at any moment.

"Are you hungry?" David asked.

"No."

"Come sit with us anyway. After all you've been through, you need something in you."

His patronizing tone irritated her, but she nodded and followed him to the table, which was already set for three. Arlene was placing several steaming bowls on the table from a serving tray, and when she saw Courtney, she offered her a somber smile.

"Well, good evening. I'm glad you're up and about again."

"Thank you for helping me."

"Don't mention it. Least I could do."

Jan showed no sign of being in pain as she walked toward the table, and Courtney found the lack of any overt sign of the dire abuse she had suffered the previous night almost startling. "Are you all right?" she asked, noting that the dark bruises on her friend's face had faded to barely-defined shadows.

Jan nodded, her eyes only flickering toward Courtney's. "Arlene took good care of me."

"Me too."

"We'll be fine."

"Yes."

"Shall we sit down?" David said, gesturing at the chairs. "Let's see what Arlene has made for us tonight."

Courtney settled into her chair at the ridiculously opulent table and found herself shuddering at the thought that, twenty-four hours earlier, she had been embroiled in the most fantastic nightmare she could ever imagine —excepting her daughter's murder, perhaps. But even *that* had been a work of purely human evil, and she could still not wrap her mind around it. Somehow, all this seemed a charade, a display of pageantry that in reality was leading up to an even more personal, still darker revelation. She wanted to pick up the fine china and hurl it — at both Jan and David — but her more rational impulses prevailed, and she sat like an automaton and waited politely while Arlene began to serve them.

Fresh spinach salad with grape tomatoes, rare prime rib *au jus,* stewed white corn, sugar snap peas, mashed potatoes with gravy, and cornbread. A full glass of Cabernet Franc, already poured. But even though she had eaten nothing since early the day before, she could barely choke down more than a few forkfuls. The table, the room, everyone present here, all were dominated by an unseen presence: the ominous, overbearing presence of the old woman hiding in the rooms above. Courtney mostly picked at her food and sipped her wine, and she saw that Jan was doing the same.

The poor, wretched thing, she thought. Brutalized, victimized, and then physically healed as if by magic — and quite unable to come to grips with any of it.

Was she *any different?*

Surely, she thought, Jan must have previously experienced some variation of the "magic" that resided here and should have an idea how to cope with its instigators. Still, of the three of them, Jan had suffered the most grievous hurt, the most intimate violation, and though her body might overcome its physical injuries, her mind could hardly have been prepared to cope with such a horrendous ordeal.

Courtney understood this and should have accepted it, for Jan was her friend. Yet she felt little other than anger and resentment.

Anger because Jan had brought her into this ungodly fold in the first place.

It was a table of grim, mostly silent strangers, each of them subjugated by his or her own secrets and inner turmoil, each cowering behind a protective wall of silence. Only David displayed any animation, mostly extolling Arlene's culinary talents, but it was forced, and his voice rang shrill in her ears.

Still, now and then, his eyes met hers, and something passed between them: a look of shared knowledge and experience, almost comforting, yet somehow still deficient, devoid of true empathy.

Because they all feared for their lives, she thought. No; more than that, even. Their souls. Death she might have tasted, but Hell she had yet to sample.

Finally, her wine gone and her nerves unable to tolerate the awkward, imperfect silence, she looked at her two companions and said, "Okay. What now? Do we have dessert? Go sit at the bar and get drunk? Wait here like sheep to be summoned by our master's voice?"

A gentle hand came to rest on her shoulder, and she looked around to see Arlene smiling sadly down at her. "No, Courtney. Why don't you come with me now? All right?"

"Just me?"

"Just you."

At first, she felt some sense of relief that the awful waiting was ending, but when she scooted her chair back and tried to stand up, her legs nearly gave way. She tried to convince herself it was just weakness, an inevitable leftover from the previous night's exertions and injuries, but then her right hand then began to tremble uncontrollably. She tucked it under her other arm, angry with her body for succumbing to such deep-rooted dread. So she made anger her focus and reveled in it, because anger was the one thing that could ward away fear. Damning the cold that still gripped her muscles, she followed Arlene to the front hall and mounted the stairs that led to the old woman's private keep.

Courtney thought back to the morning she had met Martha for the first time in the kitchen, when she had considered the woman a merely irritable old crab who took pleasure in intimidating others. While that much may have been true, how could she have imagined the depth of the ancient crone's power, the mysterious motives that drove her? There were so many things Courtney wanted to ask her, but after last night, she wasn't sure she could work up the nerve to even address her. Still, she thought, new knowledge surely awaited her, and whether or not it might prove healthy for her, this helped bolster her nerve.

As they reached the top of the stairs, Arlene said, "Don't show any fear, Courtney. She's not going to hurt you. But you listen to her."

"I don't have any choice."

Arlene stopped in front of Martha's closed door. "I'll be waiting for you out here."

She nodded. "Thank you for being so kind to me."

Arlene looked up at the ceiling for a moment, her eyes seeming to gaze back through many years. "We all need something to keep our sanity," she said. Then she chuckled, drew a deep breath, and knocked on the wooden door. "Ms. Martha? It's Ms. Courtney and me."

The voice from the other side of the door sounded like a buzz saw. "Enter."

Arlene twisted the crystal knob and the door swung open with a harsh rasp. The opening revealed only a well of dark shadows, and in spite of her newly forged resolve, Courtney's stomach felt as if it had dropped as far as her knees. Arlene's hand squeezed her shoulder, and then the older woman backed away and left her to her fate.

Shrugging off everything but her desire to learn truth, she drew herself up so her body would convey nothing but assurance and stepped into the black pit.

Behind her, the door swung shut.

#

Chapter 22

"I see Arlene nursed you right back to good health," came the sharp voice from the shadows. "She is useful, don't you think?"

A few streamers of silver moonlight wriggled through the window blinds, providing the room's only illumination. As Courtney's eyes adjusted, she could see Martha sitting at the far end of the room, in a tall, throne-like wooden chair, like the ones in the great room downstairs. A stage obviously designed to intimidate her, she thought. She must not yield to its trappings. Still, the air felt frigid, and she automatically wrapped her arms around herself.

"I'm much improved. Thank you."

"Step toward me, girl."

Carefully, so she wouldn't stumble in the dark, she took a few steps toward the bizarre figure and then halted when it raised its hand.

The old woman lifted something to her lips, and Courtney almost laughed to see that it was a can of Mountain Dew. Here, face to face with the withered-looking old witch, she found some of the casual contempt she had felt for Martha before she had learned of the Monarch. She must be careful.

"Yes, Arlene has her uses. You owe her a debt of gratitude."

"I realize that."

"No, actually, you don't. But anyway. You still feel the cold, I gather?"

"Yes."

"It is a reminder." The woman's eyes glinted in the moonlight. "Whether or not it stays with you is up to you."

"Oh?"

For a time, Martha said nothing further but continued to stare at her, the frigid eyes betraying none of the working of that virtually alien brain. Courtney tried to meet her gaze, but it was like looking into the eyes of a dog that might suddenly attack. When the woman did speak, she sounded like an old, chatty neighbor. "Why don't you tell me about your feelings for David?"

Surprised, she shrugged. "He's a mystery to me. But I suppose I owe him as well. He's been mostly kind to me — if not entirely honest."

"Surely, you feel more than just gratitude. You let him fuck you, didn't you?"

Her jaw fell, and she lowered her head, torn between taking offense at Martha's bluntness and shriveling before the stare that seemed to bore straight into her soul. "We shared our bodies. I don't know if it was more than that."

"I do." Martha chuckled. "You gave yourself to him because he represents power. Security. As when you married the man who was to kill your daughter. As when you submitted to your father."

"How do you know —?"

"Your lack of self-esteem has led you down some unpleasant paths, wouldn't you say?"

Damn it. Damn the woman. She could not find her voice, and she stared dumbly at Martha, whose eyes continued to blaze at her. She felt a twinge of rage and fought it down.

"What about Jan? Do you care about her?"

Her voice returned to her, though it was weak. "Of course I do. She's been my friend for a long time."

"But you feel as much contempt for her as you do for me."

"That's not —"

"You are angry at her." The sharp voice drilled into her eardrums. "More than that, you believe she is weak and simpleminded, and that she willfully brought you here, into danger."

She could not deny her feelings. She lowered her head again, the glaring eyes too much for her to take. "I felt she was reckless."

Martha's voice softened. "It was not Jan who invited you here."

"What?"

"I'm surprised you didn't guess on your own. It was David."

"David!"

"To be fair, Jan *thought* it was her idea, and that she was doing you a favor. But David is the one who is truly interested in you."

She remembered how, from the first day she arrived here, how David had dominated her thoughts, her time. By his design?

"You do understand."

"Why did you want to know if he had made me pregnant?"

For a moment, Martha remained silent, evidently deliberating whether she should deign to respond. At last, with a little nod to herself, she did. "David is not the master of this house, as much as he believes it is his right. There will be no new life brought into it without my leave. He knows that."

A thought then occurred to her. "Is that why you had Jan's fiancé killed?"

Martha laughed, the sound like a crow's caw. "Why would I do such a thing?"

"Yes." Courtney's eyes dared the icy gaze. "Why would you?"

"Would you say Jan is loyal to me?"

"She's afraid of you."

"That's not an answer."

She shook her head in exasperation. "I don't know. I can't answer that. I think she does what you want her to do."

"Perhaps." The old woman tapped her claw-like fingers on the arm of her chair. "She might obey, willingly or not. But she does not *think* for herself as she ought. That man of hers was not acceptable. She still has many lessons to learn before she may mother a child."

"Your kind of lessons."

She laughed again. "She learned a valuable one last night."

"You mean those men?"

"Those men. Who do you suppose provided them with all the information they needed to prove they had been cheated?"

"No," Courtney said, shaking her head, rage bubbling up in her esophagus. "You wouldn't have."

Martha turned, reached behind her, and picked up something from the nearby table. A book. *The ledger that Ray Surber had showed her last night.*

"That was left back at the cabin. How did you —?"

"A silly question from a silly girl."

"You orchestrated those things?"

"Don't be a fool. Let's just say I set certain events in motion, and they ran their natural course."

"Well, I'm sure my life means nothing to you. But what if they had killed Jan?"

"Then there would be one less heir for me to worry about. Jan is her mother's daughter and her behavior proves it. She would have seen our entire fortune given away to the likes of those vermin. Now she knows better."

"That thing did kill her parents," Courtney whispered. In her heart, she had known as much, but until now, her mind had refused to accept it. "They had promised to make amends for what they had done. So you had that thing kill them."

The eyes gleamed at her.

"Your own flesh and blood. You'd see them dead before they went against your wishes."

"You have your own lessons still to learn, girl. To fritter away everything this family has built for itself over nearly two hundred years…I would not have it from Herbert and his woman, and I will not have it from their children. David, at least, understands this."

"Then he's no better than you. I thought he might be."

“Let me see, let me see. You killed a man last night. Is that right?”

Her voice faltered for a few seconds. “I defended myself. He was going to kill me.”

“Herbert and his wife were going to destroy me.” Martha’s tone was mocking. “Tell me the difference.”

“Losing money isn’t the same thing as losing a life. They were trying to set right something that *you* were responsible for.”

“Me? Responsible?” Martha put a hand to her chest, feigning bewilderment. “How would I be responsible for the way they ran their business?”

“Now you’ve shown me your true colors,” she said. “I don’t see how it could be otherwise.”

The witch’s voice turned harsh. “You assume a great deal. You never knew Jan’s father. He was a brilliant man. A tad cunning. He amassed much of the family’s fortune on his own, by whatever means he saw fit.” Martha frowned. “Patricia, though. She was a shrill thing. He kept her largely in the dark — as he should have. When she learned certain things about the business, though… well, she began to work on him. In the end, he gave his loyalty to her, rather than to me.”

“She had a conscience.”

“She had a death wish!” Martha spat the words. “She would have seen to this family’s ruination. And her daughter intended to carry on her legacy.”

“Would it have made you happy if they had killed Jan? To have one less heir to worry about?”

“Of course not, you exceptionally thick clod. Do you think I would actually wish harm on anyone in this family? When simple reasoning can be used, I use reason. Why do you think you and I are talking now? If I were the way you describe me, I’d have simply thrown you into the swamp.”

“I’m not one of your family.”

Now Martha threw her head back and cawed, loud and long. “Oh, but my dear, stupid girl, you are. You are!”

“No. I came as Jan’s guest, and that’s all.” Now she felt her nerve starting to waver, for the woman’s ancient eyes had begun to burn with a bluish light that too closely resembled the fire that lit the Monarch’s deep sockets. “Look. All I really want is to just leave here. To go away and forget everything that’s ever happened in this place.”

“Now there’s a fine little fantasy.” Martha’s voice turned deep and hard, any pretense at levity gone. “Young woman, you will never leave here. You have become a part of everything here. David still wants you. And I have decided he shall have you.”

"No," she said, or thought she did, her head beginning to reel as Martha's words sank in. The old woman was insane. They could not keep her here against her will. "No, I'm still a free person."

"But wait. Think what will happen to you if you attempt to leave. For starters, you'll be arrested for murder. Chief Flythe was an eyewitness."

"It was self-defense," Courtney said, her voice quavering. "And we can prove exactly what happened. There's plenty of evidence to show Jan and I were abducted."

Martha tapped the ledger with her fingers. "Oh, really?"

Courtney felt as if the Monarch's pitchfork fingers had closed around her again. "There has to be. Her car. The Surbers' wrecked truck. The cabin. There's DNA. And Chief Flythe saw the thing. He saw the Monarch."

"He saw you kill Ray."

"He was with them. At the very least, he knew what was going on. He could hardly prosecute me without implicating himself."

Martha smiled. "Don't be too sure. However, as long as you are here, he'll never be able to lay a hand on you."

She thought back to the previous night and then, suddenly suspicious, gave Martha a questioning look. "No. You wouldn't have called him out there."

The old woman smiled again. "Who can say?"

"And Dwayne. What about him? It wouldn't make sense for you to have called him. He was going to let us go."

Now Martha's eyes rolled in exasperation toward the ceiling. "I might as well tell you, that was Arlene's doing. But it was merely a misunderstanding. She thought she would be helping Jan, not quite grasping the big picture. She failed to realize that neither Jan nor you needed any outside help. We have since resolved that issue."

A faint vibration crept through the floor, into the soles of Courtney's feet. Then a deeper, audible thump.

Oh, Jesus.

"Tell me," Courtney said, unable to keep the tremor from her voice. "What is the Monarch? How do you control it?"

"I believe David told you as much as there is to know. I've learned over many years how to manage it. It's not easy, I might add. You're no doubt aware that the power originally came from your dear Arlene's family?"

"Power you somehow usurped."

"Oh, come now. How do you suppose we would have fared if that power had been left in the hands of slaves? What they brought with them belonged to us. *Everything* they brought."

Martha's voice drifted to her from a short time before: *You killed a man last night*. The statement echoed through her brain like a hypnotist's voice.

Yes, she had killed, but it was truly in self-defense.

As it would be if she were to kill Martha.

No. Get that out of your head.

The thumping sounds from outside were drawing nearer. What was the thing going to do? Reach in through a window and pluck her from the house, to hang her from a tree in its dark, devilish hollow?

Martha sat about twenty feet away from her. She could easily get to the old woman and throttle her before she even realized what was happening.

But she had to remember — that ancient body had already proven deceptively strong.

No, stop it. That is not me. I cannot do that.

Martha's eyes glinted distinctly blue, just like the Monarch's. "I think you need to know something. The Monarch, on its own, is a purely destructive thing. Its domain is the place beyond death. Once I've brought it out, I guide it by creating what you might call barricades. One here, one there, preventing it from going its own way. Guess what, girl. If something were to happen to me, so would go my barricades. Can you imagine what would happen then?"

"What about when you die? No matter how old you are, someday, you *will* die."

The crow's laugh rang out again. "When your body looks like mine, I will be here. Even after your body has rotted in the grave, and the Monarch has devoured your soul, I will be here. When your children are old, I will still be here. *That* is the power I usurped."

The sledgehammer footfalls came to rest just on the other side of the rear wall. Courtney looked frantically toward the window, but she could see nothing.

"Now," Martha said, her voice lowering to a froglike croak. "You have a choice to make. You may remain in this house as one of the family. You will be treated well. Like royalty, you might say. Or you may hang as a trophy in the Monarch's den. Make your decision."

Something moved in the darkness beyond the window. Then she saw it: the tall, misshapen skull, with glaring, ice-blue crystals blazing from deep in the hollow eye sockets. The antler-like stalks that sprouted from its temples. The huge, tooth-studded jaw, now half-open to reveal a cavernous gullet that might swallow her whole if the thing so desired.

"Why?" she asked, her voice cracking, her eyes locked on the massive shape beyond the glass. Its gaze bore into her like a drill, the cold intensifying deep inside her body.

"Now, now. I can't very well have you running about knowing the things you know. But David would be terribly unhappy if I just gave you to the Monarch. His loyalty should entitle him to some reward. Don't you think?"

"I'm not a bargaining chip for you to use at your whim," she whispered. "I'm not."

Martha chuckled lightly. "Think whatever you like."

The cold inside her now seemed to spread *outward*, enveloping her like a frigid web, its strands going taut around her arms and legs. She found herself sinking to her knees, unable to maintain her balance. Two brilliant, piercing stars now dominated her field of vision, and the sound of her pounding heart drowned all else. Better to die, she thought, than to accept the terms Martha offered. A life that wasn't life. A pawn to be played or discarded as the ancient witch saw fit. It was hopelessness that brought her here, she thought. The life Martha offered condemned her to hopelessness without end.

Death had tasted almost sweet.

The entire chamber appeared bathed in blue. A cavern of ice beneath a midnight sky. The eyes outside the window expanded until they were all she could see, and — oh, God — she felt the thing inside her, its tine-like fingers digging into her chest, questing for her heart. It tore through her flesh, her muscles, showing her agony, showing her death.

Showing her a little glimpse of Hell.

There were dead things all around her, but they were writhing, wormlike, inside tunnels and chasms of ice. The face of Ray Surber flashed past her eyes, his mouth open in an everlasting scream. She saw her husband, Frank, tearing at his face with claw-like fingers, his wails of agony ringing in her ears like a screeching train whistle. There was her father, his head bowed, yanking at his genitals, ejaculating blood.

Then she saw a group of white men — seven or eight of them — all wearing hats and gray longcoats, standing in a circle around a black couple, a man and a woman, bound with thick ropes and kneeling on the ground. A young blonde woman with Jan's eyes stepped into the circle of men, approached the bound pair, and knelt to peer into their faces. The sound of pounding drums echoed eerily from a distance, its cadence slow and erratic but gradually quickening, and as it settled into a rapid, pounding rhythm, young Martha began to dance, her face beaming with ecstasy, her body whirling and gyrating with wild abandon. The black man and woman began to scream, and a weird, blue light rose around them and gradually began to engulf the dancing girl. Her voice rose in the staccato, unintelligible chant that Courtney had heard from the upstairs window so many nights ago, and it looked like something long and white beginning to wriggle from the black woman's mouth.

The scene faded, and Courtney saw Sheila, her little girl — the one human being she had ever truly loved — stumbling through a corridor of ivory laced with deep shadows. Her skin was as bone-white as the Monarch's, her eyes sunken and searching. When they swiveled to meet hers, her little mouth opened and called in a reed-thin voice, "Mama…"

Then Courtney felt a terrible pressure in her chest, and the jagged end of a thick tree branch burst through her ribcage, and all she could see was the Monarch's dark hollow in the swamp, the stars laughing above, and bodies hanging there with her: all she would see for the rest of eternity.

"No, no, no," she whispered.

"Choose," Martha said.

#

Chapter 23

Chief Flythe appeared nervous as Arlene ushered him into the great room, one hand clutching his hat, the other swiping at a lock of gray hair that kept slipping down over one eye. His leathery face had turned brittle and a tad chalky, and his usual confident, almost cocky gait had given way to a meek, self-conscious shuffle. His rumpled black and gray uniform looked as if he had slept in it. Through the west-facing window, the sun's last rays found Flythe's watery eyes and glinted weakly in them.

To Courtney, from the vantage point of her new chair, situated between Jan and David's, Flythe appeared small and unimposing, his lean frame somehow deflated. Her seat on the raised floor put her eye level just above his, and he had to lift his head to meet her gaze. He did so only reluctantly. Standing before her, silent and downcast, he struck her as a sullen subject awaiting permission to speak his piece.

What a difference from the last time he had come to call.

She glanced at Jan, who sent her a thin smile. Thanks to Arlene's "old family remedy," Jan's bruises had completely faded, and her relaxed posture gave no indication that she had suffered a grave trauma less than 48 hours earlier.

"How can we help you, Chief Flythe?" Courtney finally asked, her demeanor nonchalant.

"Well," he said, fiddling with the brim of his hat, "I'm sure you're aware that there were some strange goings-on out in the swamp night before last."

"Yes, we are." Her eyes now drilled into his. "But why do you honor us with this news, Mr. Flythe?"

"Well, now. There are five men from town, all dead." He looked warily at David, as if afraid he might have spoken out of turn. He cleared his throat for effect and added, "Some mighty gruesome business out there."

"So we gathered."

"Damn shame. It means the Surber men are basically wiped out. Ray, Ben, Dwayne. And so soon after Hank getting killed that way. Dwayne's wife, Katie, she's something of a basket case."

"How did they die?"

He squinted at Courtney as if he were staring at the sun. "We think it was some kind of big critter."

"A critter?"

"Coroner's saying a bear, maybe."

"Really? I didn't realize there were bears in the Dismal Swamp."

"As a matter of fact, there are."

"Do you think it was a bear?"

He hesitated and cleared his throat. "I can't really say, ma'am. You know, I was out there, and I saw…something. But late at night, in the dark, sometimes you can't be sure what you're seeing. I suppose it might have been a bear."

"My gracious."

He worked his jaw back and forth in obvious frustration. "I also found Ray Surber, pretty well hacked up."

"Ah!" She put on a look of surprise. "Was it the critter?"

"I expect so."

Now, with a brief, approving glance at Courtney, David leaned forward and asked, "Who were the other men, Chief?"

Flythe flicked his eyes at him. "Johnny Spencer and George Tillery."

Jan spoke, her eyes frigid. "Well, that group together couldn't have been up to any good. You know the kind of people they are. Or were."

"Well, that's as maybe. But being as they're all dead, it's my job to investigate."

"Are you investigating now?" Courtney asked, her voice a razor.

For a second, Flythe's complexion went from pale to beet red. When he spoke, his voice came out as a harsh whisper. "Well, ma'am, I don't guess I really have anything to investigate here. But I thought I should come out and check on you. And share any pertinent information."

David chuckled. Then, in a measured tone, he said, "Chief, by way of sharing information, I thought I might mention how important I feel it is for people to be discerning about the company they keep. After this, perhaps folks in town will be a little more careful. Do you think?"

Flythe narrowed his eyes. "What do you mean by that, Mr. Blackburn?"

"Well, take Johnny Spencer and George Tillery. If they hadn't thrown in their lot in with the Surbers and gone into the swamp to do whatever it was they were doing, they'd probably be alive today. Wouldn't you say?"

"I suppose that stands to reason."

"I just trust you'll remember that. For yourself."

Cowed, the chief lowered his head. "Your point is taken, Mr. Blackburn."

"Good. Then may I trust that you have no issues with any members of this household?"

Flythe's eyes shifted to regard Courtney for a moment. He shook his head, but his eyes could not conceal his displeasure. “I have no issues.”

“You know, Chief, there was a time — when my father was alive — that this family could count on the law’s prompt assistance whenever we might need it. It wasn’t all that long ago. Do you know what I would like? I would like to see a return to that far more agreeable state of affairs.”

Flythe nodded to himself, realizing he had been singled out as a traitor but was being offered a possibility of reprieve. “Well, Mr. Blackburn, everyone is entitled to fair and equal treatment by the law. Your family is no exception.”

“So we have your personal guarantee, then? Of fair and equal treatment, I mean.”

He gazed somberly at David for a long time before nodding. “Yeah,” he muttered. “My personal guarantee.”

Having said his piece, David sat back in his chair and looked at Courtney. She took his cue and said, “Well, Mr. Flythe. You’ve checked on us. Are you satisfied?”

He squinted again, attempting to meet her stare. He clearly desired nothing more than to arrest her and charge her with murder, but he knew that as long as she was under the family’s protection, doing so might cost him his life. “I reckon I am. Y’all just be careful.” He jerked his head toward the window, and, more to himself than the others, he said, “There’s something bad in that swamp.”

“And I expect it knows your address,” Jan said, her gaze darker than midnight.

Flythe took a step backward, rekindled fear turning his face chalky again, his eyes searching David’s for some kind of reassurance. Finding none there, he nodded curtly to the three of them and said, “I’ll wish you all a good-night.” Then he turned and headed for the door. Unbidden, Arlene appeared from the darkness of the hall to escort him out.

“You be careful out there,” Jan called after him.

The three of them sat in the silent, deepening gloom for several minutes, gazing through the hall door in the direction the chief had exited. Jan was the first to speak.

“He’s terrified,” she said softly. “He’ll want to get back in our good graces now that his cash cow is dead.”

“Martha may make it an interesting time for him,” David said. “We shall see, won’t we?”

The two of them rose from their thrones, David going to the bar to pour himself a scotch, Jan moving to stand before Courtney, her eyes still weak, but full of a new, cold resolve that made her look almost like a stranger.

"I'm glad you'll be here with us now," Jan said, a hint of the old warmth creeping back into her features. "I know it's all a bit overwhelming. But you'll adjust. You're strong. I know you." To Courtney's surprise, Jan took her hand, lifted it to her lips, and kissed it.

"I'll be all right," she said, her voice wooden. She pulled her hand back, turned away from her friend, and looked at the portrait David had painted of her, now hanging next to the one of Jan and David's parents. From the canvas, her familiar eyes stared back, sullen and melancholy. *Without hope*.

"Arlene's still got some work to do on me," Jan said, and Courtney turned back to see her massaging her abdomen, clearly suffering some pain. "If you'll excuse me, I'm going to let her tend to me. Are you doing okay?"

"Yes. Much better. Thank you."

Jan nodded in satisfaction. "Good. I'll see you later, okay?" Then she turned and left Courtney alone with David.

He settled himself on a barstool and stared at her for a time. In a black silk shirt and silver-gray trousers, his thick hair neatly groomed, he looked so sharp that she found her body responding to his presence. He sipped his scotch and smiled his most captivating smile.

"I'm also glad you're here. I guess you know that."

She nodded, trying to keep from staring back at him. He was a liar and a conniver. A devil. He had also saved her life and committed himself to her, damning the consequences. Martha had already proved that even her own family members were hardly exempt from her unique brand of justice; Courtney knew how much courage it had taken for him to face the thing in the swamp for her.

Perhaps it would have been better if he had just let her die.

"Care for a drink?" he asked, as casually as if the two of them were lovers meeting on an innocent summer evening's tryst.

She slid out of her seat and went to the bar, where she found an open bottle of Cabernet Franc waiting for her. She poured herself a glassful and gave David a long, cool look.

"I think I'd like to be alone for a while."

"I hope the chief's visit didn't upset you."

She shook her head. "No, that was nothing."

In deep thought, he looked at the floor for a time, then nodded. "All right. You'll join me upstairs later?"

"Yes."

"Good." He placed a tender hand on her shoulder and offered her an honest smile. "You know what?"

"What?"

"I love you."

"You're too kind."

"Don't mock me. I mean it."

"I know you do. Inasmuch as you know how to love."

He looked puzzled. "Never doubt my feelings for you, Courtney."

"Oh, I don't doubt them."

He refreshed his drink and then stood up. "Well. I know your wounds are still raw. I'll leave you now, and we'll see each other in a while."

She raised a hand. "No, you don't have to leave. I'm going to my room for a little."

He gave her a long, fond look. *The way a pet owner might look at his new cat*. "Till later, then," he said.

She nodded and walked away from him, taking her glass with her.

On the far wall, her portrait was weeping.

#

Having finished her wine, she dropped the crystal goblet into the dew-frosted grass and took a few steps through the darkness in the direction of the woods.

A heavy crunching sound came from somewhere not far away, and as she peered into the black depths, she glimpsed something pale moving just beyond the latticework of the nearest tree limbs.

It was out there — watching her, shadowing her. She turned and walked slowly toward the driveway, listening to the heavy footfalls keeping pace with her.

She dropped to her knees, close to hyperventilating. Her heart thudded sickeningly in her chest, and bile burned the back of her throat.

Trapped. Like an animal.

In a gilded cage.

But a cage nonetheless.

The chill she had suffered since her arrival was gone now. The cuts in her abdomen had all but closed. Her feet no longer hurt, and her body felt as if it possessed more physical strength than when she had worked out regularly at the gym in Atlanta.

It was the magic of this place. Arlene's magic. Aunt Martha's magic.

As long as she remained here, she was protected.

"God help me," she whispered to sky, looking up at the timeless, twinkling stars. But nothing and no one was there to answer her, nothing but something that was the antithesis of everything she'd learned as a child about God.

I'm a murderess now.

No, not a murderess. She had killed because she'd had to kill. Any reasonable human being would have done the same.

Butcher.

No!

David said he loved her, and she knew that, in his way, he did. The vile creature. The liar. The devil.

Of them all, only Arlene possessed integrity, but she lived in her own cage, trapped by fear, too weak to even want to break away from the captivating power of this place. Even after Martha had stolen the soul most precious to her.

Courtney turned back to the house and looked at the upstairs window, which glowed faintly blue in the pitch-dark night. The family's guardian sat there, silhouetted in the rectangular frame, the ancient, unseen eyes watching her, probably laughing at her dilemma, the crushing weight of the hellish chains that bound her.

But what do you know, she thought. Her rage was gone. The last remaining familiar thing — the essence of her being, ever since Frank had killed her child and stolen her life — had finally deserted her.

One day, if she could be patient, and learn the secrets that Martha knew, maybe she could turn the tables. *She* would command the thing and send it away, and she would be able to escape, back to the sane world she had left behind such a long, long time ago.

But by then, maybe she wouldn't want to.

Finally, she turned her back on the horror in the woods and headed for the door, knowing that this was her home and here she would remain for as long as she lived.

Inside, David would be waiting for her.

In the hall, Arlene greeted her, eyes sad but offering her some solace. She opened her arms and Courtney fell into them, welcoming the woman's warmth, the genuine care, which was all she had to freely give.

"Oh, my precious child," Arlene whispered. Then she began to sing her lullaby.

#

About the Author

STEPHEN MARK RAINEY is author of the novels ***Balak***, ***The Lebo Coven***, ***Dark Shadows: Dreams of the Dark*** (with Elizabeth Massie), ***The Nightmare Frontier***, and ***Blue Devil Island***; over 90 published works of short fiction; five short-fiction collections; and several audio dramas for Big Finish Productions based on the ***Dark Shadows*** TV series, featuring several original cast members. For ten years, he edited the award-winning ***Deathrealm*** magazine and has edited anthologies for Chaosium, Arkham House, and Delirium Books. Mark lives in Greensboro, NC. He is an avid geocacher, which oftentimes puts him in some pretty scary settings. Visit his website at www.stephenmarkrainey.com.

www.ingramcontent.com/pod-product-compliance
Lightning Source LLC
Chambersburg PA
CBHW060608310726
48982CB00008B/1270/J

9781937530198